Lady Vivian
DEFIES a
DUKE

SAMANTHA
GRACE

sourcebooks
casablanca

Published by Sourcebooks Casablanca, an imprint of Sourcebooks, Inc.
P.O. Box 4410, Naperville, Illinois 60567-4410
(630) 961-3900
FAX: (630) 961-2168
www.sourcebooks.com

Printed and bound in the United States of America
VP 10 9 8 7 6 5 4 3 2 1

For my mom… Your support has made this experience a thousand times easier and better. I love you.

26 August 1818

Dearest Vivian,

Foxhaven assures me Lord Ellis's visit to Brighthurst House is naught but to pay his respects. Nevertheless, I suspect the duke is sending him to gather information about you. Be on your guard and provide no grounds for Foxhaven to oppose the match.

Our coach is being readied to return to the country as I compose this letter. Send word the moment Ellis departs, and do not omit any details. I must be prepared for the next interview with Foxhaven.

With deepest regards,

Ash

One

LADY VIVIAN WORTH FOLDED THE SHEET OF FOOLSCAP and sighed. Her older brother had always shown a flair for dramatics, often predicting disaster where no risk existed. He had no reason to fret over a nobleman's visit to Brighthurst House. Vivi knew perfectly well how to behave like a lady. She'd had nineteen years of practice. Observing proper manners when no one was around to impress, however, was silly.

She tossed Ash's weekly letter beside her discarded gown, petticoats, and corset, then tore off across the damp grass, her unbound hair flying behind her. The previous night's heavy rain had swollen the spring cutting through Cousin Patrice's property to the ideal depth, and Vivi had always been powerless to resist a good swim.

Reaching the rocky ledge, she leaped into the air with a whoop, drawing her knees toward her chest. She hung weightless for a second, then dropped to the spring below with a loud splash, the water sucking her to the bottom. Vivi burrowed her toes into the pebbled spring bed, then shot upward to break through the surface again as eagerly as a newborn babe bursting into a bright new world.

Ah, sweet ecstasy. This was much better than mindless needlepoint.

Smiling, she stretched out on her back to admire the white clouds soaring like mountains into the sky. Today the sun was brighter, the trees more lush, the birds harmonious in their songs.

Lucas Forest, the twelfth Duke of Foxhaven, was showing interest in her at last, even if he was sending an emissary to call on her.

Vivi had never been a patient person, and waiting for Foxhaven to claim her had been difficult indeed. Yet, she had not faulted him for postponing the final signing of their marital agreement. He had just lost his father suddenly, and she'd understood the magnitude of that kind of loss. By age seven, she was already an orphan and quickly becoming a burden to her brother.

She could also appreciate Foxhaven's shock upon learning of the secret negotiations between her brother and the former duke. She hadn't been consulted prior to their discussions either.

Nevertheless, thirteen months had proven to be a torturously long time for her to exist in a state of uncertainty. She was ready to have the matter settled between them and leave Bedfordshire behind.

When the duke's representative, Lord Ellis, arrived next week, she would give him no reason to find her lacking. She would be everything her brother had promised Foxhaven she would be: a gracious hostess, a proper lady, and an empty-headed ninny with no opinions.

Vivi flipped onto her stomach and swam with the current.

Claiming she had no opinions was perhaps unwise of her brother. Her opinions tended to sprout up like dandelions in a field, and she was often eager to share her thoughts when others were not so eager to listen. But she would hold her tongue, even if she must bite it in the process.

Swimming to shallower water, Vivi stood and wobbled on the slippery rocks, her hands thrust out at her sides to find her balance. She had best make her way back to the house. Cook was still awaiting her approval of the meals for Lord Ellis's stay. Since Cousin Patrice had taken to her bed with a chill, the task had fallen to Vivi.

Were a gentleman's occupations as mind-numbing as a lady's? Likely not. Their reading selections certainly proved more entertaining. Perhaps she could afford to sneak in another chapter of Sir Thomas Malory's *Le Morte d'Arthur* before addressing the kitchen staff.

She trudged upstream, her mind already preoccupied with the story she had abandoned earlier. She often lost herself in daydreams about handsome knights and being adored by one. It made her lonely days feel less... Well, *lonely*.

She is attending a tournament. Sir Launcelot stops his charger in front of her and declares himself as her champion. Vivi pulls the scarlet ribbon from her hair and presents it to him. Her brave knight holds her offering to his lips, his eyes shining brightly.

"My dearest Lady Vivian, you honor me with your gift. Might I beg of you a kiss as reward for my victory?"

Vivi touched her fingers to her lips. "Yes, my brave knight." She laughed, embarrassed to still be engaging in girlish fancies. Her imagination was rather brilliant, however. She had been so lost in the moment she could have sworn she'd heard the whinny of Sir Launcelot's horse.

The smooth rocks shifted and she landed in the water with a plop. As she struggled to her feet, the snort of a horse—real, not imagined—made her head snap up.

A horse and rider appeared through the tree line ahead and approached the spring's edge.

She froze.

The man sat casually in his saddle, seemingly unaware of her presence, while his horse lowered his head for a drink. She sloshed around in search of someplace to hide, but there was nowhere to go. No bush, boulder, or tree near enough to shield her.

"Damnation!" The gentleman's surprised exclamation echoed off the stone ledge lining the opposite bank.

"Oh, look away. *Please*, look away." She attempted to run for deeper water, but her chemise twisted around her knees. Pitching forward, she landed face-first into the water, then came up coughing and sputtering, her hair in her eyes. The sounds of boots hitting the gravel and splashing made her heart leap into her throat.

She staggered to her feet, sweeping aside the curtain of hair obstructing her view. Hastily, she crossed her arms over her breasts. "Stop!"

The stranger drew to a halt, the water up to his knees. Dark brows lowered over the most striking blue eyes she had ever seen. "You aren't in need of rescue?"

She snorted. "Not from swimming."

His intense stare bathed her in heat, making her forget the affront he had just served her. She slowly began to back away. Water dripped from her nose, but she didn't dare expose herself to swipe at it.

If anyone discovered her half-nude in the presence of a gentleman... Well, it would be a million times more disastrous than the situation with Owen, and that debacle could ruin her if word ever reached London.

His gaze didn't waver.

"Will you please stop gawking at me?"

"Sorry." He covered his eyes and his lips twitched upward. "Now that we have established you are in no danger, perhaps you can answer a question. Are you a water sprite or a manifestation of my overactive imagination?"

His voice sounded like he was holding back a smile. He wasn't taking their situation seriously enough in her estimation.

"The second one, so go away."

The gentleman laughed, but kept his eyes covered. "You seem real enough. Perhaps you're a milkmaid from a local farm. Does your employer know you are attempting to drown yourself instead of attending to your duties?"

"I wasn't drowning, and I haven't time to chat with unwanted trespassers."

She continued to ease toward the opposite bank, watching him for signs of pursuit. Her pulse slowed a fraction when he held his position and still didn't peek.

"Are there any other kind?" he asked.

Reaching deeper water, she submerged herself to her neck. "Any other kind of what?"

"Trespassers. Are they ever wanted? By definition trespassing implies—"

"I *know* what it means. Now good day, sir."

He laughed again and dropped his hand by his side. "You're a cheeky one. What is your name?"

Vivi's eyes widened. A true gentleman would have pretended he had never seen her, and if he did by chance discover her half-nude in a spring, he wouldn't insensitively request her name.

"I am no one of importance. Please just go away."

The last thing she needed was a guest of the neighboring estate spreading word of their embarrassing encounter. She would be the talk of Dunstable.

Again.

And Ash would be livid with her.

Again.

The man flashed a grin. "Spoiled your fun, did I? Perhaps before I go, you might assist me."

"I am certain I have no skill in whatever it is you require." She swam backward, putting more distance between them.

"It requires no skill."

He waded out of the spring, stood on one foot to tug off his boot, and poured water from it. "I just purchased these and now I've ruined them coming to your rescue."

"I didn't *need* rescuing." Truly, she was an excellent swimmer. Why wasn't he listening?

"Of course you didn't." His sarcastic tone got her back up, but before she could deliver a scathing set-down, his magnificent eyes locked on her again. "I require directions to Brighthurst House. Do you know the way?"

"Brighthurst?" All the air rushed from her in a whoosh as her gaze swept over him. His expensively cut burgundy coat was dusty and his Hessians—well, they were likely ruined as he had said—but he was attired more fashionably than most gentlemen in the county.

Dear heavens, no!

This gentleman couldn't possibly be Lord Ellis. The earl wasn't due for several more days. Perhaps she had misheard him.

She cleared her throat. "Did—did you say Brighthurst House?"

"I must be close if the blacksmith is to be trusted."

Sweet strawberry jam! He had to be the earl. What was he doing at Brighthurst House this early? And where was his coach? "Uh, I-I don't—"

He frowned as he mounted his horse. "Don't tell me you are unfamiliar with Lady Brighthurst."

She wouldn't say she was unfamiliar with her, for it was best to avoid speaking falsehoods whenever possible. "You might have gone—" She waggled her finger. "Go *that* way."

His gaze followed her wavering finger. "Which way? The way I came?"

"Yes, I think. Maybe."

"Yes or maybe?"

"Uh... Perhaps you should find someone else to ask."

He raised a brow and looked pointedly around the area. "Ask someone else? Who, pray tell?"

"Forgive me, sir, but I really must go." She swam for the opposite bank, reaching her destination and clinging to the rocky ledge.

"Just a moment. I require an answer. Do I go back the way I came or not?"

"Um, yes!" Dear Lord, she had just lied after all. To an earl. Vivi's heart pounded in her ears, blocking out his reply. She blinked. "Pardon?"

"I asked if you would like something for your trouble. A shilling or two?"

"No!" Good heavens, no. She couldn't take his money, too. Her knuckles ached as she fought against the current trying to sweep her downstream.

He walked his horse a little ways into the water. "Are you certain you don't require assistance? You appear in danger of drowning again."

"I *know* how to swim," she said through clenched teeth.

The gentleman rubbed his forehead, appearing to mull over the wisdom of leaving her.

She eyed the steep incline on her side of the creek. It would take a bit of effort, but she could scale the hill. If the gentleman would leave. "Thank you for your concern, but you may go now."

A slow smile eased across his mouth like honey dripping from a spoon. "You are too cheeky by half, chit. Take care when climbing to the top. I wouldn't like to see you hurt."

"I will be fine, but thank you again."

With a shake of his head, he flicked the reins and turned his horse back toward the trees.

Lud! She didn't have much time. As soon as rider and horse disappeared from sight, Vivi levered her elbow against the rock ledge, flopped her leg on top, and then climbed from the water with a soft grunt. Pushing to her feet, she kicked free of the chemise tangled around her legs and grabbed a large tree root dangling down the side of the embankment. She scurried up the hill hand over hand, her mind awhirl.

What was Lord Ellis doing at Brighthurst this early? And why did he have to arrive at this exact moment? She had the worst luck of any person she knew.

Her feet slipped on the dark dirt, stirring up an earthy scent. She held tighter, ignoring the burn in her palms, and continued her climb. When she made it to the top, she dashed for her clothes.

Lord Ellis couldn't reach the house before her. He just couldn't. She needed a moment to think, to sort out what to do before he arrived. She had to find a way to salvage her situation, because she couldn't bear to be a disappointment to Cousin Patrice again.

In the distance, someone called her name. It was her maid.

"Lady Vivian, here you are. I have been searching everywhere for you." Winifred marched through the meadow in her direction. "It looks like another storm is blowing in. You better come back to the house."

A gust of wind sent the meadow grass into a frantic dance. Vivi snatched up her crumpled gown from the ground. "Winnie! Come quickly. Something awful has happened."

Her maid broke into a run. "My lady, what is it? Have you been injured?"

"No, nothing of the sort, but please help me with my dress." Winnie grabbed her corset and petticoats, but Vivi waved them away. "There isn't time. You may dress me properly once we reach my chambers."

"I don't understand, my lady. What happened?"

Her maid draped the undergarments over her shoulder and tossed the gown over Vivi's head, yanking the skirts down her body inch by inch as the Indian muslin stuck to her wet skin.

When her head emerged, she saw a thick cloud dull the bright sun. The air seemed stagnant and heavy. In the distance, foreboding storm clouds hovered on the horizon as if getting into formation to launch an attack. It was moving in quickly, catching her unawares, much as Lord Ellis had.

Before her maid could fasten her gown, Vivi linked arms and dragged her through the meadow back toward Brighthurst House.

"Lady Vivian, what are you about?"

"Oh, Winnie. I'm in a real pickle. Lord Ellis will arrive at our front door in a matter of moments. We must hurry."

"Lord Ellis? But he isn't expected until next week." Winnie planted her feet, jerking Vivi to a stop. Her brow furrowed as she captured Vivi's face and peered into her eyes. "You didn't knock your head, did you?"

Vivi brushed her maid's hands away. "I haven't lost my senses. Let's go."

Fingers of lightning stretched toward the ground, and thunder made the earth below them shudder.

Her maid clung to her arm. "We should hurry, my lady."

"That is what I've been trying to say. Lord Ellis ambushed me at the spring, and he is on his way to Brighthurst House."

Winnie's eyes grew as round as shillings. "Merciful heavens, the earl discovered you in your chemise? Oh dear. This is beyond horrifying."

"You're not comforting me." Clasping hands, they ran for the dower house as the wind whipped through the meadow and plastered Vivi's wet gown against her. The first raindrops splattered the dirt as they reached the house and slipped inside.

Vivi shivered, and her maid put an arm around her shoulders. "Come upstairs, Lady Vivian, before you catch your death."

At this point, death might be the easier solution. "Ash will send me to the nunnery for certain this time."

Winnie squeezed her tight. "Well then, he will have to send me too. I'll not let you wreck havoc on those poor Sisters of Mercy alone."

Vivi almost laughed, but it was hard to find much humor in her complete ruin. "You would do that for me, Win? Perhaps it wouldn't be terrible if you were with me."

"Phoo!" Her maid flicked her hand. "We'll come up with some way to get out of this. But first, let's change you out of these wet clothes."

They ascended the stairs side by side and bustled down the corridor to Vivi's bedchamber. Once the door closed, Vivi wrestled with her damp gown. Winnie hurried forward to assist. With her soiled gown discarded and a dry one donned, Vivi rushed to the window to search for signs of Lord Ellis. The gravel drive was deserted.

"Egads. It's raining like the devil."

A blinding flash and boom caused her to jump back with a scream.

Rain pinged against the glass, deafening with its intensity, and dark clouds blotted out the sunlight.

"Tell everyone we must put lights in every window."

"Yes, my lady."

A deep rumble vibrated the windowpanes. Her heart hammered against her ribs.

Surely Lord Ellis would throttle her for deceiving him. If he survived.

26 August 1818

Dear Lady Brighthurst,

I am writing to inform you of a change in plans. Lord Ellis's journey has been delayed, so he will no longer be calling at Brighthurst House. Fortunately, there has been a change in my schedule as well, and I will be free to make Lady Vivian's acquaintance in two days' time.

I apologize in advance for my lack of forewarning, but I have only a brief period of time in which I may visit. I do hope my presence is not a burden to you.

I have also written to Lady Vivian's brother in London to apprise him of my visit.

> *Sincerely,*
> *Foxhaven*

Two

Vivi sent her maid downstairs to inform the other servants of Lord Ellis's impending arrival. Meanwhile, she wanted to check in on Cousin Patrice, who had been ill since yesterday.

She knocked on Patrice's door and strained to hear a response. Easing the door open, she slipped inside and waited for her eyes to adjust to the dusky light.

"May I come in?"

"Vivi," her cousin croaked then coughed with such violence, Vivi feared she might expel a lung.

She rushed to the side table to pour a glass of water. "Oh for heaven's sake. Where is Bea? You shouldn't be left alone."

Patrice struggled to prop herself up on the bed pillows. Her breathing sounded ragged in the silence of the chamber. Perhaps Vivi should have the doctor retrieved again. "I sent Bea away," Patrice said.

"Whatever were you thinking?" Vivi lifted the glass to her cousin's lips to allow her a small sip. "You need her help."

Patrice waved her off when she tried to give her

another drink. "Bea is just a girl and frightened out of her wits. Besides, her mumblings about me dying and coming back to haunt her were beginning to annoy me."

Vivi replaced the glass on the side table and huffed. "Silly girl and her ridiculous superstitions. Why, if you were to haunt anyone, I would think it would be that dreadful Mrs. Honeywell."

Patrice's chuckle quickly turned into another bout of hacking into her handkerchief. Vivi stepped forward to assist, but there was nothing she could do. When her cousin could breathe again, she rested her head against the pillows and closed her eyes. "You mustn't speak that way about the good lady."

Vivi saw nothing redeeming in Mrs. Honeywell. She was a tyrant who lorded her husband's status as the largest landholder in the area over everyone in the village. In addition, she had been holding Vivi's family hostage for nearly two Seasons, offering to keep Vivi's secret in exchange for an invitation to stay with Ash and his wife in London. Vivi's sister-in-law had been so angry about being burdened with the busybody's company that she had refused to allow Vivi to join them. Not that she had any desire to spend more time with Mrs. Honeywell. Vivi had had quite enough of the woman's meddling the rest of the year.

Mrs. Honeywell also possessed an unnatural interest in Patrice's affairs. What care was it of hers if Vicar Ramsey called on Vivi's cousin more than he did on his other parishioners? Didn't the Bible charge Christians with the duty to visit the widowed? She couldn't be certain—her mind did tend to wander during the vicar's uninspiring sermons—but it sounded like a reasonable charge to her. Something that *should* be in the Bible if it wasn't.

"Remember what the vicar says about turning the other cheek," Patrice said.

Vivi lowered her gaze to give the appearance of contrition, but the gossipmonger could go jump in a lake for all she cared. "Forgive me for speaking out of turn, Cousin."

"Thank you, dearest. I'm pleased my lessons in humility are not going unheeded."

She repressed a sigh. She owed much to her cousin. Humility seemed a small price to pay in return. Patrice had devoted the last ten years to Vivi's well-being, educating her and showering her with the affection she had lost after her parents died and her brother married. Vivi might have been sent to the convent as soon as her brother's bride moved into Ashden House if not for Patrice's plea to allow Vivi to live with her.

She swallowed around the large lump forming in her throat. No matter how many sacrifices Patrice made for her, they seemed to be made in vain. Vivi inherently disappointed everyone who cared for her.

Patrice weakly patted her hand. "Did you need something?"

She looked away, unable to meet her cousin's eye. Her gaze landed on a welcome distraction, a stack of unopened correspondence on the writing desk. "Would you like me to sort your post?"

She started for the desk, but Patrice stopped her with a touch to her arm. "The post can wait until I am well. I should rest now, dearest."

"Of course. Forgive me." Vivi placed a kiss on Patrice's forehead then turned for the door.

"Oh, Vivi?"

She stopped at the doorway and looked back over her shoulder. Patrice already had her eyes closed.

"Thank you for discussing next week's menu with Cook. I am certain Lord Ellis will have a pleasant stay."

"It's my pleasure," she mumbled.

Patrice sank against the pillows with a serene smile. "If your brother could see you, he would be proud."

Her brother could visit her any time he wished. He had chosen to keep his distance since the incident with Owen.

Her cousin's eyes fluttered open and she studied Vivi. "It is hard to believe you were once the high-spirited girl who arrived on my doorstep long ago. You have transformed into a beautiful lady. The duke will be delighted."

Vivi slipped into the corridor without responding. She had become too good at hiding her true nature from Patrice. She was exactly the same hoyden who had arrived on her cousin's doorstep, a pretender who had been caught in a lie by the one man she needed most to convince she was a lady.

❦

A bright, white flash and deafening crack split the air.

"Damnation!"

Luke Forest, the Duke of Foxhaven, gripped his

horse's reins tighter. The hairs on his arms stood on end and his heart raced.

Another bolt of lightning struck a nearby tree, splintering the upper trunk. Thor jerked and nearly unseated him. He held fast, his legs clutching the horse's quivering sides.

"You're not afraid of a little lightning, are you?"

Deep-throated thunder rumbled the ground, earning an uneasy whinny from the horse.

"I'm not fond of it either." Luke straightened in the saddle and urged Thor into a trot. It might be treacherous to hurry along the rutted lane in fading light, but no more dangerous than riding in a thunderstorm.

A gust of wind ripped his hat from his head, but another blinding flash and concurrent explosion discouraged him from turning back for it. Rain saturated what had been left of his dry hair and dripped into his ear. He must look like a drowned rat by this point. Certainly, he was less appealing than the water sprite he had come across earlier.

Silly chit. She either had no sense of direction, or else she had purposefully misled him as punishment for disturbing her swim. It was a good thing he had come across another gentleman on the road who was able to provide better instructions than "go that way."

Of course, if Luke had followed her directions, he would be safely ensconced in the White Wolf Inn enjoying a thick steak and a tankard of ale. But where was the thrill in playing it safe? If he were to die, at least it would be on his terms. No chance of death catching him unaware today.

Lights flickered through the trees; shelter from the

storm was close. As they rounded the bend, a house lit up like a fireworks display loomed in the distance. He grinned. This must be Brighthurst House, and the likely employer of the mischievous water sprite.

Too bad he wouldn't have enough time to deal with the impertinent wench, but he was at Brighthurst for one purpose only. He would see this arrangement between him and the Marquess of Ashden's sister dissolved as quickly as possible and return to London to finalize his arrangements with Captain Pendry. His task, however, was of a sensitive nature and required finesse. It was better for him to speak with Lady Vivian in person rather than entrusting his friend, Ellis, to handle the matter.

He had his father's legacy to consider, but Lady Vivian's welfare was at stake as well. She was an innocent in this situation. She didn't deserve to be caught in the middle of a battle between Luke and her brother. In their last audience, her brother had vowed to call Luke out and declare his father a liar if he refused to honor the marriage settlement, a worthless threat given Ashden was more versed in Latin and antiquities than weaponry. Luke would win in a duel easily, his father would be exonerated, and yet Lady Vivian's reputation would be in tatters.

What had his father been thinking to enter into negotiations with a man who would put his pride before his sister?

Luke had been mulling over his father's covert actions often lately, and he was inclined to agree with his mother's companion, Johanna Truax. This arranged marriage had been one more attempt by his father to force him into becoming what he was incapable of being. Father had refused to accept the truth about him. Luke hadn't been the same since his accident, and no amount of browbeating could make him regain what he had lost. If not for his brother, Richard, at the helm this last year, Luke didn't know what would have become of his family.

He didn't wish to drag another person into his disordered life. This ridiculous betrothal could go away quietly if Lady Vivian's brother was a reasonable man, but he wasn't. The marquess had refused to listen to reason, but perhaps an appeal from his sister would sway him.

As Luke rode up to the house, a groom ran to greet him. He shouted instructions and handed over Thor's reins. The driving rain drowned out the man's response as he led Thor to the stables straightaway.

Luke bounded up the stairs, and the front door of Brighthurst House swung open. A butler waved him inside.

He bowed low. "Welcome to Brighthurst—"

"I'm flooding Lady Brighthurst's floor, my good man. Save the pleasantries for another day."

The man drew back, clearly aghast at his brusque manner. Luke was more concerned about ruining his hostess's home than observing the pomp and circumstance associated with his station or shocking the butler.

He tugged off his gloves and handed them to the servant. Two footmen hurried forward, one to remove his drenched jacket and the other to extend a towel.

"Thank you. Now if you would kindly show me to my quarters so I might make myself presentable."

The butler's shaggy gray brows shot upward, but

he nodded to one of the footmen. "Do you have no trunks, sir?"

Had he arrived before his valet and trunks again? Luke must have a discussion with his driver about dallying. Now he was in a predicament. He couldn't request an audience with Lady Brighthurst and her charge in his sorry state, but he didn't wish to tarry longer than necessary either. "Perhaps my staff took shelter from the storm. I expect my personal belongings will arrive tomorrow."

The butler's gaze swept over him as if he was trying to puzzle out what type of man traveled in the middle of a thunderstorm. The servant's placating smile indicated he thought Luke was a tad unhinged.

"Very good, sir. I will locate a change of clothing for you to wear for dinner. Lady Brighthurst kept her late husband's wardrobe."

Luke hesitated rather than follow the footman above stairs. Perhaps before the loss of his father, he wouldn't have blinked an eye at the butler's suggestion. "Are there no other options for attire? I don't wish to give the good lady a shock by arriving for our interview in Lord Brighthurst's jacket."

The servant nodded his understanding. "I fear her ladyship is indisposed and unable to receive you this evening."

Luke suppressed a sigh. He had hoped to get to the business at hand and return to Town no later than tomorrow. "How long do you expect Lady Brighthurst will be unavailable?"

"It is difficult to say. She has taken to her bed with a chill."

Devil take it. "I see. Please, extend my wishes for a speedy recovery."

"Lady Vivian will fulfill her ladyship's hostess duties this evening. She has asked me to inform you dinner will be served at eight."

"Extend my appreciation to Lady Vivian. I look forward to dining with the lady this evening."

He had desired her kinswoman's blessing before speaking alone with Lady Vivian, but obviously she had been accommodating enough to procure it for him.

Accommodating and amiable. Luke had no objections to those qualities. It was the words *obedient, docile,* and *domesticated* her brother had used to describe her that left him unsettled. If Luke valued those characteristics, he could get a dog.

Three

VIVI'S MAID TIPPED HER HEAD TO THE SIDE AS SHE studied Vivi's reflection in the looking glass. "If Lady Brighthurst thought she didn't recognize you earlier…"

The conversation with Patrice had given Vivi an idea. She had to try something to salvage her situation, and she had nothing more to lose.

At best, Lord Ellis would return to London with reports of her eccentricity. Being considered eccentric, however, was preferable to being labeled a scandalous hoyden who swam in her unmentionables and sent gentlemen to their deaths by stranding them in storms.

As long as she didn't take things too far… She didn't want the distinguished title of Batty Lady Vivian bestowed on her either. She turned to the side to view her disguise from a different angle and frowned. She walked a thin line. Donning the former Lady Brighthurst's red pouf wig practically screamed Bedlam candidate.

"What is your opinion?"

Her maid shrugged. "It's not bad."

In truth, the coiffure was hideous. But after searching

every old trunk in the attic, the pouf—adorned with a life-size faux peahen nestled in the curls as if the bird took to roost—was the closest to normal she and Winnie could find. How very telling of the former countess's fashion sense, or lack thereof.

"Should I trim the top again?" her maid asked.

Vivi shook her head and knocked herself off balance. She grabbed on to Winnie to steady herself, and they both had a fit of nervous giggles.

Earlier Winnie had wrestled the bird from its perch then trimmed two inches from the height of the pouf with a set of garden shears borrowed from the greenhouse. It was still a ridiculous creation that shot into the air like the Tower of Babel, but any more alterations and the wire frame underneath would show.

Their laughter died down and Vivi turned around slowly, testing the weight of the hair monstrosity. "If this abomination doesn't hide my identity, at least it will distract Lord Ellis from looking too closely at my face."

Winnie grinned. "And if not, falling flat on your bum should divert his attention. Although I am not sure you want him looking too closely down there either."

Vivi moved to her dressing table to hide her embarrassment. "I told you, he didn't see anything."

"Indeed. He was a perfect gentleman."

"He was."

She didn't know the reason she defended the man, but he had behaved with gentlemanly restraint, for the most part.

Winnie pried the lid off a tin of Patrice's rouge, poked her finger into the jar, and with a grimace, applied the color to Vivi's lips. "If this *doesn't* work, your betrothed will receive an earful from the earl."

"It has to work." Vivi rose from her seat and smoothed her hands over her skirts. "Lord Ellis cannot realize it was me he saw today."

Her maid held out a fan. "Wave it in front of your face often to obscure his view."

"Brilliant suggestion." She accepted the offering and walked from her chambers as quickly as the wig would allow.

As she glided down the curved staircase, she refused to acknowledge Saunders's quizzical glance. The butler would likely report her odd fashion choice to Patrice later, but he knew his place and kept his opinions quiet. She would tell Patrice the truth once her cousin was well.

If she asked.

Or if Vivi's plan failed.

Picking up her pace, she made her way to the formal dining room, her skirts whispering around her ankles. She had never cared for the dining room. It was self-important and stuffy, but appropriate for a visiting nobleman. Most importantly, the dining room housed a long table that was unsuited for prolonged discussions or thorough inspections of one's dining partner. If she made it through the meal without Lord Ellis becoming wise to her, she would collapse with relief once she reached her chambers again. The moment the earl continued on his journey couldn't come soon enough.

Dim light spilled from the opened doorway of the dining room and onto the polished marble floor. At the threshold, she paused. The servants had followed her directions nicely, leaving the room cast in shadows.

She ventured into the dining room, intent upon reaching the seat farthest from the door so her guest had no need to pass by her. Her gaze traveled to the mantel clock. She had fifteen minutes left to gather her wits.

"Lady Vivian, I presume?" The rich timbre vibrated within her chest, sending shock waves quaking through her arms and legs.

"Oh!" Vivi recoiled then shot her hands out for balance.

Lord Ellis was standing beside his chair. His quick blue eyes narrowed. "You are Lady Vivian, are you not?"

"Yes." She snapped the fan open and fluttered it in front of her face as much to hide her identity as to cool her scorched cheeks. He was early again! A most unbecoming habit. "I didn't see you there."

She lowered her head and dashed past his seat.

"Perhaps the servants should light the chandelier," he said.

Her lips strained with the effort of forcing a smile as she assumed her place at the table. "That would be wasteful, wouldn't you agree?"

He nodded thoughtfully. "Quite right, Lady Vivian. How sensible of you."

A frisson of pleasure rippled through her until she recognized his compliment was tainted by sarcasm. Sinking into her seat, she noted with satisfaction that the massive arrangement erected between them blocked him from her view. The earl would have a devil of a time seeing her through the floral jungle.

"Lady Vivian?" Lord Ellis leaned to the side to peer around the peonies. His black hair gleamed in the candlelight and his eyes sparkled. "Ah, there you are. I feared I had lost you for a moment."

She lifted her arms to allow a footman to drape a napkin over her lap. "I suppose a man of your station expects more of a fuss, but as it is my cousin's larder and not my own, I didn't feel at liberty to prepare a lavish affair. Please forgive the oversight."

"On the contrary. I have been made to feel comfortable at Brighthurst. Your cousin is most gracious." He disappeared behind the arrangement again as a second footman reached his end of the table with a bottle of wine. He murmured something to the servant before returning his attention to her. "I'm sorry to hear Lady Brighthurst is unable to dine with us this evening."

"I will convey your regrets. She will be sorry to have missed making your acquaintance."

The footman serving Lord Ellis headed in her direction, stopped halfway, and then plucked the arrangement from the table.

Vivi stifled a gasp and snatched up her glass of lemonade. She took a long sip, trying to hide and likely failing.

A corner of Lord Ellis's mouth kicked up. He nodded to the footman. "Lady Vivian appears thirsty. Please refill her glass."

Once her glass had been refilled, he raised his for a toast. "To Lady Brighthurst and her entertaining kinswoman. May fortune smile upon Brighthurst House and her occupants from this day forward."

Vivi pressed her lips together before she said something

she would regret. He was laughing at her. Maybe not outright, but the humorous ring to his voice and glittering blue eyes were evidence he made sport of her. Her jaw twitched, and she barely noticed the footman placing the bowl of soup in front of her through the red clouding her vision.

Entertaining kinswoman indeed. "I'm not mad," she blurted.

"No?" He lobbed a crooked grin toward her end of the table. "How delightful to know, my lady."

⤜⤏

A servant hurried forward to refill Luke's wine goblet, but he waved him away. His gaze remained on Lady Vivian. Her answers to his questions had grown cooler and more clipped during the first course. She refused to meet his gaze and often seemed to be attempting to shield her face with a delicate touch of her napkin to her lips or a well-placed hand to her brow.

Did she think him too dense to recognize her from their afternoon encounter?

He didn't wish to shatter her fantasy, but Lady Vivian would be recognizable even in a beaver hat and mustachio. The relic she wore on her head couldn't disguise her in the least, if that indeed was her aim.

She was an Incomparable.

And unforgettable.

Had he realized when he had come upon her swimming that she was a lady instead of a maid, he would have practiced more restraint and not peeked. But he had. Long enough to make his blood run hot again as he recalled the vision: The creamy swells of her breasts. The gentle curve of her shoulders. A honey-colored curl plastered to her round cheek.

His body hummed at the prospect of pursuing her. Not that he must pursue the lady, since her brother offered her like a gift to a sultan with no regard for what she might think. The daft man. Luke would never treat his sisters with such callousness.

He loosened his grip on the carved wooden armrests where his finger had molded to the deep grooves and cleared his throat. "Your cousin's cook is to be praised for this exquisite fare. Is this duck or goose?"

Lady Vivian looked up with a wry smile twisting her full lips.

He glanced down at his plate, realizing too late that he hadn't touched his braised *beef*.

"I will pass along your compliment, my lord." She was kind enough not to call him a dimwit, at least to his face.

He speared a carrot and tried to sort out what was happening here at Brighthurst. Ashden's sister—if she was indeed his sister and not a maid pretending to be Lady Vivian, which seemed unlikely given her poise and the other servants' deference to her—did not meet any of his expectations.

She was nothing like the simpering daughters of the *ton* he had been sidestepping these last few years.

He had wanted to be done with the matter quickly when he had arrived, but damn if he could walk away from the riddle Lady Vivian Worth posed. Captain Pendry's expedition couldn't go forward until Luke saw to a few matters, but he couldn't leave Brighthurst until he had some answers.

He pinched the bridge of his nose and sighed heavily. "Are you ill?"

Her slightly harassed tone reminded him of his manners. Smoothing his hands over the napkin on his lap, he regained his composure. "Lady Vivian, perhaps we might adjourn to the drawing room after dinner. I have a few inquiries I wish to make."

"Inquiries?" Even from a distance, the lady's cheeks looked flushed. She whipped out her ivory fan and waved it, sending tendrils of bronzed hair fluttering at her temples.

"Just a few questions, if you please." He flashed a smile to show he meant no harm.

She grabbed her drink and slowly drained the contents. When she set the glass down again, she took a long time blotting the napkin to her reddened lips.

Tension coiled in his lower belly. She was either stalling or attempting to drive him to distraction.

"I am afraid I must beg off, sir. My cousin should take part in our interview, and she is abed with a chill. I hope you understand."

She smiled, appearing too smug by half at deflecting him handily.

"I understand, Lady Vivian." He would not allow her to dismiss him, however. "I will wait until Lady Brighthurst recovers before conducting my interview."

The lady's eyes flew open wide. "Wait? But it could be days. Perhaps a week."

"Then I must find ways to occupy my time while Lady Brighthurst recovers." He propped his elbow on the padded armrest. "I'm an early riser. Perhaps I will pay a visit to the dairy barn tomorrow."

"Why?"

"There is a matter I would like to discuss with one of Lady Brighthurst's servants, a milkmaid, I believe." He was teasing her; surely she would realize he knew who she was and give up her ruse. "Of course if I can't find the chit, I will have to ask Lady Brighthurst in what area of the house she works."

"Oh." Lady Vivian stared at him with lips parted. "Oh," she said again then pushed away from the table.

Luke stood too.

She started for the door. "Forgive me. I really must look in on my kin now."

The fear in her expression made his stomach pitch. He hadn't meant to frighten her.

"Lady Vivian."

She veered away from his outstretched hand. "The servants will provide you with whatever you require. Good evening."

She dashed through the doorway and disappeared, leaving nothing but the lingering scent of her sweet perfume and the echo of her footsteps as she ran down the corridor.

He sighed and sank into his seat. Now what was he to do? Lifting his goblet, he signaled for the footman to refill his wine.

He wished he could consult with Miss Truax on how to handle Lady Vivian. He trusted his mother's companion when it came to the workings of the female mind. She had been pivotal in coming to understand his sisters and reconnect with them after their father's passing. But Luke was on his own this time. He would have to draw on what little he had learned about ladies' minds from spending time with his mother and sisters this past year.

Of course, with Lady Vivian, no amount of experience or study of the fairer gender might help him. She was a mystery. One he intended to solve.

Four

"LADY VIVIAN, WAKE UP."

A warm hand grasped Vivi's shoulder and shook her. Her eyes flew open and she blinked, her surroundings slowly coming into focus.

Floral bed curtains.

Quilted counterpane.

Her window seat.

Her location sunk in. Rolling onto her back, she stared up into Winnie's frowning face, which was entirely too close with her leaning over the bed. "It's time to get up, my lady."

"But it is dark outside." Vivi's voice sounded gravelly, like an old man's after forty years of pipe smoking.

Her lady's maid straightened and nibbled her fingernail. "When did you *think* the cows were milked, my lady?"

Not at this ungodly hour. "They can't desire to be awake any more than I do." She curled on her side, pulling the sheet up to her neck. "Let the poor creatures sleep in today."

"But if Lord Ellis wakes and ventures outside…" Winnie shook her again. "What if he goes to your cousin?"

She flopped on her back with a groan. *Infuriating man!* "I'm getting up."

"You had best hurry, my lady. The milkmaid is already in the barn." Winnie tossed a spare maid's dress on the bed, then grabbed both of Vivi's hands to pull her into a seated position.

Vivi rubbed her eyes with the back of her hand and yawned. This whole pretense was likely a waste of time. "I think he recognized me already." The thought had kept her awake late into the night.

Her maid retreated to a tea cart and poured steaming chocolate from a pot. "Then why didn't he say something at dinner?"

She shrugged and climbed from the bed before accepting the cup of chocolate. "Maybe he wants to be certain before he carries back a report to the duke." She sipped the drink and welcomed the warmth on her scratchy throat. "I have been thinking, perhaps life in the nunnery won't be as horrid as I have imagined. Not exciting, mind you, what with no one but the sisters to talk to and such a drab wardrobe. But I am coming to accept my fate."

"Since when?" Winnie said with a scoff.

"Since the clock struck two this morning, Miss Impertinent."

"Then please forgive me for speaking out of turn, my lady." Her maid didn't appear the least bit contrite with a small smile upon her lips. "Would you be so kind as to lift your arms?"

Vivi placed her cup on her dressing table and did as her maid requested so her nightrail could be removed. "Perhaps I can convince Lord Ellis to keep our meeting at the creek a secret. I would hate for Patrice to know the true reason behind the duke's rejection."

"I've never known you to surrender without a fight," Winnie said while Vivi was still buried under her nightclothes. "Maybe Lord Ellis only wishes to scold you for sending him out of the way in the middle of a storm."

Vivi's heart lifted a fraction. If her maid was correct, Lord Ellis might say his piece and forget all about their encounter at the creek. She could still free Patrice to marry the man she loved without dooming herself to live in the convent. This was incentive enough to don the serviceable dress and pretend she knew the first thing about milking cows.

She smoothed her hands over the rough fustian gown, readjusted the white cap covering her loosely bound hair, and then turned away from her reflection. "Wish me luck at fooling the earl."

"Oh, my lady. Can't I wish for something more likely to come true?"

She tossed a wry smile over her shoulder. "Again, you are no comfort, dear Winnie."

"My apologies, my lady."

Vivi eased the door open, determined the corridor was clear, and sped toward the servants' stairwell. A lamp at the foot of the stairs cast elongated shadows on the walls as she made her way to the ground floor. She retrieved a spare lantern hanging from a peg and lit it before opening the back door.

Outside, the cool morning air held the promise of autumn with the smell of freshly cut hay hanging on the breeze. She both loved and dreaded the season, knowing cold weather chased on its heels. Yet, on the other side of winter, there was always a new beginning. Vivi tried to keep this foremost in her mind. There was still a chance she could get out of this mess.

Worst case, Vivi wasn't above groveling for mercy.

❧

The chamber was dark when Luke woke. An unfamiliar creak as someone passed outside the door reminded him of where he was. *Brighthurst*. The home of his would-be betrothed. A surge of alertness swept through him, and he tossed the counterpane aside to sit on the side of the bed.

Lady Vivian wasn't making his task easy, and not because she lived up to her brother's definition of the perfect lady. She was a scandal waiting to happen. Most gentlemen would find it within their rights to sever the betrothal after discovering her half-nude in the creek. Luke wasn't like most gentlemen, however.

Lady Vivian's unorthodox pursuits provided no reason to destroy her future, and he wouldn't consider using his discovery against her. She must make an appeal to her brother. If her brother released them from the agreement before anyone learned of it, she wouldn't suffer. But first Luke must garner her cooperation, which required the audience he had yet to be granted.

He grumbled under his breath as he climbed from bed and made his way to the mantel to retrieve the tinderbox. There was no telling how long he would be delayed while Lady Vivian's cousin recovered, and his business with Captain Pendry couldn't wait. Luke's man of business had forwarded him the ship's manifest and an accounting of the costs required for supplies. He needed to review the documents before authorizing payment, but he had hoped to ask his friend for help. Captain Daniel Hillary could complete the task in his sleep after years of sea travel, but Hillary was leaving for Brighton at the end of the week. Luke's hopes of catching him before he left London were dwindling. He would have to complete the work himself.

The char cloth sparked and caught fire. He lit a candle, dressed, and then pulled the documents from an inside coat pocket. Sitting down at the small desk, he resigned to get the task behind him. A tightening in his jaws began before he read half the page. Rubbing the back of his neck, he discovered bunched muscles already forming. Another blasted headache. By the second page, his vision began to blur and a band squeezed his head like an ill-fitting hat. He blinked and tried to clear his sight, but the ink remained a hazy mess on the page.

Devil take it. He threw the papers aside and pushed to his feet. The movement set off a dull drumming in his skull. He cursed aloud. Captain Pendry was at a standstill until Luke responded to his request. Why couldn't he perform even the simplest tasks without these headaches plaguing him?

He moved to the window and shoved the drapes aside, disgusted. Dawn had begun her subtle painting of the sky. He'd watched many sunrises lately. Even before his father's death he had been an early riser, but this past year had seen him awake more hours than asleep.

He'd lost his chance to make his father proud,

and no amount of wishing would ever bring him back. Before his father's death, Luke had been too busy raising hell. He needed adventure, craved the thrill of putting his life on the line. Sitting in a study going over ledgers was boring, and he'd avoided his father—and his duties—every chance he could.

After Luke's accident he avoided his father for another reason. Shame. What if the duke found out he could barely read without debilitating headaches? How could he care for the estate? He would be the ruination of their family.

Sometimes fury over his father's death expanded inside him, pushing words from his mind. How could he have died? How could he have left him alone?

This morning his usual disgust with himself was nudged aside by puzzlement as he recalled his encounters with Lady Vivian.

"Why her?"

Of course, his father couldn't have been aware of the lady's true nature. Her high spirits would earn his father's disapproval, even though they appealed to Luke more than he cared to admit.

A figure passed below the window, dragging him from his reverie. It was a woman, and she held a lantern aloft, lighting amber curls spilling down her back.

His pulse quickened. "Lady Vivian?"

Without a chaperone again.

He shook his head, not believing what he was seeing. What was the minx up to now? He grabbed his jacket and left his chambers in pursuit.

He found the corridor for a back staircase, hoping for a quicker route to the barn. He held himself in check as he stepped outside, his muscles tense and his stomach churning with anticipation. He was about to engage Lady Vivian in round three.

The mewling of a calf intermingled with Lady Vivian's rich laughter and drifted through the open door of the dairy barn as he neared. The lady expressed her mirth with hearty vigor, the smoky sound drawing him inside. He hurried his step, eager to see her again.

The smells of sweet hay and musky animal hit him as he entered. He spotted her at once, but Lady Vivian had her back to him. She was scratching behind the ears of a spotted calf tethered to a post. The baby nudged her hand and elicited another heart-stopping chuckle from the lady.

"Patience, little one. You may have your mama in a minute."

She rose on her toes and leaned her crossed arms on the top railing of a stall to peer at a full-grown milker. The cow flicked a bored gaze in his direction, but Lady Vivian seemed unaware of his presence.

Luke cleared his throat.

She swung around with a soft gasp. The rhythmic swish, swish of milk squirting into a bucket ceased.

He meant to appear unaffected, but he couldn't help grinning. The lady was as charming in maid's attire as she had been soaking wet yesterday.

She dipped into a deep curtsy. "How relieved I am no harm came to you yesterday, sir."

"Life is full of surprises, is it not?" Of course Lady Vivian was the biggest surprise, along with her tenacity. That she clung to her pretense fascinated him.

Luke approached her, caring not that he stared.

Lady Vivian's cheeks colored. She backed around the calf, her half boots stirring the hay. He didn't slow his advance. Not when he would reach her in two strides and earn the reward of gazing at her up close.

"Time to milk." She dashed into the stall, avoiding direct eye contact. Avoiding *him*. "I am sorry for providing unclear directions yesterday, but you found Brighthurst."

Unclear directions? The chit had purposefully misled him. He followed her into the stall. "Apology accepted."

She tossed a look back over her shoulder. Her pale blue eyes softened. "Thank you. You are a generous soul, Lord Ellis."

He balked. *Lord Ellis?* She thought *he* was Ellis? How could that be when he had sent word?

The servant girl—likely the true milkmaid—scooted from the stool to allow Lady Vivian to sit, then shimmed past him to exit the stall.

"Thank you, Kimberly. I will finish the task," Lady Vivian said.

The milkmaid bobbed her head and left him alone with her mistress.

Lady Vivian offered a tight smile when he crossed his arms and regarded her. "I wish you a safe journey as you continue your travels. Good day, my lord."

She thought to send him on his way, did she? Well, she had misjudged him. He was fond of games of strategy, and he couldn't resist engaging with her, though he didn't know the rules or what the winner's spoils would be.

"I'm in no hurry to leave. I informed Lady Vivian last night I intend to stay until Lady Brighthurst recovers."

She flinched. It was barely noticeable, but Luke

hadn't taken his eyes from her since he had entered the barn. It was a near impossible feat.

"Go on with your work. I don't want to interrupt you." Luke squatted beside her. "I have often wondered how one goes about milking a cow."

"Uh…"

A becoming shade of pink climbed her neck and infused her round cheeks. He shouldn't tease her before revealing he knew her identity, but the lengths she would go to in order to fool him were impressive. He awaited her next move with great anticipation.

"You don't mind if I watch, do you?" he asked.

She hesitated, but then shook her head. The curls gathered at her nape swung in a gentle arc along her back. He itched to loosen the tie confining her hair and run his fingers through the fine strands. He made a fist and held it against his thigh. It wouldn't do to treat her with anything other than the respect her station deserved.

"Go on. Don't be shy on account of my presence."

She closed her eyes, her darker lashes lying against her rosy skin. Perhaps she hoped when she opened them again, he would be gone.

No such luck.

She stole a quick sideways glance at him then directed her attention back to the milker. "There, there, Maggie." Patting the animal's side, she eased her hand under the cow, her lip curling. When the tips of her fingers touched the creature's udders, she snatched her hand back with a soft squeal.

Luke concealed his amusement behind a fake cough. "Are the udders cold?"

Lady Vivian frowned, expressing her disdain with a lift of her nose. "They feel like flesh, my lord, but I wouldn't expect someone like you to be privy to such information."

"Fascinating. Just like flesh, you say? Please continue, unless you have changed your mind about milking."

Her mouth set in a grim line. "I haven't changed my mind."

He admired her determination.

Taking a deep, halting breath first, she shot out her arm and seized one of the udders. A strangled moo ripped from the cow, and the animal stomped close to Lady Vivian's foot. The lady jerked back with a cry and kicked over the pail of milk.

"Oh, drat it all anyway!"

Luke chuckled and reached out to stroke her shoulder in a comforting gesture before realizing what he was doing.

Her body grew rigid under his touch. "My lord! What, pray tell, are you doing?"

Luke dropped his hand. "My apologies. I didn't mean—" He took a deep breath to regain control over his rapid heartbeat. "Lady Vivian, let's end all pretenses, shall we? You are not a servant any more than I am, and I would hazard a guess that you have never milked a cow."

Ice blue eyes, so light they reminded him of melted silver, turned on him. The defiant spark he had seen moments earlier dimmed. "You knew at dinner."

"Yes, I'm afraid I did." When her shoulders drooped forward, he took her hand in his. The need to ease her discomfort welled up inside him, confusing and yet too strong to ignore. "It is an honor to make your acquaintance, my lady."

Raising her hand, he placed a chaste kiss on her fingers. Her skin was soft and warm against his lips. He hesitated to release her from his light grasp. This was an intimacy he had never experienced upon an introduction, the feel of a lady's bare skin. Pushing the limits of propriety, he gently turned her arm to bare her wrist and grazed his mouth over the sensitive spot.

Lady Vivian trembled, her eyes wide. "Lord Ellis, release me. *Please*." She yanked her arm from his hold.

Luke's stomach dipped. What the hell was he doing? He aimed a cool smile at her. "Allow me to correct a misconception, Lady Vivian. I'm not Lord Ellis. I sent word to Lady Brighthurst three days ago. I am your intended."

He didn't know why he introduced himself in such a manner. When he had set out for Brighthurst House, he'd had no intention of fulfilling his father's promise. Nothing had changed, except his unconscionable impulse to take liberties not belonging to him. Luke eased away from her, remembering himself.

Lady Vivian twisted on the stool to face him. She held her tongue, but an array of emotions flickered across her countenance until impatience threatened to claw through him.

"What are you thinking, Lady Vivian?"

She licked her lips, chipping away at his determination to release her from this farce of a betrothal.

"Do you wish for complete honesty, Your Grace?"

He grinned for real this time, relieved that his disclosure and inappropriateness hadn't rattled her as much as he had feared. "Even partial honesty would be appreciated, my lady."

Her gaze dropped to the ground. "Right," she mumbled. "A little censorship might be in order."

He captured her hands again and urged her to look at him. "On second thought, be fiercely honest. What were you thinking a moment ago?"

She tried to ease her hands from his grasp, but he held on tight. Whether it was by instinct or will, he didn't know, but she curled her fingers around his and secured the link between them.

Her swallow was audible. "I was thinking how much I regret messing up our agreement. I never imagined you would be so handsome, Your Grace."

Luke laughed, reveling in the warmth swirling around in his chest. He was not naive when it came to marriage. Mutual attraction couldn't sustain a happy union over the years, and there was no question that he was unusually attracted to the lady. Nevertheless, he had witnessed the subsequent misery of many gentlemen who were swept up by lustful urges then disappointed when the bloom of beauty faded. These were the gents sleeping at White's every evening, complaining about their greedy mistresses and harpy wives.

He still took pleasure in Lady Vivian's admission.

"I have no intention of dishonoring my father's word, my lady." He noted the lifting of her arched brows. "But perhaps you will do me the honor of speaking with your brother so we may both be freed."

Five

VIVI JERKED HER HANDS FROM FOXHAVEN'S GRASP, jumped up, and tripped backward over the stool. The duke lunged for her, but she fell hard on her backside in the dirt.

The cow swung her head toward Vivi and fixed a sad brown eye on her.

"Don't you dare feel sorry for me," she blurted.

Foxhaven stepped over the stool and hauled her from the ground. "Why would I feel sorry for you?"

"Not you." Vivi dusted off her hands and jabbed a finger toward the cow. "Maggie. I don't want *her* pity."

His gaze shot between Maggie and her. His forehead wrinkled. "I see this has been a shock, Lady Vivian. Perhaps you should go lie down and we can resume our discussion later."

There was no discussion to be had. She couldn't ask her brother to release her from the agreement.

Foxhaven bobbed his head so he was in her line of vision again. The lines between his brows deepened. "Are you all right? You didn't sustain an injury, did you?"

Aside from a throbbing bum, no. Unless she counted

her wounded pride. Tears burned at the back of her eyes. "I have no need to lie down, Your Grace. Now, if you will excuse me, I am changing my attire and going for my morning ride. You—you have turned everything topsy-turvy with your arrival, and I'll not stand for it any longer."

She tried to step around Foxhaven before she blubbered a river, but he blocked her retreat. "Wait a moment. I didn't mean to upset you."

Upset her? *Ha!* She was not upset. Try devastated. Reeling. Desperate. "I have no say in our betrothal, Your Grace. My brother has made his decision."

"Every lady should have a voice in whom she marries. Surely Ashden will listen if you try to reason with him. Your brother is too stubborn to listen to my arguments, but no good can come from this match."

Vivi drew back. How blunt he was, and hurtful. He had made a judgment as to her suitability before he had even arrived. She pulled herself up to full height, determined to hang on to the last scraps of her dignity.

"I cannot speak with my brother. I bid you good day."

Again she tried to escape the stall, but he lightly captured her shoulders. His touch muddled her mind and set every nerve ending aflame.

"Lady Vivian, please be reasonable. We don't even know each other."

"Then take your hands from my person before I remove them from *your* person."

Foxhaven's eyes rounded. He had vivid blue eyes. Bluer than anything she had ever seen. Perhaps as blue as the sea. Oh, why had she admitted she found him handsome? This was humiliating beyond the pale.

He exhaled forcefully, stirring the curls on his forehead. "Lady Vivian, could we please start anew? I will release you if you promise not to run."

"I want to go for a ride," she murmured. "Please."

Foxhaven sighed and relaxed his hold. "Of course, my lady. I don't wish to disturb your routine any more than I already have." He dropped his hands to his sides and stepped aside. "Go prepare for your ride."

Vivi dashed past him and out of the barn, running when she cleared the doors. Ash would never allow her to back out, and if Foxhaven refused to sign the contract, her life would be ruined. Worse, her cousin's life would be ruined, and Vivi couldn't live with that guilt.

She needed a long, heart-pounding ride to clear her thoughts. Maybe she would just keep going until she reached the seaside. Perhaps then she could determine if Foxhaven's eyes were indeed the same shade of blue.

❧

After changing into her riding habit, Vivi looked in on Patrice. No violent coughing greeted her this time, and her cousin's breathing was steady and calm. Reassured that Patrice was recovering, Vivi headed outside and stopped short. Foxhaven was standing in the circle drive with the groom, who'd saddled two horses, hers and the duke's.

She ran a hand over the split skirt Winnie had fashioned for her at the beginning of summer. She should have requested a sidesaddle instead of providing the duke with even more reason to oppose their match, but she hadn't expected him to join her. Hadn't she said she wanted to be alone?

Before she could escape unnoticed, Foxhaven looked up and smiled, revealing a small gap between his straight white teeth. "Lady Vivian, your man here assures me you can handle this massive beast."

She took a deep breath, adjusted her bonnet, and approached her bay gelding. Romie's coat shimmered like polished mahogany under the morning sun. "I've had him for years. He was a gift from my brother on my fifteenth birthday." That year had been her best birthday since their parents had died.

Foxhaven stepped forward before the groom to offer assistance mounting her horse. "Ashden must have a lot of faith in you."

Vivi frowned as she accepted the reins from the servant and placed her boot in the duke's cupped hands. "He has faith in my ability to handle a horse, Your Grace." His belief in her was another matter, but she had no one to blame but herself.

Foxhaven lifted her in the air, his muscled chest flexing under his waistcoat. Grasping Romie's mane, she swung her leg over his back and settled into the saddle. She looked away quickly to hide the blush she sensed flooding her cheeks.

He patted her horse's neck; his side brushed against her leg. "I sense a hidden meaning behind your words," he said softly. "Does your brother think you require help with bringing a gentleman up to scratch?"

Her fingers tightened on the reins. "I cannot read thoughts, nor do I possess special insight into the workings of Ashden's mind. Thank you for the leg up."

"My pleasure, Lady Vivian."

When he turned to approach his horse, she seized the moment.

She brought Romie's head around and left Foxhaven in the drive.

❧

"Devil take it!" Luke scrambled to mount Thor and give chase. The lady had an aggravating habit of running away from him, but this time she would not escape. Lady Vivian would grant him an audience even if he must wrestle her to the ground and sit on her.

He snorted. What manner of duke had to beg anyone for an audience or resort to such measures? Not his father.

Ahead, the lady veered off the lane and urged her horse into a gallop across a field. The gelding's hooves threw up clods of grass and dirt in his wake. Luke's body tensed, his vision narrowing on her. She handled her horse better than most men, and looked a hell of a lot better with her bottom lifted inches above the saddle.

His determination to catch her grew, his muscles quivering from the rush. At the edge of the field, he let Thor have his head. The stallion broke into a gallop, his strides long and graceful, eating up the lead she had on him. Just as he and Thor were drawing closer, she slowed her horse to a canter, preparing to stop in deference to a fence ahead.

Luke eased back on his horse's reins. Now was his chance to corner the lady and make her see reason. But she didn't stop. She dropped her heels, rose up in the stirrups, and sailed her horse over the fence. The magnificent animal stuck the landing and raced up the hill without pause.

A delicious shiver chased down Luke's back. He had never had a woman run from him before, and Lady Vivian proved to be a worthy opponent. He pushed his borrowed hat low on his head, squared his horse to the fence, and sailed him over the barrier too. Thor's hooves landed as Lady Vivian and her steed crested the small hill, scattering the sheep, and then disappeared down the other side.

When he reached the top, she and her horse were headed toward a fat ribbon of water twisting through the pasture. It appeared she planned to allow her horse a drink after his impressive performance, but Luke wouldn't put it past her to pick up speed and barrel through the water to race up the next hill.

He refused to abandon the chase until Lady Vivian stopped and dismounted. She led her horse to the water's edge, then released him. The bay walked into the spring, immersing his front hooves, while she wandered along the bank. She bent to pick up stones and flung them along the surface of the water.

One. Two. Three. Four. Five skips.

He drew Thor to a halt a few feet away. "Noteworthy performance, my lady." In truth, she impressed the hell out of him. "Who taught you to ride in that manner?"

She picked up another flat stone and whipped it across the water's surface. "My brother."

"And skipping stones? Did he teach you this as well?"

Looking into the distance, she nodded. "I feel it is only fair to inform you he taught me to shoot and fence too."

Luke chuckled as he dismounted and joined her at the water's edge. "Do you mean to run me through with a sword or put a ball in my chest?"

She spun around, her mouth opened in horror. "Oh no, I didn't mean to imply—"

"Foil or saber?"

Her expression softened, her lips curving up into a half smile. "Foil. Ash thought it unwise to teach me anything beyond the basics, and only when my sister-in-law remained behind at Ashden Manor."

"Your brother never mentioned any of your more interesting accomplishments when we spoke."

She dropped the stone she held and walked toward a willow tree resting along the bank. Its canopy of branches draped over the spring, trailing into the water. "I had intended to give up these pursuits when I married. I don't suppose it matters now."

She sat on a patch of grass and leaned back against the tree trunk. He secured Thor then assumed the place next to her, drawn to her like a hummingbird to a flower.

"I owe you an apology, Your Grace."

"Indeed?" For which transgression?

She picked up a stick and scribbled in the dirt. "I understand your reason for wanting to dishonor our marriage settlement, and I will accept the consequences of my actions. But if any part of you is considering granting me another chance, I promise to abandon my undesirable habits. No more swimming, or riding astride, or shooting."

"And fencing? Will you surrender this endeavor as well?"

She leaned toward him, her expression earnest. "I will devote myself entirely to ladylike occupations, so as not to embarrass you. I give my word."

All the lightness she had awakened in him yesterday dimmed. If their circumstances were different and he could marry her, he would never ask for the concessions she was offering. She shouldn't be forced into giving up who she was to become any man's wife.

Your title would protect her. He scowled at the voice whispering inside his head.

"Lady Vivian, you mustn't think you are responsible for my request to dissolve our betrothal. I possess many faults that render me a poor candidate for a husband."

She drew back, her eyes seeming to double in size. "You do not intend to marry anyone then?"

He shrugged. His future would be determined by whether he returned safely from the voyage.

"But you are a duke. You will have need of an heir, which means you will require a wife at some point."

"That is the current thought among our equals."

"Then reconsider marrying me. *I* will provide you with an heir."

Luke grinned, enchanted by the thought of her in his bed, but he couldn't be foolish and allow desire to make choices on his behalf. He couldn't guarantee she would even be with child before he left England.

She drew her knees to her chest and hugged them against her body as if retreating from a battle. "You seem amused by my suggestion."

"Not at all."

She studied him a long time and nibbled her lip. He knew the instant she decided to press forward. Her eyes assumed a zealous gleam. "Once I have given you a son, you need never see me again."

"I don't think—"

"I could live alone," she said in a rush. "You must have several homes where I could choose to reside. I would want our children to live with me, of course, at least until our son is old enough to attend school. Young children need a mother's love. I vow I would be no trouble for you. Could we have an understanding, Your Grace?"

She appeared to be holding her breath as she awaited his answer.

His shoulders sagged; weariness invaded his body and spirits. She spoke of a future not meant for either of them. "Do you truly wish to live alone in the country?"

Her hopeful light faded and she turned her face away from him. "I could adjust my expectations."

Yet, she shouldn't have to compromise on what she wanted. She was young and beautiful. She would have her choice of gentlemen in London. He had assumed the lady hadn't been given a Season because she was shy, but clearly he had been mistaken. Why did her brother keep her hidden away?

He cleared his throat, hating that he must disappoint her. "I'm certain you would make a lovely wife. Unfortunately, I am not the husband you seek. Please tell me you will speak with your brother."

She looked out over the water, her jaw hardening. "I am sorry to disappoint you, but I won't ask my brother to release you. If you, on the other hand, choose to cry off after having made my acquaintance, I won't hold a grudge. For long."

Luke gritted his teeth. Why must she be this stubborn? "Your brother said you were amiable," he grumbled.

"He has been known to stretch the truth, Your Grace."

Dear Lady Vivian,

Please know I am praying for a speedy recovery on your behalf. No need to fret that I might take my leave before we have had an opportunity to further our discussion. I will remain at Brighthurst as long as necessary.

Best wishes,
Foxhaven

Six

VIVI HAD BEEN AVOIDING FOXHAVEN FOR THREE DAYS, pretending to have caught Patrice's chill and taking to her bed. When he had asked for an audience again yesterday, she had been too pretend-ill to grant his request, of course. His written reply today made her truly sick.

Sugar biscuits! She couldn't hide forever, even if that was what cowards did. And Vivi was a coward to be sure. A restless, bored-out-of-her-wits one. Unable to tolerate another minute of staring at her ceiling, she tossed the covers aside and rang for her maid.

Winnie didn't keep her waiting long. "You're up at last."

"I made a miraculous recovery a minute ago. I suppose I should join Foxhaven and Patrice for dinner."

"Lady Brighthurst will be pleased, no doubt." Her maid ducked her head as she set to her task, but not before Vivi saw her smile.

Once she was dressed and Winnie was satisfied with her toilette, Vivi made her way to the family dining room. Foxhaven's and Patrice's voices carried into the corridor as she approached, their words indistinct, but tone friendly. It appeared the duke hadn't yet announced he wouldn't marry Vivi. Thoughts of the scene that awaited her made her stomach flip-flop. She hesitated outside the doorway.

Why couldn't the duke have saved her the indignity of being rejected in person? A letter would have sufficed. He obviously knew how to put quill to foolscap.

Vivi sighed. When Ash paid her a call in the near future, he would blister her ears so well they might never heal.

"I wish Vivi could join us, but she is quite ill." Patrice spoke haltingly as if it required effort to uphold her part of the conversation. "I am afraid you'll have naught but my companionship this evening."

Guilt sank its teeth into Vivi and gnawed. How could she have considered leaving her cousin to entertain the duke alone? She hadn't been thinking of her kinswoman at all.

Plastering on a bright smile, she swept into the room. "Here I am. I apologize for my lateness."

Patrice startled. "Vivi, I thought you were still sick."

"I woke this afternoon feeling back to my old self." Moving to Patrice's side, she placed a kiss on her sallow cheek. Bluish half circles under her cousin's eyes made her appear as if she'd lost a round of fisticuffs. Her illness had battered but thankfully not beaten her. Vivi hoped the duke's revelation wouldn't send her cousin back to her bed.

She curtsied. "Your Grace."

"Lady Vivian, what a delightful surprise." He bestowed a charming smile upon her. "How lovely to see you again."

Vivi didn't know whether to admire his jolly nature or be irritated by it. Their situation hardly called for smiles and pleasantries.

Foxhaven remained standing until she took her seat. When he sat, he angled his head to one side. "Lady Vivian, have you done something different with your hair this evening?"

Her heart skipped. "You are likely noticing the string of pearls."

"Ah, yes. Quite right, my lady." He sipped his wine, watching her over the gilded rim of his goblet with twinkling blue eyes. "You are a vision."

Vivi froze with her glass of lemonade halfway to her mouth. He had accused her of being a figment of his imagination at the spring, a *vision*. She placed her drink back on the table and silently pleaded with him not to tell her cousin about their first encounter. "Thank you, Your Grace."

Foxhaven nodded, his expression unreadable as he studied her. What thoughts churned behind his keen eyes? Perhaps he was simply organizing a list of her faults to justify his rejection. It shouldn't be a difficult task.

Her hand shook as she reached for her fork, her focus on her plate for fear she might burst into tears if he glanced crossways at her. Patrice had worked tirelessly to raise her to be a lady, and Vivi had repaid her cousin's kindness by tossing everything she had learned aside.

Patrice cleared her throat. "Please tell us of your plans for autumn, Your Grace. Will you travel north?"

"I will make a brief appearance in Northumberland,

but then I must return to London. I have an appoint-
ment with an associate, Captain Pendry."

Vivi's interest was piqued despite her troubling
thoughts. "A military man?"

"Master of a ship. *My* ship." Foxhaven's chest
puffed up like Vicar Ramsey's did when Patrice
complimented him on one of his sermons.

"What need do you have of a ship?" Vivi asked.

Patrice raised her eyebrows, but she dismissed her
cousin's subtle warning. Hearing what Foxhaven
had to say was worth any gentle scolding she would
receive later.

"Why shouldn't I have a ship, Lady Vivian? I cannot
think of a single reason I shouldn't." The duke reminded
her of a boy who had just received a new toy.

She frowned. "Don't tell me you dabble in trade."

They both pretended not to hear Patrice's quiet gasp.

"I dabble in exploration, Lady Vivian. Admittedly
I have yet to set out on a true expedition, but all will
be remedied soon. The *Isla* sets sail in October, and I
will be onboard. We will sail where no man has gone
before us."

Vivi's pulse quickened. He spoke with humor, but
could he be serious about leaving England? "Where is
it you intend to explore?"

"The Antarctic. It is believed there is an entire continent south of the Sandwich Islands. There is a race of
sorts to see who will discover it first: America, Russia,
Britain. I'm placing my money on the Crown."

"The Sandwich Islands. Do you mean Captain
Cook's islands? But his discovery was fifty years ago."

"Forty-five."

She laid her fork and knife aside, forgetting about her meal. "Close enough."

Patrice threw her another warning look. "Please recall that His Grace is a guest, my dear."

"Thank you, Lady Brighthurst, but please allow her to speak freely. It is rare to meet a lady with much knowledge of history." The duke's manner was kind even as he overruled her cousin. "Your time frame was not out of a reasonable range, Lady Vivian. Forgive my uncouth manners. Please, continue with your thought."

"Thank you." Truly, the duke surprised her at every turn. She had never known a gentleman to acknowledge she had anything worthwhile to add to a conversation. Her rigid posture relaxed a smidge. "As I was saying, it has been a long time since Captain Cook's discovery. Why hasn't the continent already been found if it exists?"

Foxhaven tapped his fingers against the tabletop, appearing to consider her argument. "I suspect no one was looking. The threat of war then war itself was foremost in everyone's minds. Only peace allows for discovery."

"And you wish to discover the Antarctic?" She wanted to ask how he could entertain such outrageous ideas when he was a duke, but she feared sounding like her brother. Still, if Foxhaven was like most men of his station, his entire family relied on him to provide for them. How could he set out to discover a hypothetical continent when he had real responsibilities at home?

Gads. She sounded exactly like Ash.

"I enjoy a good adventure," he said. "Captain Pendry holds an interest in the Antarctic. I have simply provided him with a means of accomplishing his task."

This was the most preposterous thing she had ever heard. Did her brother know of the duke's plans?

"It seems like a risky venture, Your Grace. Are you certain this expedition is wise?"

Foxhaven's lips thinned and curved into a parody of a smile. "You needn't worry, my lady."

She needn't worry because she would not become his wife. She braced to hear the words spoken aloud.

"Sunday is the church picnic," Patrice said, guiding them toward a more benign topic of conversation. "I don't know if I'll be strong enough to venture out. I'm not quite feeling myself yet."

Vivi was more than happy to shift the focus of the dinner conversation. Despite the duke's observations, she could be amiable when she chose. She aimed a teasing grin at her cousin. "Mrs. Honeywell will be disappointed you won't be able to attend. Who will she accuse of cheating when she loses the pie baking contest this time?"

Patrice's cheeks flushed pink. "Now, Vivi."

Vicar Ramsey judged the contest and without fail had awarded the first place ribbon to Patrice and her perfect peach pie every year she had entered. In fact, he loved Patrice's pie so much he had called at Brighthurst every day for a week upon his return from America last summer. Each morning her cousin had risen at dawn to bake a pie for the minister, which bespoke of her mutual affection.

Vivi hoped her cousin might someday find happiness with the vicar, even though she had refused his offer of marriage once before. Patrice insisted she must see Vivi settled before she entertained thoughts of matrimony.

She'll be free when you join the convent. Vivi tried to shake that depressing thought from her mind. That life wasn't for her.

"I can just imagine the look of horror on Mrs. Honeywell's face when someone else bests her in the contest this year," she said, hoping she sounded more cheerful than she felt. "I hate to miss it."

"If you linger by the judging table, you will not miss a thing."

Vivi balked. "You want me to go without you? Shouldn't I stay home, too?"

"Oh, dear. I thought you appeared peaked yet. You are still unwell, aren't you?" Before Patrice did something foolish, like test her forehead for fever, Vivi waved her off.

"I feel fine."

Patrice's forehead scrunched. "We can't be too careful. I know you refused to see Dr. Fredrick, but—"

Vivi held up her palm to stop her cousin's unnecessary fretting. "I swear I am fully recovered. The picnic will be just the thing to make me feel better."

"If you are certain…" Vivi nodded and Patrice's worry lines faded. "Thank you. Vicar Ramsey relies on friendly faces in the sanctuary when he is delivering the liturgy. The vicar gets nervous when he speaks to a crowd."

Foxhaven's brows shot up. "What an unfortunate choice of vocation for the man."

"He was never cut out for the cloth, but his father insisted. Vicar Ramsey's sojourn to America did not reap the benefits he had hoped it might. I'm afraid he is stuck with his vocation."

Vivi had never known Vicar Ramsey's history. In truth, she had never given much thought to him beyond his association with Patrice, but this explained his lack of rousing sermons. "How awful for the vicar."

"I am certain he would appreciate your sympathy, Vivian, but please say nothing to him." Patrice was beginning to sound hoarse.

"Perhaps we should call it an evening," Vivi said. "You need your rest."

Her cousin stifled a yawn. "I am rather tired this evening." Leaning her elbows against the table, she pushed to her feet. Foxhaven stood to assist then tucked her hand into the crook of his arm and escorted her toward the door.

"The vicar may count on another friendly face Sunday, Lady Brighthurst. I'll make certain Lady Vivian arrives to the church on time."

Pardon? Vivi scrambled from her seat.

"I would be grateful if you ensured her safe arrival, Your Grace."

"It would be my pleasure. Lady Vivian shall come to no harm under my watch."

They spoke of her as if she were a child or a dimwit in need of supervision.

"I don't require an escort." As soon as the words left her mouth, she realized how ludicrous she sounded.

Foxhaven halted at the threshold and looked back over his shoulder. Patrice turned to stare at her too.

"I meant to say, I would employ the services of a footman."

Foxhaven's smug grin chafed. "It's no trouble, my lady. A day of picnicking sounds delightful."

A full day of the duke toying with her sounded anything but delightful to her.

❧

Luke frowned when Lady Vivian scooted farther to the edge of the bench of Lady Brighthurst's curricle as they drove to church Sunday morning. Any farther and she might tumble out.

He held out the ribbons to her, but she stared at them as if he offered her poison. "Don't you know how to drive?" he asked.

His condescending tone had the effect he hoped for.

"Of course I know how to drive." She snatched the ribbons from him, gripping them tightly in her kid gloves.

With his hands free, Luke wrapped his arms around her waist and hauled her toward the middle of the seat. She stiffened in his embrace.

"I promised your cousin you would come to no harm under my protection. Now do stop risking your neck by sitting close to the edge."

He meant to release her, but her warmth and the sugary scent of her perfume made him hesitate for several pounding heartbeats. Telling himself he didn't trust her to stay put, he kept one arm around her back. She tried to scoot away, but his fingers curved around her narrow waist, the seams of her corset imprinting his palm.

"Release me, Your Grace." Her voice held a sharp edge.

"I thought you wished to marry me, my dear. I shall embrace you often once we speak our vows." He was goading her, trying to represent the facts clearly. If she despised his touch, as it seemed she did, the lady should speak with her brother.

She took a deep breath, glared at him briefly, and then returned her attention to the lane. "If you think to frighten me into doing your bidding, you are wrong. You're not that scary."

Luke smiled to hide his surprise. Lady Vivian had even more pluck than he'd imagined.

She shifted the reins to one hand and placed her free one on his thigh. His breath whistled on an inhale. She slanted a smirk in his direction and squeezed.

"Jiminy!" Luke captured her hand and forcefully returned it to her lap. He shifted away before she noticed the rise in his breeches.

"Two can play your game," she said. "If you touch me, I will touch you right back."

He smothered a groan. It would be a long day if they spent it groping one another. Thank God they were attending a church affair. Otherwise, Lady Vivian might come out the victor. Her touch ignited a flame inside him while his only served to harass her.

Seven

LUKE MAINTAINED A RESPECTABLE DISTANCE BETWEEN himself and Lady Vivian on the hard church pew. As he should have anticipated, there had been many curious looks upon their arrival together. Even now, there was a prickling sensation at his nape he often felt when someone was watching him.

The vicar would have nothing to worry about on this Sunday, as all eyes seemed to be trained on Lady Vivian and Luke. For her part, she didn't seem to notice. A faraway smile played upon her full, pink lips. She boasted a perfect, kissable mouth, the kind that made a man forget his troubles when it was pressed against his.

She glanced in his direction and caught him staring. Her smile slipped.

Damn. Luke snapped his gaze forward. Crossing his arms, he settled in to listen to the vicar's sermon, his blood cooling simultaneously. Nothing killed a man's passion swifter than the sight of another man in a dress. Luke shifted away from Lady Vivian to resist the temptation of ogling her again. Nevertheless, his thoughts drifted back to her.

Not only was she breathtaking, she possessed high spirits and boldness. Most impressively, she could converse on his current topic of interest, and she'd had no qualms about putting him in his place when he had been patronizing. She was also refreshingly transparent. She disapproved of his expedition, although she hadn't spoken out against his plans like his younger brother had.

He had tried explaining his troubles to Richard once, but his brother had shaken his head like he'd pitied him. Luke's shame wound tightly around him and a light sheen blanketed his skin. He wasn't even able to look at the pages of a book without a blinding headache coming over him. How was he to take care of his family when he couldn't focus on anything but the pain? He was no longer cut out to assume his father's title, so what purpose did his life serve?

He glanced at Lady Vivian again. She wanted to marry, bear children, and live a normal life, but Luke was incapable of being normal now. A sedate life alone in the country wouldn't satisfy a young and lively woman for long, no matter Lady Vivian's claims. She would desire seasons in London, the opera, and gentlemanly attentions.

His spine stiffened. *Gentlemanly attentions, my arse.*

The thought of bloody rakehells providing her with comfort rubbed him raw. He turned to glare at the other men in the church for good measure and realized everyone was standing.

He bolted from his seat as the first bars of "Amazing Grace" piped from the organ. Lady Vivian offered to share her hymnal. Luke gazed warily at the book before taking hold of his half.

Her strong, sensual voice surprised him. After sitting through countless musicales featuring his three younger sisters and various family friends, he had come to believe only actresses could carry a tune.

Lady Vivian's fingers brushed his as she adjusted her position and sent a jolt up his arm. He glanced to see if she had touched him on purpose, but her attention stayed focused on the notes and lyrics.

Luke couldn't sing any better than his sisters, so he mouthed the words. An impertinent actress had once compared his singing to the caterwauling of an alley cat. He didn't believe his musical talent to be quite as lacking, but no one would mistake him for a nightingale.

Lady Vivian's hip lightly bumped against his. Again, she gave no indication of being aware of what she had done. On the third stanza, he swayed to the side and bumped her back. She lifted her face, mischief dancing in her eyes. She *had* touched him on purpose. Holding his gaze, she finished the verse, a corner of her mouth curling up. Luke's throat constricted as her voice washed over him, casting a spell unbroken even when she looked away. Was this her attempt at revenge for his unabashed staring earlier?

When the toe of her half boot angled to touch his foot, desire flooded through him. How could he become aroused by such innocent contact? In church, no less. Pretending to sing all seven verses of "Amazing Grace."

Seven, for the love of God!

Curse Mr. Newton and his severely debauched life requiring seven verses to prove his rehabilitation.

As the last bars of music faded into the rafters, she took the hymnbook from him and smiled innocently up at him. "Your Grace."

He wanted to wring her neck. Or kiss her until she babbled nonsense. Or bend her over the—

"Lady Vivian!" A shrill voice ripped into his fantasy and gave him a start.

A ruddy-cheeked older lady was frowning at them from the aisle, her heavy bosoms stressing the seams of her gown.

"Mrs. Honeywell, how nice to see you again. Did you have an enjoyable Season in London?" Lady Vivian's polite greeting reminded him that she was a lady of good breeding. He had to stop daydreaming about compromising her.

"Where is Lady Brighthurst?" The woman's nose wrinkled as she spoke of the viscountess. "Is your brother aware of her lax approach to chaperoning you?"

Lady Vivian stiffened beside him.

Mrs. Honeywell nailed her with a disdainful glower. "Surely, Lord Ashden would want to know of your behavior in today's service. He would likely thank me for informing him."

Luke eyed the woman in return. This was the harridan Lady Vivian had spoken of at dinner last night.

"Lady Vivian," he said. "Please introduce me to your friend."

He thought she might have snorted softly, but he kept his focus on Mrs. Honeywell.

"As you wish. Please allow me to present Mrs. Honeywell, the local—uh…"

The lady raised her severe eyebrows. "Mr. Honeywell

is the largest landowner in Bedfordshire." She paused as if waiting for Luke to say something.

"Indeed? Congratulations, Madame. You must be proud."

"Yes, I am proud..." She blinked, bemusement fluttering across her round face.

Lady Vivian pressed her lips tightly together, struggling to school her features.

Mrs. Honeywell dismissed his comment with a flick of her wrist and regained speed, her glower focused on Lady Vivian. "When *your* brother hears of your brazen display today—"

"Forgive me, dear lady." Luke smiled, aiming to charm her, although his tone left no room for mistake. She had no leave to chastise Lady Vivian, especially in his presence. "I must accept the blame. You see, I'm quite taken with my betrothed, but infatuation is no excuse for bad manners."

"Betrothed?" Mrs. Honeywell almost choked on the word, her face blazing redder. "His lordship never mentioned finding a husband for *her*."

Luke's jaw twitched, but otherwise he hid his anger. He'd had years of practice. It would be unwise to lay claim to Lady Vivian. The negotiations between his father and Ashden were not common knowledge. Yet, the drive to protect her from this harpy was too strong. When he glanced down at Lady Vivian, he smiled. "Your brother hasn't publicized our joyful news yet, has he?"

"I'm afraid not, Your Grace. But it is a sudden development, wouldn't you agree?"

All color leeched from Mrs. Honeywell's complexion. "Your Grace?"

Lady Vivian linked arms with him, playing the role of besotted maiden with relish. Lifting her face toward him, she fanned her thick lashes and beamed. Gads, his insides quivered when she gazed at him in admiration. What would it do to him if it were real?

"Mrs. Honeywell, allow me to present the Duke of Foxhaven, my very newly betrothed."

"Oh my. The Duke of Foxhaven?" The older lady fanned her glossy cheeks.

Luke gave a perfunctory bow. "At your service. Now, if you will excuse us, Madame. I promised to escort this charming young lady to the church picnic."

As they made to step around her, she moved to block their way. "Your Grace, perhaps you should seek me out at the picnic. I may be privy to something you might wish to know."

"I possess everything I need to know. Good day, Madame."

And he did. Lady Vivian would not go unscathed after their performance today. If Mrs. Honeywell was representative of the good townsfolk of Dunstable, they were a judgmental lot. He couldn't leave Lady Vivian to face the consequences alone, but he didn't know what to do about her either. His plan to set her free was growing more complicated every moment he spent in her presence.

❧

A rush of affection for Foxhaven urged Vivi to squeeze his arm as they descended the church stairs. He had surprised her again, this time with his gallant defense. Was he reconsidering marriage to her? His response to Mrs. Honeywell seemed to indicate so.

Vivi had thought her offer the other day was sound, and to have him reject her outright had bruised her pride. Perhaps he was beginning to see the advantages of marrying a lady who would place few demands on him.

"Thank you for protecting me from the dragon back there."

He tsked. "Lady Vivian, clearly Mrs. Honeywell is descended from Gorgons, not dragons."

She giggled. The duke was as irreverent as she was, and she liked it.

Her behavior in church caused her a bit of embarrassment, though. Pretending to accidentally touch him had been brazen, even for her, but Foxhaven's response when she had squeezed his leg in the carriage had left her giddy. Shameful as it was, she liked ruffling his calm. It made him seem more human.

His hand covered hers and applied pressure. "Is the woman likely to contact Ashden? I would be happy to write to him and explain."

Some of her confidence faded. Perhaps she wasn't bringing him up to scratch after all.

"I have learned to never underestimate Mrs. Honeywell. If Ash should hear about the incident, I will graciously accept your offer, but there is no need for action at this point." She cocked her head to the side. "Has anyone ever told you that you play the doting suitor well?"

"Do I? Excellent. My inspiration is very…*inspiring*." He winked and drew her closer. "But now you must stay by my side all afternoon so no one figures us out."

They wandered arm-in-arm to the field behind the

stone church where colorful blankets dotted the green
grass like beds of flowers. Tables had been set up close
to the church building, each loaded with like items for
the contests—pies, lace, drawings, embroidery.

Foxhaven nodded toward the tables. "Do you
enter contests?"

"Heavens, no. Although I should. To provide a
boost of confidence to the other ladies."

"Then you have never had the pleasure of taking
home a ribbon to mark your achievement?"

"One must achieve something to earn a ribbon of
achievement, Your Grace."

They moved to the queue forming in front of two
long tables draped in white cloths and covered with
platters of chicken and cold ham, bowls of fruit, and
sugar biscuits. Foxhaven passed a plate to her then
allowed her to precede him through the buffet. Vivi
selected what she wanted and left him at the table
while she found a spot where they could sit.

A group of young ladies she had once considered
friends saw her approaching and looked the other
way, presenting their backs to her. The ache of lone-
liness had dulled over time, but their snub pricked
her more sharply today. She located a blanket set
apart from the others and claimed it. In a moment,
Foxhaven joined her.

He pointed to a group of men stringing a finish line
from one stake hammered into the ground to another.
Mr. Fry, a church deacon, held strips of cloth in his fist
as he supervised the placement of the finish line. The
tails flapped in the breeze.

Foxhaven turned to her. "I think we could take the

ribbon in the three-legged race. You're a fast runner. Would you partner with me?"

Her first impulse was to accept, but she held back an enthusiastic yes. Checking to make certain no one sat close enough to overhear, she spoke softly. "We are already a source of gossip. If you have no intention of marrying me, I fear I have already given the townsfolk enough cause to speculate on the reason."

His thick, black brows dropped low over his eyes. "You must know I cannot refuse, especially now. You would be ruined. Only you may cry off at this point."

She suppressed a sigh. They were back to the same place they had begun. "If I may be frank, I have been more trouble to my cousin than I'm worth. I cannot ask her to assume responsibility for me any longer. I realize you don't deserve to be saddled with me either, and for that, I apologize. But you are my last hope—"

"Lady Vivian."

"Please, hear me out. All I ask is that you seriously consider my offer. Give me your name then you may do whatever you like. Discover Antarctica or search for the lost city of Atlantis, and I will lead a quiet life in the country. You wouldn't have to be bothered by me again."

"Stop speaking nonsense." His blue gaze burned into her. "Your father was a nobleman, and some gentleman will make you an excellent husband. Why are you willing to settle?"

Vivi blinked back the tears threatening to embarrass her. He didn't understand. To settle implied one had choices. "If I don't marry you, my brother has resigned himself to send me to a convent in Scotland.

My sister-in-law has been harping on the idea for at least two years now."

Foxhaven recoiled. "A convent? Whatever for? You would do well in London. Is your brother mad?"

She shrugged. "I have often wondered the same thing about Ash. As far as his wife goes, I know for a fact she is a bit touched in the head." She swiped at an escaping tear and forced a laugh that sounded hollow. "On second thought, Your Grace, you are probably wise to put distance between yourself and my family. The madness could be catching."

The hardness around his mouth melted away and his foot brushed against hers. "You're not mad. I clearly recall you telling me as much at dinner the other evening."

She winced. "Is there any chance you might forget the other night?"

"Not even a sliver of a chance," he said with a smirk.

"Splendid."

"Listen. Don't fret over anything at the moment. I may have an idea on how we can work this out."

She turned a hopeful gaze on him. He smiled in return, showing off the small gap between his teeth. She could fall in love with that smile, so perfectly imperfect.

Setting his plate on the blanket, he stood then offered her a hand up. "Today is meant to be fun. No more gloomy talk."

"Agreed."

"Now, come along. I wish to take home a ribbon, but I need your assistance."

Vivi set her food aside and took his hand. How could she deny him when he needed her?

Mr. Fry put his fingers in his mouth and let loose a sharp whistle. Most conversations halted as heads turned toward the deacon.

"Ladies and gentlemen, the three-legged race is about to begin. Come this way and select a partner."

She and Foxhaven were the first competitors to step up to the line, but other participants soon joined them. Lastly, the reluctant stragglers came forward. Miss Heaton blushed as red as Christmas when Lord Goodrich pulled her toward the starting line, paying no notice to her fiercely whispered protests.

Mr. Fry marched down the line handing out strips of cloth. Foxhaven knelt beside Vivi and lashed their ankles together. When he stood, he slipped his arm around her waist. Her body tingled from her ankle to her hip where his hand rested lightly.

"You must hold on too," he murmured in her ear. "You did promise to touch me back if I touched you."

Heat flashed up her neck, but she placed her arm around his waist.

His fingers coiled into a fist against her hip and pulled her against him. She had never considered the scandalous nature of this particular race until that moment. It was a wonder the vicar and deacons allowed such goings-on. Perhaps they were unaware of the delicious sensations generated by the close proximity of a man and woman, their hips pressed together.

"Let's try to walk," he said. "Middle leg first. One, two, three."

They stepped together, circling around some of the other couples for practice.

Mr. Fry waved everyone to the starting line. "On

the count of three. The first team to cross the line is the winner."

Foxhaven's muscles shifted and tensed. Vivi glanced up at him. His jaw was set in a determined line, his gaze focused on their destination. In that moment, she recognized nothing would stop him from getting what he wanted. A ripple of unease went through her, but she set it aside. Today she wanted what he desired, and she would help him achieve it. Tomorrow was another story.

Mr. Fry held his brown beaver hat aloft. "One, two, three." He swung his arm down. "Go!"

Two young boys lurched ahead, their screeches making her laugh. Foxhaven hugged her and matched her pace. The leaders missed a step and fell in a tangle of legs. She and Foxhaven angled away from them and continued at a steady run. Each footfall landed at the same time and they surged ahead.

Looking to her right, she caught sight of Miss Heaton and Lord Goodrich.

"Faster!" the baron shouted as if he drove a team of horses.

Vivi focused on the string a few feet ahead. She couldn't observe the competition if she wished to see where she was going.

"Just a little farther, my dear. You're doing magnificent." Foxhaven's compliment boosted her spirits. Truly, she could run like this forever at his side.

Lord Goodrich continued to shout behind them, his voice taking on an angry edge. Miss Heaton cried out in despair as they fell farther behind.

Vivi and Foxhaven crossed the line first, laughing and a little out of breath.

"Brava, Lady Vivian!" He hugged her once more then bent to sever the tie binding them.

⤜∾

Vivi fanned the winning ribbons out on her lap. There were three in total: the one she and Foxhaven had earned in the three-legged race and two the duke had won for shooting and archery.

She squinted against the blazing afternoon sun when Foxhaven steered the curricle up the lane leading to Brighthurst House. He had a comfortable confidence about him in the way he handled the grays, his legs propped wide and his hat tipped at a jaunty angle. He possessed all the self-assurance of nobility and yet surprisingly little arrogance.

She liked his nose. Not too commanding and not too perfect with a raised ridge that spoke of a past trauma. "You lost the footrace on purpose, did you not?"

He kept his eyes on the lane in front of them. A corner of his lips twitched. "What makes you think I would lose on purpose?"

"I outran Adam Randolph three summers past when he challenged me to a race at Dottie Kennicot's garden party." How she missed her dearest friend, Dottie. She shook off her sadness. She hadn't had fun in a long while, and she wouldn't spoil the moment thinking on things that couldn't be changed. "Mr. Randolph was in a sulk for two weeks afterward. He refused all but the curtest acknowledgment of me at church."

Foxhaven laughed. "Poor Mr. Randolph wasn't allowed to claim his prize. It is no wonder he was brooding."

"What prize? There were no stakes involved."

Foxhaven must have a fountain of happiness inside him for he never seemed to run out of smiles. "A kiss, Lady Vivian. That's what I would have demanded in his position."

She swung away before he spotted the telling flush searing her cheeks. "You would not, Your Grace. What a terrible tease you are."

"I assure you, I would have."

Gathering the ribbons in a pile, she lined up the edges. Vivi didn't know how to respond. In the art of coquettishness, she had always remained an observer. She settled for practicality. "If you kissed me, you would feel honor bound to marry me, and we both know you desire no such association."

He pulled the carriage off the lane and parked under a tree. Brighthurst House remained in the distance, its pitched roof peeking over a hill.

Grabbing her hand, he scooted from the seat. "Come with me."

"Why?" Vivi's voice squeaked. She scrambled to follow lest he drag her. Good heavens, he didn't intend to prove himself, did he?

His hands circled her waist before she tumbled from the carriage and lowered her to the ground. But even after her half boots were securely on the grass, he held on.

Oh, my molasses! She had never been kissed and she didn't know what to do. Her eyes drifted shut, but she wasn't sure what to do with her mouth. She licked her lips then puckered up, waiting.

A woodpecker's rapid hammering sounded from a nearby tree. A breeze ruffled the sleeves of her gown. His fingers tightened on her waist and urged her closer.

"Blast it all." He released her.

She blinked into the empty space where he had just been. She spotted him rounding the horses and stared as he approached an ancient, gnarled oak. Its branches twisted like arthritic fingers with unsightly knots like swollen knuckles. Pinching the bridge of his nose, he blew out a noisy breath but said nothing.

"That is a good climbing tree," she said in place of witty repartee, anything to fill the strained silence.

He looked up at the branches. "Do you climb trees?"

She trailed after him. Admitting to yet another unladylike habit would prove how unsuited she was to be his duchess, but it wasn't her odd endeavors that seemed to bother him.

"I have been known on occasion to climb a tree, but only if I'm wearing trousers."

His eyes lit when he looked at her. "You're nothing like I anticipated."

"Thank you, Your Grace. I think." She lowered to the grass, tucked her knees up under her skirts, and rested her forearms across her knees.

"You may refer to me as Luke if you wish, Foxhaven if my Christian name feels too familiar and offends your sensibilities. But our association warrants discarding such formalities as Your Grace."

She looked up at him with a cautious slant of her head. "And what is the nature of our association?"

He crouched down in front of her as if indulging a child. "We are becoming fast friends, I believe."

"You want something from me I can't give you. I

expect our friendship will be short-lived. Perhaps we shouldn't abandon our manners too hastily."

Plucking a blade of grass, he twirled it between his fingers. His lips thinned briefly, but then he bestowed another generous smile. His smile dazzled and did something unsettling to her insides, but she was beginning to distrust it. He used his smile as a cloak, she suspected, to hide what stirred behind his serious eyes.

"Tell me how you envision your future," he said. "Not the one you are willing to settle for in order to avoid the convent, but the one you truly desire."

She could easily desire what knelt in front of her. Foxhaven seemed kind and tolerant. She could grow to love him, to be a good wife, to honor him. But she couldn't admit this to him.

"I'm no different from most ladies. I wish to make a good match. If my husband is smart with his money, not too strict, and possesses all his teeth, I will be happy."

Foxhaven tossed his head back with a hearty, openmouthed laugh, proving he met her last requirement nicely. "Is that *all*? I find it hard to believe you wouldn't want more."

"I am hardly in a position to ask for more. You must know a woman has little say in such matters."

He sobered and nodded thoughtfully. "What about children? You mentioned providing an heir, but don't you wish for a family life?"

She studied the blade of grass he wound around his finger. The tip turned scarlet then bordered on plum before he released it. Did he feel like his finger, bound tightly and dying off inch by inch? She knew the pressures his station in life carried with it. Her brother often suffered under the weight of his responsibilities, and then there was Muriel. His wife's periodic bouts of illness were a leash 'round her brother's neck. What if Vivi's dreams of family were a burden to Foxhaven like Muriel's illness was to Ash?

"You don't desire a family life, do you?" she said. "You might have a need for an heir, but you do not want a family."

He rocked back on his heels. "I haven't given the possibility much consideration, truthfully."

Vivi bit her bottom lip. She could release him. The act would cost her a great deal, but being the cause of another's suffering seemed worse than enduring misery she had brought on herself.

She swallowed hard and wished she were braver.

"I have a proposition, Lady Vivian. A solution, perhaps. I want to escort you to a house party in Northumberland."

"A house party?" What type of daft solution was he proposing?

"My mother hosts a party every year. The entire affair is respectable and more than suited for our purpose."

"Forgive me if I sound ungrateful. I do appreciate the invitation, but how is a house party suited to our purpose?" And what purpose would that be?

"There will be many eligible bachelors attending." He raised his eyebrows and gestured to her as if to ask, *isn't it obvious?*

It wasn't, at least not to her.

When she didn't respond, he sighed. "I could provide information about each gentleman—his disposition, family, financial standing—then facilitate an introduction. You could find a replacement husband then break off our agreement without anyone knowing we never intended to marry."

"I see you have given this thought." He may have meant no harm, but his desire to foist her off onto another gent stung. Especially after the lovely day they had shared.

He smiled broadly, appearing proud. "A respectable match should keep your brother happy and you out of the convent, and I would be released from my father's promise without breaking his word or tarnishing your reputation. I don't know why I didn't think of it sooner."

Tightness coiled in her chest, and she absently smoothed a hand over her heart. "I'm not sure Ash would grant his permission. He thought it best to secure a betrothal without presenting me."

"Did he now?" Foxhaven's intense blue eyes bore into her. "For what reason?"

She shrugged one shoulder and looked away. It was wrong to hide the truth, but she had been unfairly judged and she needed this match with him. "You must admit I am different from other young ladies. I could never expect to have a successful Season with my tendency to act before thinking."

This had been a problem for her since she was a child. Patrice had promised she would outgrow it, but she never had.

His jaw lost its hard edge and warmth radiated from his smile. "You are a breath of fresh air, Lady Vivian. Gentlemen will issue challenges to win your favor."

"Liar," she teased, her cheeks flushing with pleasure despite knowing he falsely flattered her. "When it comes to a choice between death and marriage to a hoyden, no one is winning in this scenario."

"You underestimate your charms."

And he underestimated other gentlemen's ability to be like him. He might not run away in horror, but that didn't mean other men wouldn't.

"Perhaps I could persuade your brother to allow you to attend the party, but only if you give your consent. I won't ask you to do this if it isn't what you want."

"Oh." No one had ever requested her opinion on anything pertaining to her future, and she had certainly never been asked to give her permission. Tears stung the back of her eyes.

"What is your answer, my lady? Will you allow me to find a husband for you?"

She nodded slowly, repressing her silly sentiments. It meant nothing that he was showing her kindness. He still wanted to be rid of her.

"Splendid," he said. "I will dictate a letter to your brother this evening."

She accepted his outstretched hand and climbed to her feet. His fingers linked with hers, and he held on as they strolled to the curricle. She glanced sideways at him, trying to puzzle him out. With every word, he said he wanted to be free of her, but his actions conveyed his reluctance.

A stirring began in her heart; a question. What if he wasn't yet aware he wanted her for his wife?

Her relentless imagination refused to slumber as he lifted her into the carriage, his touch lingering on her waist. Courtship of a man—a duke—required bravery and more than a trace of foolishness. Fortunately, she possessed the later in abundance.

"Thank you, Luke."

His nostrils flared briefly before his neutral mask slipped back in place. Now that he wasn't attempting to persuade her, perhaps he wanted to retract the offer to further their intimacy.

She took her place on the bench. "Do I still have leave to use your Christian name?"

"Of course, Lady Vivian." He bounded into the carriage as sure-footed as an acrobat, sank down beside her, and retrieved the reins.

"You may call me Vivian if you like."

Luke nodded once then signaled the grays to return to the lane. As the carriage bumped over a rut, her attention turned to a possible hitch in her plan.

She had no idea how to go about courting a man.

Eight

Luke had discovered a number of pleasant ways to pass the time at Brighthurst House while awaiting his youngest brother and sister-in-law's arrival. His family would be assuming chaperone duties for the coming journey to Irvine Castle since Vivian's cousin hadn't fully recovered from her illness.

Much of the past week had been spent in Vivian's company, beginning with invigorating morning rides and ending with battles over the chessboard. Occasionally, she even beat him soundly. She was much more than her brother had promised, and Luke had begun to wonder if Ashden knew his sister at all.

This afternoon he had retreated to the small orchard with his valet, eager to test the accuracy of his newest acquisition, a Harper's Ferry flintlock pistol. One of the best advantages to a holiday in the country was no one complained about noise when one fired a barking iron.

He nodded to Thomas to place the target then waited for his servant to move to safety.

After rotating the flint to full cock, Luke aimed and

squeezed the trigger. The gun gave a satisfying flash and kick. He had dreamed of owning this particular firearm ever since he had seen an American officer carrying one three years ago. His friend, Daniel, had procured it during one of his trips to America and gave it to Luke as thanks for assisting his family in a matter.

The gun felt right in his hand. The aim was off by a fraction, though, and shot to the left of his target. He reloaded, compensated for the inaccuracy, and fired again. The rotting apple exploded.

"Solid shot, Your Grace," Thomas said.

The sound of applause startled Luke, and he wheeled around to discover Vivian approaching with her maid. "Bravo, Your Grace. I was walking in the gardens when I heard a gunshot."

How like the lady to be undeterred by shots fired.

He held out the pistol for her inspection. "It's my pride and joy."

Reaching out to brush her hand over the polished handle, her fingers made contact with his. The slow-burning fire that had been smoldering inside him for days sparked to life.

"How beautiful," she said. "Ash has nothing as fine."

That was untrue. Ashden had a sister of the finest quality, even if the man didn't recognize her value. Finding another gentleman eager to marry her would be no challenge.

He cleared his thickened throat and moved away to reload. He couldn't think on another gentleman enjoying her companionship, or he might do something stupid. "Would you like to fire it?"

"Me?"

"Place another apple," he called to Thomas before returning his attention to the lady. "I believe early in our association you admitted to a talent for shooting. I will reload and you can give a demonstration."

"I said I know *how* to shoot, not that I could hit an apple at ten paces."

He winked. "Lucky for you the apple doesn't shoot back then." Half-cocking the flint, he retrieved a paper cartridge, bit off the end, and poured black powder into the priming pan. "Do you know how to load a firearm, too, or just how to discharge one?" he asked as he closed the frizzen.

"I have watched my brother reload many times, but he never allows me to handle the powder." She leaned closer to observe his work.

Luke grinned and funneled the remaining powder into the barrel. "That will never do. A lady who wields a barking iron must learn how to arm herself properly. After you take the shot, I'll show you how." He pushed the lead ball and paper as far as it would go into the barrel, returned the ramrod to its home, and offered her the gun. "Before you fire, I wish to see your stance."

She took the pistol and held it in both hands with arms outstretched and the appropriate amount of tension in her limbs. Good. She was experienced enough to be prepared when firing an unfamiliar weapon. He had no cause to worry about a bruised cheekbone or broken nose from the piece kicking back at her.

"Aim a bit to your right to hit your target."

"It has no sight. How am I to aim?"

"I'll show you." He stood behind her to wrap his arms around her. She jumped, her bottom brushing against his groin. He sucked in a sharp breath.

"Oh! Sorry. I didn't mean…" She trailed off, a pink flush climbing the back of her neck.

His blood ran hot and rushed to places that held a special fondness for her. He tightened his grip around her hands, sensing the tremor moving up her arm. "You must hold steady."

"I'm trying," she said on a wisp of breath.

He placed his head beside hers, tempted beyond reason to taste the delicate place behind her ear. She always smelled sweet, like vanilla and sugar. "Close one eye then look down the length of the barrel."

His tumultuous breaths stirred tendrils of hair curling around her delicate ear. His lips parted as he contemplated gliding his mouth along her slender neck to coax a pleasurable sigh from her. He wanted to trace the hollow of her collarbone with his tongue then release the fastenings of her gown and peel away the muslin from her shoulders. His fingers longed to free her perfect breasts from the vicious corset holding her prisoner and caress her skin.

"Good luck!" Her maid's shrill call brought him crashing back into the moment.

He shuffled back a step, creating space between him and Vivian. "Whenever you are ready, my lady. Squeeze gently." His voice had grown husky.

Her finger hugged the trigger, and a flash of light and heat preceded the sharp crack. The top left half of the apple was obliterated.

"I did it!"

The servants cheered, and a wide grin split Thomas's face. "Excellent shot, my lady."

"Thank you." She spun toward Luke, her eyes shining like jewels. "May I try again?"

"Only if you reload it. I'll tell you what to do." He captured her hand and led her to the supplies. She took the cartridge from him and sniffed it.

"Must I bite it?"

"If you are ever in danger, you must, but allow me." He closed his hand around hers and brought the cartridge to his mouth, ripping the top with his teeth. Her lips parted on a soft gasp, and he couldn't hold back a satisfied grin.

To realize he affected her as much as she did him gave him a jolt of shameful pleasure. He had no right to engage in a flirtation with the lady when she belonged to another gentleman, or would belong to another gentleman.

His mood sobered. "Now open the frizzen so you can pour a little in the pan."

She followed his directions, her slender fingers sure and proficient. Once she had the firearm primed and loaded, she moved into position. Luke kept his distance this time, curious to see what she was capable of.

Her shot missed.

She turned to him with a frown. "May I try again?"

"As many times as you wish. Just wipe the flint with your thumb each time to keep it clean." He hung back as she prepared to reload. This time she bit the cartridge with no hesitation.

Her next shot sent fragments of apple flying and earned an exhilarated yelp from the servants.

He lowered to the grass, enjoying the view as she hurried to reload the pistol again. She hit her targets three more times and likely would have continued target practice if a commotion on the front drive hadn't deterred her. A carriage was pulling up to Brighthurst House.

That would be Drew and Lana.

Luke rose, dusted off his trousers, and went to collect his gun. "Shall we go greet the new arrivals?" He set the pistol on a stump and offered his arm. As they started toward the front drive, a high-pitched caterwaul rent the air followed by another.

A crease appeared between Vivian's brows. "Good heavens. Was that a cat?"

"Worse. My brother has arrived with his ladies."

"Ladies? How many ladies?" The quiver of her voice suggested her imagination might be less proper than one would expect of an innocent maiden.

"Just three."

Specifically, Drew's spirited wife and lively ginger-haired daughters. His mother referred to the little ones as twin handfuls.

"Only three? And they don't mind?"

He chuckled and squeezed her hand affectionately. "There's no cause for alarm. It's only my brother's wife and daughters."

Her grip relaxed and she released a breathy laugh. "You tease me horribly, Your Grace."

As they neared the drive, they encountered a flurry of activity. A footman was loosening the last of the trunks while another hoisted one on his shoulder and toted it inside.

His brother waved and reached back inside the carriage to assist his wife down the stairs. Lana emerged with tousled hair and a wrinkled travel gown.

Another scream blasted from the confines of the coach.

"Chloe, please," she chided as she alighted with a painfully amused grin.

Vivian's cousin floated from the house and waited by the entrance to greet Luke's family. The lady appeared as fragile and pale as a ghost, but Vivian had assured him she was beginning to look more like her former self.

Luke slanted an appreciative gaze at Vivian on his arm. She possessed a healthy glow and didn't look one missed meal away from starvation. She would be soft and full of life in the marital bed.

Another high-pitched squeal came from the carriage, shattering his improper musings, not to mention his eardrums. "Shall I make introductions, my lady, or should we run away while we still have a chance to escape?"

Before Vivian could answer, his sister-in-law spotted them and rushed forward with a wide smile. She ignored Luke and clasped hands with Vivian. "You must be Lady Vivian. How lovely to meet you. I'm Lana, and we are sure to be great friends."

Vivian received Lana's enthusiastic greeting with bright smile. "Welcome to Brighthurst, my lady. Will you allow me to introduce you to my cousin?"

"With pleasure." The ladies walked away arm in arm, their heads drifting close together as Lana whispered something to Vivian.

Drew approached with his daughter, Chloe,

squirming in his arms. She released a loud burst of frustration and he flinched. "Now, now."

He sat her on his shoulder and her screams transformed from angry outbursts to screeches of glee. Her sister, Claire, appeared accustomed to her twin's boisterousness and continued to sleep curled up into a ball against her nurse's chest, a fistful of sunshine hair tangled in her chubby fingers.

A rush of affection flooded through Luke for his brother's offspring. Some might consider it justice that his youngest brother, a former rake, was given not one but two girls to protect, but Drew had become a different man since he'd married. He appeared softer when he looked at his daughters with affection. He wasn't so changed that it would be wise to cross him, however. Luke pitied any gent foolish enough to glance sideways at his nieces once they came of age.

"Your wife gave me the cut direct," he said.

"I'll take her to task later."

"That is blasted unlikely." Luke's brother was uncommonly permissive with his wife, but Luke was only teasing. A lady with a mind of her own didn't require guidance on how to use it.

He and Drew fell into step together as the ladies disappeared inside the house. "What is Lana about, whisking Lady Vivian away?"

Drew smirked. "What makes you think I know anything about what goes through her mind?"

"Perhaps because she speaks freely, and you have been enclosed in a carriage with her all day."

"Who says we talked? It's hard enough to think with darling Chloe monopolizing the conversation."

Drew's grin widened as he settled his daughter back in his arms and kissed her forehead. "But there may have been talk between the Forest women last week about a grand wedding breakfast following your leg-shackling. Did you know Mother has commissioned a goldsmith to fashion your leg iron?"

"Very funny. You had best inform Lana to cease making any plans."

Drew's brows shot up. "Oh?"

They entered the darkened foyer, and Luke paused inside the threshold to allow his eyes to adjust. Of course his brother would have questions. Perhaps he could even assist with selecting an appropriate suitor for Vivian.

"I can explain everything once we have some privacy. I'm sure Lady Brighthurst would allow us the use of her parlor. Shall we?"

7 September 1818

Dear Sister,

I am pleased to learn you were able to bring Foxhaven up to scratch. Now if you can only control yourself until the deed is done. This Season proved to be a tedious affair. Lady Ashden is eager to be rid of Mrs. Honeywell's companionship. Her ladyship missed several of the Season's most popular balls when the stress of entertaining the woman drove her to bed with a headache. Yet, as it is unlikely Mrs. Honeywell will keep her own counsel without incentive, it was impossible to send her away early.

Vivi, if you fail in this endeavor, there is nothing more I can do to assist you. I am sorry. I wish you safe travels and regret I cannot be present to see you off.

> *Sincerely,*
> *Ash*

Nine

LUKE'S FAMILY WAITED AT THE EDGE OF THE FOYER while Vivi made her good-byes.

"I hate for you to travel alone." Patrice spoke into her ear to be heard over the rambunctious screeching of the tiny girls. They reminded Vivi of eager puppies wriggling to break free from their parents' arms.

"I fear I may never be alone on this journey," she murmured in reply, but all in good fun.

Luke's nieces provided ample entertainment. Their fervent exploration of anything breakable or deadly kept Lord Andrew on his toes. Vivi had grown quite accustomed to Luke's brother launching from his chair, leaping obstacles if necessary, to snatch one of his girls back from the edge of disaster. Who knew babies were so nimble on hands and knees?

Patrice's hug lacked its usual vigor.

Vivi held on to her and tried to force down the knot of apprehension forming in her throat. "I'll miss you. Do you promise to rest and eat at mealtimes?"

Patrice patted her back. "You mustn't worry about me. Just be happy. You're to be a duchess soon."

As part of her understanding with Luke, no one was to know of the agreement. Everyone was supposed to believe Vivi had tossed him over once it was all said and done. Were she not humoring him by pretending to participate in his scheme, guilt might compel her to be honest with her cousin. As it was, Vivi expected to be the Duchess of Foxhaven within the month, two at most.

Luke appeared in the threshold, his cheeks rosy from his morning stroll. "The carriages are ready. Have you had enough time with Lady Brighthurst to bid her farewell?"

Patrice squeezed her hand. "Go on, my dear."

"I sent word to Vicar Ramsey requesting he look in on you while I am gone."

Her cousin's gaze darted to Luke, and his family gathered at the entrance. "Vivi," she demurred. A blush climbed her neck.

Vivi smiled cheekily and sashayed toward the door. Now that Patrice no longer had to worry about her, a gentle nudge might be all her cousin needed to make a match.

Luke gave Vivi a secret wink and escorted her outside. He had just returned from carrying word to the vicar on her behalf.

Outside, her maid was waiting beside Lord Andrew's carriage. Winnie, dressed in a dark-blue traveling gown that had once belonged to Vivi, giggled as they approached. This morning they had both admitted to being giddy at the prospect of attending a real house party.

Lord Andrew assisted the nurse with settling his daughters into his carriage while she and Lana—they had been on a first-name basis since the day the lady had arrived—prepared to climb into the ducal travel coach. Vivi accepted Luke's help on the stairs and settled on the plush ivory seat. The gold coach lace at the windows swayed in the light breeze. With Lana seated beside her and the gentlemen situated at last, the carriage started with a small jerk.

Lana smiled at her. "I understand you're seeking a husband among the gentlemen at Irvine Castle."

"*Lana*," Lord Andrew protested a second before he received an elbow in the ribs. "Ow! What the—"

Luke glowered at his brother. "I thought we spoke in confidence."

"I thought you meant I shouldn't say anything to Lady Vivian. I tell Lana everything." He attempted a stern expression, but gazing at his wife seemed to have a strange effect on him. Lord Andrew broke into a dimpled grin that had probably shattered a thousand hearts. "You weren't supposed to say anything."

"Oh, dear." The young woman touched Vivi's arm. "You did know already, didn't you? Luke didn't mislead you about the journey, I hope."

"Good Lord." Luke dropped his head against his palm with a smack.

Vivi chuckled. It was refreshing to encounter a lady who practiced candor. "I am aware of His Grace's plan and gave my consent. And please, don't trouble yourself, any of you. I prefer having the situation in the open. There is less pressure on me to keep a secret."

"Splendid." Lana adjusted her skirts and folded her hands in her lap. "We must discuss strategy at once."

"Strategy? This isn't war," Luke said.

Lana rolled her eyes in his direction. "Pay him no mind. He knows nothing about matchmaking. Had you known of his lack of expertise, I am certain you would have declined his offer. I, on the other hand, have a leg up when it comes to facilitating unions, and thereby offer my assistance."

"You can't argue with her record," Lord Andrew said when Luke opened his mouth to protest. "Lana had a hand in several betrothals, all love matches."

Luke scoffed and looked out the window.

"You may laugh, old man, but love matches do exist." Lord Andrew winked at his wife, activating a radiant glow on her porcelain complexion. "Lana has created a list of prospective gentlemen attending the party. All upstanding gents."

"Lady Vivian doesn't require a list," Luke grumbled. "I will assist her."

Vivi absorbed the knowing looks exchanged between Luke's brother and sister-in-law. They were up to mischief, and she couldn't resist aligning with them. "Do you have the list with you, my lady?"

"Why, yes. I do." She opened her reticule and extracted a folded piece of paper.

Luke crossed his arms and turned a bored look out the window. Not the reaction Vivi had hoped for.

"First, I must apologize," Lana said. "I married the most acceptable of the lot, but there are a few unattached gentlemen who meet with my approval."

"Thank you, my dear," Lord Andrew said.

"Certainly." Clearing her throat, Lana rattled the page for maximum drama. "There is the tenth Marquis of Corby."

The muscles in Luke's jaw shifted, but his gaze stayed frozen to the passing landscape.

"He is such a lovely man, Vivi. I'm certain you will like him. In addition, Lord Corby has a nice title and significant property holdings with a handsome yearly income."

"He's too short," Luke said.

Lana peered over the list. "Too short?"

"Yes, he is two inches shorter than Lady Vivian."

"I hardly think his stature should have any bearing on his suitability." She turned to Vivi. "Would you be troubled by marrying a shorter man?"

"Only if I must gaze down on his bald pate."

Lana nodded. "Rightly so. I hadn't considered that viewpoint. Lord Corby has a full head of hair at the moment, but one never knows."

Luke gestured to Vivi. "And if you wished to run in another three-legged race, your stride would be off."

"Oh, yes," she said. "Excellent point, Your Grace. Perhaps we should eliminate Lord Corby."

Lana lowered the paper to her lap. "Then I am afraid Lord Mitcham must come off the list, too. Did I hear you and Luke took the first-place ribbon for the three-legged race at the church picnic?"

"We did."

"I see. Then we require a gentleman of similar height to Foxhaven."

Vivi ran her gaze from his head to his toes as if assessing him. "Indeed. His Grace is perfect."

Luke smiled smugly.

She leaned over the paper to see it better. "Do you have someone of similar stature on the list?"

Luke sat up straight. "Let me see the blasted thing."

Lana held it out to him, her thin brows arching upward.

He snatched the list from his sister-in-law and read it aloud. "Mr. Pickering. Lord Blackmont. Ellis?" His hand fell to his side. "Why is Anthony on the list?"

"What issue do you have with Ellis?" Lord Andrew asked.

"If you must know, his interests lie elsewhere, namely with our little sister."

"Exactly. Just performing my brotherly responsibilities. Gabby despises him."

"He's a decent chap. And he is coming off the list." Luke perused the rest of the names and flicked it back toward Lana. "None of these gentlemen will do. No more lists. I'll assist Lady Vivian in her search."

Lana huffed and shoved the paper back into her reticule, but Vivi's heart danced in victory. There were at least ten names on the list. It seemed the Duke of Foxhaven wasn't so eager to be rid of her after all.

❦

Luke adjusted his position on the bench and brushed against Vivian's calf.

Damnation. No matter where he attempted to move his legs, she already seemed to be occupying the space. He had begun to suspect her of purposefully getting in his way.

He held rigid to keep from touching her again, because each contact sent a jagged current straight to his lower abdomen. He closed his eyes and attempted to think of anything other than touching her all over.

He was accustomed to riding in the saddle for hours at a time, not folded into a cramped carriage with a woman who aroused him merely with her proximity. The muscles in his lower back and thighs were knotted and on fire.

Gads. He had to move again.

He checked the placement of her legs before stretching, but somehow he grazed her ankle anyway. He glowered in her direction, but she was staring out the window with a peaceful half smile.

"We just passed a mill," she said. "The village cannot be much farther."

He sighed with relief. This was their destination for the night. Traveling with young children made it necessary to stop at a decent hour, and Luke would not complain.

When the carriage entered the coaching yard of The Bull Inn, he scooted to the edge of the bench. He had to get out of there. He alighted without waiting for the stairs, then stretched.

Vivian was grinning at him from the doorway when he turned around. Perhaps the minx knew what she was doing after all. He offered a hand to assist her from the carriage.

"Thank you, Your Grace." The warmth of her smile enveloped him as she entwined her arm with his. His nerves buzzed like a hive of honeybees. Her action was possessive and presumptuous, but instead of wishing to extract himself, he pulled her closer.

The nurse and Vivian's maid exited the other carriage with Chloe and Claire, and Lana and Drew went to collect them.

"Wouldn't a stroll be lovely?" Vivian said. "I haven't sat that long for ages."

Lana held her arms out for Chloe and nuzzled her

plump cheek when her daughter went to her. "*I* want nothing more than a warm bath before dinner."

"I'm sure that can be arranged." Drew hurried ahead and disappeared inside the inn.

Lana's gaze darted between the inn and Vivian, resting on the inn longer. "You will need an escort if you go for a stroll."

"There is no need to alter your plans." Vivian nodded to her maid. "Winnie will accompany me."

Luke missed her warmth the moment she released his arm. "It's unsafe to wander the village without a male escort," he said.

"I see." She nibbled her bottom lip, hands on her slender hips. Her silver-blue eyes flashed with a stroke of brilliance. "Perhaps one of your footmen would lend his assistance."

John halted in the middle of loosening a strap and gazed at Vivian with calf-eyes.

Luke shook his head. The servant snapped his attention back to his task with a dark frown.

"My men are occupied with their duties. Perhaps you will accept my escort instead."

Lana tossed an overly bright smile at them. She was plotting something. He could see the mischief in her eyes. "What a splendid solution. Now I may rest without worry."

She wandered toward the inn with the nurse and her girls, leaving him alone with Vivian and her maid.

"Shall we?" Vivian took his arm. Her eyes crinkled at the corners and her smooth cheeks plumped when she smiled up at him.

He tried to dismiss the skip of his heart as a result

of too much inactivity. He was a man of action, not given to lazing about for the better part of a day. His body needed activity. When Vivian's breast brushed against his arm, the type of activity his body desired became apparent. Perhaps he should have enlisted the footman's services after all, but since it was too late to bow out, he led her from the coaching yard. Vivian's maid trailed behind them but paused to allow a new arrival into the yard.

Luke stifled a groan when he spotted the crest. The carriage door flew open, and Viscount Brookhaven spilled out in a disheveled tumble of satin. A chorus of high-pitched cackles echoed inside the conveyance.

"Brookhaven, where's the bloody fire?" Jonathan Collier appeared in the doorway, weaved, and barely grabbed the door frame before he dove headfirst on top of the viscount. Even foxed, Collier's ability to sniff out a beauty functioned with maddening accuracy. His gaze landed on Vivian and a grin spread across his cherubic face.

Luke drew her closer to his side.

A frizz of brown hair ducked under Collier's arm. Another head-shattering cackle burst from the owner's crimson lips. "Foxhaven! Yoo-hoo!" Her lily-white arm shot into the air and flailed. It was the only lily-white attribute the woman possessed. "We are traveling to Irvine Castle. Is that not a happy coincidence?"

"Mrs. Price." Luke nodded out of politeness as he directed Vivian away from the scoundrels and their entertainment for their journey.

"Pay a call later, Your Grace, if you would care for a treat."

He would be paying a call indeed, to Brookhaven to clear up the mistaken belief that an invitation to his mother's house party extended to trollops and ne'er-do-wells like Collier.

Vivian's maid rounded the carriage, gaping.

"Come along, Winifred," he said.

The girl scurried around Brookhaven, who was sitting cross-legged on the ground, and made a huge arc to escape his grasping reach.

"Help me up, wench."

She quickened her step to catch up to her mistress.

Neither Luke nor Vivian spoke as they strolled along the pathway. Honeysuckle dripped over a meandering stone wall, and narrow strips of grass nestled up to the thatch-roofed cottages.

Vivian stared up at him with her direct blue gaze. "You failed to introduce me to your friends."

"Lord Brookhaven and his guests are old acquaintances. I don't classify them as friends."

"It appears Mrs. Price would like to become reacquainted, Your Grace. You may return to speak with her if you wish."

Her formality in addressing him rankled. A few days ago his name had rolled from her tongue as sweetly as if she had crooned it. Perhaps more galling was her lack of concern over who received his attentions.

Damnation! Why should he care? Her nonchalance meant he held no place of importance in her heart, which would facilitate his mission. If she had no tender feelings for him, she would be more apt to choose a replacement husband quickly. Another wave of irrational anger swept over him.

"It seems Mrs. Price—"

"We are finished discussing Mrs. Price," he snapped.

Vivian planted her feet, and her maid bumped into her with a surprised cry. She opened her reticule, withdrew a coin, and wheeled around to press it into her maid's palm. "Winnie, would you be a dear and retrieve a sweet for us?"

The servant's forehead creased in bewilderment as she searched for and then spotted the sweet shop across the lane. "As you wish, milady."

"Don't forget one for yourself."

Once Winifred crossed the lane and disappeared through the shop's door in a tinkling of bells, Vivian looked up at him.

"Do you like sweets, Luke?"

"Pardon?"

Her eyes gleamed with a touch of wildness now that she stood toe to toe with him. "I asked if you liked sweets. It's a simple question."

There was nothing simple about her inquiry. Or Vivian.

He couldn't hold back a pleased grin.

Ten

VIVI HATED THE TIGHTNESS IN HER THROAT AND THE way her voice broke. Jealousy was an unbecoming attribute. It reminded her of a mad creature with bulging, bloodshot eyes and spittle dripping from yellowed fangs. But she didn't like Mrs. Price or the way the woman had allowed her gaze to roam up and down Luke's body like she wanted nothing more than to toss him on the lane and do unspeakable things with him. Or how the woman tried to lure him to her bedchamber with the promise of a treat.

"Well, *are* you fond of sweets, Your Grace?"

There was a slight narrowing of his sparkling blue eyes. "Do you reference baked goods, or are you schooled in code and espionage?"

He was laughing at her again, finding her a source of amusement and adding to her humiliation.

"Forget I inquired." She turned her back to him, her toe tapping against the cobbled walk before she realized it. She forced her body to be still and fought against the urge to fidget as she waited for her maid to return.

His hand on her shoulder gave her a start. "I suppose it depends on the baker, Vivian." The softly spoken words were like a tonic, smoothing her ruffled feathers. Tingles radiated from the spot where his hand rested. She wished she really were his betrothed, so she could turn into his embrace and snuggle her cheek against him. Instead, she reluctantly shifted away from his touch.

He sighed. "I have heard it said Mrs. Price is too free with her baked goods. I can assure you I have no desire to be a recipient of her generosity."

"I see." Heat singed her cheeks. She was not so ignorant as to be unaware of Mrs. Price's position in society. Yet, it was overwhelming for a country girl, having never been exposed to the sophisticated life of the *ton*. She glanced toward the coaching yard, uncertain what her response should be. More than anything, she wanted to avoid appearing like a naive girl in Luke's eyes. She was a woman, and she wanted to be his wife.

He urged her to face him. "I have never been fond of bakers being too free with their sweets. I intend to speak with Lord Brookhaven about reconsidering his traveling party if he wishes to stay at Irvine Castle."

Vivi turned back toward the sweet shop, trying to hide her relieved smile.

A bell jangled as Winnie emerged. She looked both ways then crossed the dusty lane. When her maid reached her side, she held out the treats. "The shop had your favorite."

"Thank you." Vivi took the bundle, handed a chocolate biscuit to Winnie, and selected one. She wrapped up the third treat and placed it in her reticule.

Luke fell into step beside her as they resumed their stroll. "You're not going to share with me?"

Vivi bit into the biscuit and made him wait for an answer. After drawing out the silence, she flashed a teasing smile. "You made it clear you don't appreciate sweets given out too freely, Your Grace."

His deep chuckle lifted her spirits. He seemed to have forgotten her unseemly display of jealousy already. "I really must question your brother on your education, Lady Vivian, for I have the distinct impression you were tutored in codes."

When they returned to the inn, she and Winnie retired upstairs so Vivi could change into a fresh gown before dinner.

Luke rapped on her door minutes after her maid had set her to rights. He too had donned clean attire and appeared very ducal standing outside her door, except for his wide grin. Her papa had never made an appearance without his stern frown, and her brother always looked as serious as a case of smallpox. Perhaps someone had neglected to inform the Duke of Foxhaven men of aristocratic birth were not jovial creatures.

"Has anyone ever remarked that you are too happy, Your Grace?"

"Never." He didn't seem taken aback by her question in the least. Nothing ever seemed to ruffle him.

He bowed then held out his arm. "Lady Vivian, shall I escort you below stairs?"

She returned his smile as she slipped her arm through the crook of his elbow. "If any gentleman ever suggests you should behave like a stuffy old duke,

I hope you will recommend he take a leap from the Westminster Bridge."

"I shall take your advice under consideration, my lady."

"As you should, Your Grace."

A throat clearing behind her made her jump. Glancing over her shoulder, she discovered Lord Andrew and Lana were standing in the corridor. Surely they hadn't been there the entire time.

"They are irritatingly formal," Lana muttered to her husband. "Lady This, Lord That."

"Your Grace," Lord Andrew added in a falsetto. "With their high-handed manners, one might mistake them for nobility."

Vivi laughed. Her travel companions behaved more like friends than chaperones, which made for a pleasant journey thus far.

As Luke led her below stairs, she reveled in his warmth. There were not enough opportunities to be close to him, so she would relish each one. Inside the private dining room, she didn't release him until he pulled out her chair at the long, linen-covered table. Lana and Lord Andrew assumed places on the opposite side.

Luke snatched up the bottle of wine resting in the middle of the table. "Allow me to do the honors."

Vivi started to request lemonade, thought better of it, and held her tongue. She would only draw attention to her lack of social experience if she refused the wine. Ash and Muriel always had wine with their meals. Cousin Patrice was an exception, but she preferred life in the country and probably had forgotten how to be sophisticated.

"Thank you, Your Grace."

"My pleasure." He raised his glass into the air. "To new adventures."

"To new adventures." She touched her glass to each of her dining partners' glasses.

Lord Andrew arched a brow. "At your age, old man, what new adventures can one hope to have?"

Luke's smile dimmed, and he lost some of the liveliness Vivi admired.

She sat up straighter and squared her shoulders. "Every *day* is new, my lord. One must simply look for adventure to find it."

"Well spoken, my lady," Lord Andrew said and exchanged a look with his wife. "You are amazing, Lana. How do you do it?"

She shrugged and sipped her wine, a smug grin in place.

"Do what?" Vivi and Luke asked at the same time. Before Lana could respond, there was a commotion at the dining room entrance.

The two gentlemen from the coaching yard barreled into the room with Mrs. Price.

One of the men lifted a hand in greeting. "Foxhaven and Forest." His smooth cheeks and unsteady gait reminded her of an overgrown baby.

"Mr. Collier. Lord Brookhaven." Luke's tone revealed nothing of what he thought of sharing the dining room with the gentlemen and their companion, even though Vivi was almost certain paramours and ladies did not mingle.

She studied Lana for a cue on how to react to the other woman's presence, but her chaperone's expression was blank. Not helpful in the least. In fact, Luke and Lord Andrew's granite faces were just as useless at assisting her in navigating this awkward situation.

Vivi inclined her head in greeting when the silence became too much to bear. "Good evening, Mrs. Price. Gentlemen."

The woman drew back, blinking as if a speck of dust had flown into her eye. "Good evening, Miss…"

"Vivian Worth."

Luke set his wine down hard, almost sloshing some out of the glass. "*Lady* Vivian, the Marquess of Ashden's sister."

Vivi cringed. The first words from her mouth and she had made a cake of herself.

"Ashden has a sister?" Mr. Collier asked. "I thought he was an only child."

Was her brother so ashamed of her he kept her existence a secret? She notched her chin up to hide her hurt.

Mrs. Price smiled politely. "It is an honor to meet you, my lady."

"Wine," Mr. Collier declared before moving for the seat beside Vivi and colliding with Lord Brookhaven. Mr. Collier proved more agile and plopped down beside her while his friend stumbled into the wall.

She averted her gaze, embarrassed on the gentleman's behalf.

"Please, help yourself," Lord Andrew drawled when Mr. Collier grabbed the bottle of wine.

Mrs. Price selected the chair beside Luke's brother and fluffed her plum skirts. "Good evening, Lord Andrew," she said without looking at him.

Luke's brother jerked upright in his chair then turned an incredulous look on his wife. "Hell's teeth, peach. Did you just pinch me?"

"How does she know your name?" Lana's harsh whisper carried across the table.

Mrs. Price peered around him. "Lord Norwick spoke of your husband upon occasion, my lady. I hope all is well with the earl. It has been a long time since he has called."

"Oh. Yes well, I imagine his new countess keeps him busy." Lana adjusted her position, a pretty, pink blush flooding her cheeks. "My apologies, my lord. I only meant to get your attention."

Lord Andrew grinned. "Effective, but unnecessary. I assure you."

"I cannot believe Ashden has a sister," Mr. Collier announced. "He never mentioned having a sister."

Vivi really didn't appreciate being reminded she was a shameful secret.

Lord Andrew sent her a sympathetic smile. "No gent wants you two knowing he has a sister. Brookhaven, you look like a trout out of water. It's not an attractive sight."

The gentleman snapped his mouth closed, dragged up a chair, and sat at the end of the table. A heavy silence blanketed the dining room. Everyone seemed to be as lost as she was when it came to knowing what was proper etiquette when dining with a courtesan.

Vivi took a sip of her drink, hoping someone would break the silence soon, and her face nearly folded in on itself. Her wine was bitter beyond the pale.

"I-I think it has gone bad," she sputtered.

Luke tested the wine. "It tastes fine to me."

"Oh." *Gads*. How did anyone consume the beverage without choking?

"Would you prefer something else to drink? Perhaps lemonade or cordial water?" Luke asked.

She shook her head, took another sip, and stifled a grimace. It seemed all eyes were trained on her, all except Mrs. Price's. The woman was too preoccupied with ogling Luke.

Vivi's jealous side bared its fangs again. "His Grace doesn't have a taste for sweets, Mrs. Price."

Every person at the table gaped at her as if she had lost her wits.

"I beg your pardon, my lady?"

Vivi's smile stretched tightly. "In the coaching yard, you mentioned having carried treats with you, and since His Grace doesn't care for sweets, he will surely decline to sample any of yours."

A shadow of horror darkened Lana's face. Mrs. Price uttered several incomprehensible sounds, her cheeks flushing as crimson as her lip rouge.

Oh, dear Lord! Why hadn't Vivi stopped to think before she had spoken? Mrs. Price hadn't been trying to lure Luke to her room with the promise of a sweet. She *was* the treat. Embarrassment crawled up Vivi's skin.

Luke stood. "We should go."

Mrs. Price met Vivian's eyes across the table. "Forgive me, my lady. I spoke out of turn when we arrived at the inn. Please stay and enjoy your meal." She pushed away from the table and tried to escape the dining room, but Mr. Collier grabbed her arm.

"Where are you going? We haven't eaten yet."

"We should dine in the tavern."

Collier grinned at Vivi. "I am staying right here."

"Behave yourself, sir," Mrs. Price said then added under her breath, "or you will go without biscuits or milk this evening."

Her travel companions roared, slapping their knees. Mr. Collier threw his head back with a hearty cackle, tipped to the side, and fell to the ground. From what Vivi had witnessed thus far, Lord Brookhaven and Mr. Collier spent more time on their backsides than their feet.

She leaned close to Luke. "Perhaps I *should* ask for lemonade," she whispered. "I think too much wine addles the mind."

A small smile played upon his lips. "Brookhaven was born an addlepate. Collier may have been dropped on his head."

"Oh, I see." Maybe her worry was for naught. She took another drink of her wine. The bitterness was dissipating and her body began to melt against the chair. It was not an altogether unpleasant sensation. She took another sip, noting with pleasure that Mrs. Price and at least one of the gentlemen were taking their leave.

❧

Luke acknowledged the folly in serving Vivian wine the moment she tossed her head back with a husky laugh that displayed her slender neck. Her voice held every ounce of the dynamic spirit that infused her, drawing him closer. There was something uncommonly engaging about her. She was the

juxtaposition of innocence and lustful joy for life.
She stirred his desire unlike any woman ever had,
but he resisted her call. He couldn't offer her what
she deserved, and he cared enough for Vivian to deny
his selfish urges.

Ashden was a fool. The marquess's sister possessed
no fault to render her undesirable, as evidenced by the
bloody rake salivating at her left.

Collier—having declined to leave when Brookhaven
and Mrs. Price made their exit—shared in Vivian's
merriment. His hungry gaze roamed over her, lingering
too long on her modest décolletage. "Lady Vivian,
you are enchanting beyond compare. I do hope we
may further our acquaintance in Northumberland."

Like hell they would. Collier would never be on
Luke's approved list of suitors for Vivian. Not that he
had compiled a list.

Collier laughed at something else she said—likely
something charming Luke had missed while wrapped
up in his thoughts of throttling the blackguard—and
placed his arm on the back of her chair. One glare
from Luke made him jerk back.

"You only needed to stake your claim, Foxhaven,"
he mumbled. "Don't know why you didn't make an
indication earlier."

Vivian's silver gaze, twinkling with mischief, lifted
toward Luke. Her cheeks were flushed and her lips
moist and red from the wine. He would enjoy staking
his claim. The realization rattled him.

"Mr. Collier, you mistake His Grace's intentions,"
Vivian said with a sweet smile. "He only wishes to
play matchmaker on my behalf."

Luke held his grimace in check. Serving Vivian wine had been more than folly. It was a bloody disaster.

She turned back to Collier and lowered her voice. "He seems particular, I'm afraid. Perhaps he thinks you are an unsuitable match."

"The devil, you say!" Collier glowered at Luke over the top of her golden head. "What objection do you have to my person?"

"The shorter list would be what he doesn't object to about your person," Drew piped up from his side of the table. He looked too amused by half. "You're a rakehell of the first order."

"I am *not*." Collier tried to hammer his fist on the table, missed, and smacked his thigh. "Where did the blasted table go?"

Vivian laughed again, drawing the man's attention back to the creamy swells of flesh jiggling too damned enticingly above the neckline of her gown.

Luke pushed back from the table. This had gone on long enough. In another minute, he would issue a challenge to Collier and ruin their chances for an early start the morrow. "Lady Vivian is correct. I don't approve of you."

Collier narrowed his eyes. "Are you her guardian or something?"

"I'm something." A hard knot formed in Luke's belly. As appealing as she was to him, he must give her up once they reached Northumberland. But they were not in Northumberland yet, and he would rather beat Collier silly than surrender Vivian to him.

Luke offered her a hand up. "My lady, I will return you to the care of your maid now."

She placed her hand in his, her intense stare never wavering. "Thank you, Your Grace."

"Good evening, Collier," Drew said as he assisted Lana from her seat.

"No need to cut the evening short. It's early, gents."

No one paid him any notice.

Once their party reached the upper floor of the inn, Luke nodded to Drew to signal he wished to be alone with Vivian. His brother swept Lana into the room across the corridor before she could protest, and from her surprised cry once the door closed, his brother had found a way to distract her.

Vivian captured Luke's hands and urged him to follow as she backed against the wall. "Have you ever courted a lady, Your Grace?"

Before he could answer, she frowned. Her forehead wrinkled in concentration as she reached her fingers to touch his bottom lip and tugged it down to peer into his mouth. "Is there a name for that little gap between your teeth?"

He playfully nipped her finger. She jerked her hand back with a squeal.

"You can't handle your spirits, darling."

Her hand settled on his chest. "I have never had wine before tonight."

When she swayed to the left, he captured her around the waist. She twined her arms around his neck and tipped her face up, her eyes closed.

He savored her heat and perfume. Her scent reminded him of a confection. She was the only sweet he wanted. He leaned forward, tempted to taste her. Their lips hovered close, her warm breath flowing over his chin and along his neck. His fingers curled into her skirts, easing her closer. Her body pressed against his and she sighed, melting into him.

Devil take it. She was the most tempting creature on earth, but she wasn't in any state to know what she was doing. And damned if he could kiss her if he had no intention of making her his wife.

She is yours. Luke gritted his teeth and forced down his primal instincts. Lady Vivian wasn't his. Yet, unable to deny himself fully, he placed tremulous lips against her forehead. She was so soft. He lingered. When he pulled back, he tasted a trace of salt on his lips. He trembled from the strain of resisting her.

Vivian's long lashes fluttered before her gaze met his. She seemed to be puzzling out what had just occurred. He had no answers for her. He had never been more befuddled in his life.

"Vivian, I'm sorry for exposing you to Collier. You deserve better than the likes of him."

Her smile returned slowly, a happy glow illuminating her face. "I couldn't agree more, Your Grace. And I shall have him."

He released her with a frown. Did she have someone in mind already? Not Brookhaven, surely.

Her grin grew wider. "With your assistance, of course."

It appeared Vivian was satisfied with their pact. She would travel with him, tempt him with every breath, and then she would make a match with another gentleman just as he had planned. His chest was too tight all of a sudden. He longed to escape to his chamber and loosen his waistcoat.

He released her to open the door to her chamber. "Turn the lock. I'll come for you in the morning."

Once he saw her safely inside and heard the tumble of the lock, he slumped against the wall to gather his wits.

Vivian would marry someone else, perhaps someone he knew well. And she expected his assistance. Unfortunately, her trust might be misplaced, for he couldn't think of a single gentleman deserving of the incomparable Lady Vivian Worth, nor one to which he could imagine surrendering her.

A creak sounded from the stairwell. Collier trudged up the stairs and paused on the top step to smirk in Luke's direction. "I see. You are Lady Vivian's guard, not her guardian. Did you have to become a eunuch for the position?"

He glared in return. "She is mine. Stay away."

Collier climbed the last step and swaggered toward him. "That isn't what the lady said. It seems to me she is fair game."

Luke met him halfway down the corridor. "My betrothed has a peculiar sense of humor. I don't."

Collier balked. "You are affianced to Lady Vivian?"

"I already said she's mine. If that is unclear, I will be more than happy to meet you early tomorrow to clear up the matter."

"There is no need to resort to threats, Foxhaven. One lady is no great loss when there are many others waiting for my attentions."

"With bated breath, I'm sure."

Collier scowled. "You always were a jackass."

"If you come anywhere close to Lady Vivian again,

I'll remind you just how big a jackass I can be." He felt a twinge of regret for his past treatment of Collier, but he was serious about protecting Vivian from the rake.

The other man bumped Luke's shoulder as he passed by, knocked himself off balance, and careened into the wall. Luke stood rooted in place until Collier recovered and stormed to his chamber.

What the hell was he doing? Every moment in Vivian's company drained him of his good sense, but he was growing less enamored with the thought of giving her to another man. Unfortunately, even if he could marry her, she no longer wanted him. At least not as a husband. She had seemed agreeable to kissing him, however.

He should have just kissed the lady until her legs couldn't hold her up any more, then given her no choice but to accept him.

Devil take it. He had completely lost his senses. He had to give her up.

Eleven

VIVI DROPPED HER HEAD AND SHOT PAST LUKE TO climb into the carriage. Tucking into a corner, she wished for the thousandth time that morning she could disappear. Had she truly grabbed his lip and looked at his teeth like he was a horse? Never had she done anything so humiliating, and that was saying a lot, for she had done *many* things she had later regretted.

Lana joined her in the coach and took the seat across from her. Thankfully, the gentlemen would be on horseback the first leg of the journey. Nonetheless, while Vivi didn't want to be confined to a small space with Luke, his choice to put distance between them this morning made her jumpy inside. She had probably ruined everything with her misguided attempt at seduction.

The carriage jerked forward and initiated a throbbing in her head. "I will never drink wine again."

Lana looked up from the book lying open on her lap. "Why ever not?"

"Because I behaved like an idiot last night."

Her companion laughed. "You were a charming dining partner, and entertaining."

"I don't *want* to be entertaining," she said on a near wail. "I want to be beautiful and alluring and irresistible. Not the court jester."

"You are all of those things in addition to being amusing. I daresay Luke found you charming."

Vivi shifted her gaze out the window and held her tongue. It would be unladylike to accuse her chaperone of handing out lies. He had refused to kiss her, even when nothing in her conduct suggested she was opposed. This was not the action of a gentleman who had been charmed. Although any gentleman capable of being enchanted by her jealous outburst and dimwitted actions was suspect, in her opinion.

When she glanced back at Lana, her chaperone regarded her with a half smile. "If something is troubling you, I know how to keep a secret. You may tell me anything without fear."

"I understood Lord Andrew to say there are no secrets between you."

Lana winked. "See how capable I am of keeping secrets? Even my husband has no idea."

Vivi wavered between blurting everything out and keeping her own counsel. It would be nice to have a confidant again. Once Mrs. Honeywell had made enough innuendos and hinted to the residents of Dunstable that she was a terrible influence on their daughters, Vivi had lost her friends. She missed Dottie Kennicot most of all, but her bosom friend had been threatened with a severe beating if she sought Vivi's company again.

Patrice had been livid and written to Ash about the woman's betrayal, but he had been unsympathetic. As long as no one of consequence learned of her ruin at the hands of a servant, no harm had been done. Instead of threatening the woman, Vivi's brother had asked her price for silence. How lucky they were that Mrs. Honeywell's desire for prestige and lavish parties in Town outweighed her craving to spread gossip beyond the small village.

Lana leaned across the carriage to touch Vivi's knee. All traces of teasing and merriment were gone. "I promise to never share your secrets with Drew unless you grant your permission."

Vivi nodded and studied a speck of dried mud on her skirts rather than chance seeing Lana's displeasure. "I have misled His Grace. I entered this arrangement with no intention of releasing him from the betrothal. I don't want another suitor. I want him."

She risked a quick glance to see how badly her deceit and selfishness appalled her new friend, but Lana simply stared back at her with an enigmatic smile. Vivi's body melted against the cushions.

"He is unlike other gentlemen," Vivi explained in a rush. "He doesn't berate me for swimming or riding astride. And he not only allowed me to fire his pistol, he encouraged me to load it. How am I to let go of a man so perfectly suited to me?"

"It would seem you are a good match for him as well, but Luke is more complex than other gentlemen."

"How so?"

She shook her head. "It's not for me to speak of his personal affairs."

"But do I have a chance of winning him? Please, be honest. I may have made a fool of myself already, but I don't want to be humiliated."

Lana drummed her fingers against the book page, a line appearing between her arched brows. "I wish I could tell you there is no risk involved in love, Vivian, but that would be dishonest. Nevertheless, you may have the best odds of bringing him up to scratch than any lady who has tried thus far."

Vivi sank back against the seat with a sigh. She had hoped to hear something less discouraging. "Are you implying he might never marry?"

"I don't know what is in my brother-in-law's mind. I would venture to say few people do. If he confides in Drew, that is one thing my husband keeps from me." She tipped her head to the side. "If I may ask, how did you learn to ride astride and shoot a firearm?"

"My brother taught me, but that was before he knew better. It was just the two of us after our parents died. Ash was barely old enough to be my guardian, but he tried."

Lana chuckled. "The lessons our brothers teach us can come in handy at the most unexpected times. I have four older brothers of my own, and I daresay my education as a lady was enhanced, thanks to them."

"Well, Ash's wife does not view my unorthodox education the same. She was raised with sisters only, and my rowdiness often sent her into the vapors. My poor brother didn't know what to do when she took to her bed for days after he defended me."

She nibbled her bottom lip and glanced out the window. How it had broken her heart to see her brother conflicted. When Muriel was with child, Vivi knew she would be sent away. Even in her nine-year-old heart, she realized this was for the best. If her sister-in-law had lost Ash's issue after a spell brought on by her antics, Vivi might have lost her brother, too. She had been saddened by the news of Muriel's miscarriage, but also relieved she wasn't to blame. She had been living at Brighthurst House for weeks at the time.

Now, Muriel despised her for forcing her to endure Mrs. Honeywell's companionship. "I fear my brother's wife and I will never be on friendly terms."

Lana clucked her tongue. "Please don't take offense, my dear, but I shouldn't think I would like to make Lady Ashden's acquaintance. Is there a way to avoid inviting her to yours and Luke's wedding?"

Lana's optimism buoyed her spirits until memories of what Vivi now dubbed "the tooth blunder" resurfaced. She groaned under her breath.

Lord, help her. She made for an abysmal seductress, but she must try or else surrender.

And surrender had never had a place in her vocabulary.

"Lana, how does a lady court a gentleman exactly?"

"Just continue to be yourself." When she frowned, her friend laughed. "Oh, very well. I may have a couple of suggestions, but I warn you to use them wisely and be prepared."

"Prepared for what?"

"For *anything*. The Forest men are an unpredictable lot."

❧

Luke shifted in the saddle and peered over his shoulder toward the carriage where Vivian was safely ensconced. Safe from what, exactly, he didn't know. Perhaps safe from him.

After a sleepless night of fantasizing about removing

each article of her clothing and kissing every inch of her body, he didn't trust himself to remain a gentleman if he found himself alone with her again this evening.

Being in close proximity all day would only make matters worse. Yet he missed her wit and laughter. The heat of her skin as his leg accidentally brushed against hers in the carriage. His body ached for her.

This is insanity. He swallowed a groan and returned his attention to the rutted road.

Drew chuckled.

"Speak your mind and be done with it," Luke said. "You know you will eventually, so spare me the suspense."

"You only need to give the word if you want to join the ladies."

"I don't." But he did. He wanted it with great intensity, which was the reason he was riding his damned horse.

Drew's black stallion plodded along beside Thor in companionable silence. Luke wished he could say the same for his brother.

"Lady Vivian is a beautiful young woman. Father chose well."

Luke pulled his hat lower to shade his eyes. "I'm certain Father had no idea what he was agreeing to when he entered into negotiations with Ashden."

"What do you mean? Lady Vivian is lively, intelligent, and not a bit hard on the eyes. What fault do you find with her?"

"She has no faults in my eyes. Father, on the other hand, would not have approved of her high spirits."

"Hmm," Drew muttered noncommittally.

"Have you ever met a lady who wields a foil and

can sit a horse better than most men? You should have seen her clear the fence at Brighthurst. It required hardly any effort."

A surge of energy chased away the sluggish feeling that had been dogging him since he had climbed from bed that morning. Vivian excited him; she made him feel intensely alive, like the day he had been caught in the thunderstorm. The first day he had laid eyes on her.

"If Lady Vivian is an accomplished equestrienne," Drew said, "you should have invited her to join you instead."

"She is perfectly fine in the carriage. I can barely keep my hands off her as it is."

Drew's brows drew together. "And why can't you touch her?"

Luke had never known his youngest brother to abstain from anything he desired, which likely accounted for his bemusement. "If I'm to help Vivian make a match, I cannot ruin her, now can I?"

"I see no reason you should hand her over to another gent, especially if you're entertaining thoughts of bedding her."

"I am *not* thinking of bedding her." At least the thought hadn't invaded his mind for the past ten minutes, but it was back like an annoying itch he couldn't scratch. "I promised to help her find a husband, and I honor my word."

Drew shrugged. "Lana had some decent gentlemen on her list, but you dismissed them all. Who do you think would be a good match for Lady Vivian?"

"I haven't decided, but none of those will do."

The thought of Vivian marrying Lord Corby

or Mitcham did not sit well with him, even if the gentlemen did boast sterling reputations. Nor did he care for Lord Ledbery or Mr. Theobald. And what in God's name made Lana believe Osborn, Kirby, or Gillingham would make a decent match for Vivian? She needed a husband who understood and embraced her nature. Luke wasn't certain if any gentlemen of his acquaintance would meet his standards.

Drew cleared his throat. "What are your intentions for yourself once you have ensured the lady is well settled in marriage? I hate to sound like Rich, but you are the duke now. Neither our brother nor I may assume the role."

Luke's lips thinned. That was the rub. Only he could bear the title, but he was least suited to fulfill the duties. At one time, he had been ready to embrace his role, but that was before his accident.

He had been engaging in tomfoolery with his Oxford classmates in the dormitory corridor. He remembered almost nothing beyond that moment, aside from the crash of glass and cold air on his face. The impact remained a forgotten memory, one he didn't care to recall. Yet, sometimes the fall came back to him in flashes as he drifted to sleep at night, causing him to jerk awake and his heart to slam against his ribs.

"Let's see how the expedition goes before we begin settling my future," he said. "Later I will concern myself with finding a wife. If I make it back."

"Stop talking that way. Of course you'll make it back, but Lady Vivian will be lost to you by then."

Luke's stomach lurched and he swallowed against

the bitter taste at the back of his throat. "*If* I return, I'll find someone else."

Drew scowled but said nothing.

"Marriage is about mutual benefit for both parties, and a title wouldn't be enough for Lady Vivian."

Was that true? She had said she could be content living a life apart from one another.

"Marriage is about mutual benefit, is it?" Drew said. "How foolish of me to believe love might play a small role."

"One can't deny you are foolish in the extreme." In truth, both of Luke's younger brothers were besotted fools. Richard was just as arsey varsey over his wife as Drew was for Lana, but one could not deny they were in the minority. Gentlemen of means and title married for many different reasons. Love was an illogical one.

"Don't become too smug, brother," Drew said with a smirk. "You're in danger of joining the rank of fools, too. I have noticed how you regard Lady Vivian."

Just the mention of her name stirred Luke's body. "This conversation has grown tedious. First one to reach the bend ahead is the winner."

Drew's horse shot forward. "Loser buys the ale," he shouted over his shoulder.

Luke squinted against the fine dust cloud stirred up by the other horse's hooves and lightly kicked Thor into a gallop. His horse reached full stride in moments and closed the lead.

Drew's whoop carried on the wind as he antici-pated victory. His hat whipped from his head. Luke ducked before it hit his face.

Thor reached the other horse's hindquarters just as

they rounded the bend, his brother besting him as he usually did when they raced.

Luke and Drew eased back on the reins to slow their horses. Luke's heart beat heavily and he laughed, exhilarated by racing neck-or-nothing against his brother.

Drew's cheeks were red and his hair was tousled. "The ale is on you tonight, old man."

"You had an early start."

Drew grinned, that same cocky smirk he'd sported since he had worn short pants. "My only advantage was that I'm a superior specimen of man."

"Not to mention modest."

In truth, Luke didn't mind losing to his youngest brother. At least Drew was willing to indulge him and take his mind off his troubles. Had Richard been traveling with him, Luke would have been tearing down the lane alone. Situated squarely between Luke and Drew in birth order, Richard behaved as if he were in his dotage. They had uncles less crotchety.

Luke raised his brows. "Aren't you riding one of Father's horses? That would make him mine, you realize."

"Demetrius? Sorry to disappoint you, but Father gave him to me long ago."

"That wasn't how I heard it. I think the tale went something like you absconded to London with Father's prized Thoroughbred."

"Borrowed? Gifted? Is there truly any difference?"

"Not to you, I guess."

Their banter continued as Luke turned his horse back down the lane and made to return to the ladies. As he rounded the bend, he spotted another carriage closing in on their small caravan.

"Damnation. It's Brookhaven and Collier again."

Drew rode up on his side. "We are traveling to the same destination. It should come as no surprise that our paths have crossed again. I imagine we will be breaking bread with them this evening."

Luke's fingers tightened on the reins. "If I take the ribbons and drive the team, it should be easy enough to lose them."

"You most certainly will not. My wife and children are in the carriage."

Luke shook the foolish notion from his head. "I wasn't seriously contemplating it."

Any risk of harm coming to Vivian or his kin would never do, even though putting distance between themselves and the rogues was tempting. He dreaded another dinner with the drooling mongrels, especially when the tasty morsel they would be eyeing was Vivian.

Drew walked his horse to where his hat lay tipped over in the lane, dismounted, and slapped it against his trouser leg before popping it on his head. He swung back into the saddle as Luke's carriage approached.

As the conveyance passed, Luke took up position alongside it. Vivian flattened a palm against the glass, as if waving, and smiled. She had removed her gloves and bonnet, and wisps of hair had slipped down around her face.

God, she was breathtaking.

A tug of longing from deep inside caused him to bolt upright in the saddle. The feeling was unexpected, startling him, just like the falling sensation that jerked him awake at night.

Twelve

VIVI WELCOMED THE STOP TO CHANGE HORSES AND hastened to exit the carriage when Lord Andrew opened the door. Not only had her backside grown numb from the prolonged period of sitting, but her mind was also turning to mush. Although Lana's conversational skills were exceptional, there was only so much Vivi could contribute before she grew restless. She was the type of lady who preferred doing to discussing.

She swept her gaze over the coaching yard and didn't see Luke. Where could he have gone? She had spotted him only moments before their arrival.

Lord Andrew assisted his wife down the steps next then tucked her hand into the crook of his arm. "Shall we retrieve the girls?"

"Yes," Lana said on a rush of breath.

Vivi bit her bottom lip as she watched her companion hurry to gather her daughters from the nurse. How difficult it must be for Lana to be separated from her children all day. If Vivi were any kind of friend, she would invite the girls to join them in

Luke's carriage. She opened her mouth to make the suggestion, and a loud shriek caused her to jump.

Egads. That child had a voice. Perhaps she would wait until they reached the next coaching inn before extending an invitation.

"Would you like to take refreshment, Lady Vivian? Luke will join us in a moment." Lord Andrew cuddled his daughter against his chest and placed a kiss on her red curls. Chloe, or perhaps it was Claire—she had a difficult time telling the little ones apart—seemed mesmerized by his moving mouth and grabbed for his lips.

It was an unwelcome reminder of her encounter with Luke last night. Vivi wheeled around before anyone could see the hot blush climbing her neck and stealing into her cheeks. "I-I believe fresh air will benefit me most. Please, don't allow me to keep you from taking refreshment, though."

"If you are certain…"

She kept her back to her chaperones, feigning interest in the mundane tasks performed by the servants. "I'm quite certain, thank you."

"Very well."

Her maid hung behind as the brood entered the inn, Lana's happy chatter becoming muffled with the closing of the door. Winnie's shoulders drooped on a loud sigh. "Do you wish to take another stroll, my lady?"

The poor dear. Being confined to a small space with two forces of nature and their frazzled nurse must require great fortitude.

"Not this time, Winnie. You may find a quiet place to rest. I promise not to wander away."

Winnie's thin brows shot upward. "You? Not wander?"

Vivi sniffed; her earlier compassion for her maid was dissipating a bit. "I will confine my wanderings to the stable yard. Does that put your mind at rest?"

"Not by much, my lady." Her maid glanced around the coaching yard with her fingers laced. The area was deserted, except for the ostler, stable boys, and Luke's servants. There was no danger present. "Will you stay close to His Grace's servants?"

"I have already given my word. Now, go. Enjoy the rest. I am sure you have earned it."

Winnie slowly shook her head. "I don't know. Lady Brighthurst said I should look after you, my lady."

"Win, I'm not making a request. Take some refreshment and rest. No more arguments."

Winnie turned on her heel and plodded up the stairs in a sulk.

Vivi released a pent-up breath when the door to the inn closed behind her maid. Vivi didn't require a keeper, and she certainly didn't need one on the brink of keeling over from exhaustion.

She began a leisurely circle of the stable yard, grateful for a moment alone. She stayed close to the outer perimeter so as not to interfere with the men's work. The fenced area proved uninspiring in the extreme. Nothing but horses, harnesses, and sweaty men.

And the smell…

She pretended to scratch her nose to block the stench, not wishing to insult anyone.

Stopping at a wooden gate, she eyed the pebbled path beyond it. A trail wound alongside the inn and disappeared behind the building. Perhaps she would find quiet and escape the smell if she followed it. Another carriage drove into the yard. While everyone was occupied with the new arrival, she unlatched the gate and hurried through it. The gate banged back in place behind her.

Unexplored paths had always been irresistible to Vivi. An unknown trail filled her with anticipation for what she might find at the other end. A cozy cottage? A swing shaded by the lush branches of an oak? A hidden garden or tranquil pond? How was anyone to resist the temptation of discovery?

The trail wound alongside a copse of trees, and tall grass grew up to the path's edge. She could still hear the rattling of harnesses and the deep, mumbled voices of the men in the distance, but civilization receded for the moment. Tension escaped her on every breath, and she tipped her face up to feel the warm sun on her skin. This was exactly what she had needed: a chance to convene with nature.

Rounding the building, she entered a clearing where a kitchen garden grew. Vegetables weren't nearly as romantic as flowers, but it was more pleasant than the stable yard. She walked between rows of lettuces, attempting to identify the different varieties. She paused before a weed that had sprouted up between the lacy leaves.

"You don't belong here." She removed her gloves and bent over to pull the interloper from the dark soil. Straightening with a smile, she resumed her walk. A few paces down the row she spotted another weed and frowned. She plucked it from the ground, and upon standing, she found two more.

For heaven's sake. Someone had been neglecting her duties. The invading pests seemed to pop up from no place as soon as she turned her back. She tossed both gloves toward the edge of the garden and set to work pulling the weeds. She would have this row looking quite the thing in no time.

Pleasing warmth invaded her cheeks and her breathing grew heavier as she extracted weed after weed. Her heart practically sang with joy as it pushed blood through her veins. Her hat slipped forward and she shoved it back on her head. Halfway down the row, she encountered an especially stubborn fellow and tugged on it with both hands, throwing her hips into wrestling the weed from the spot where it had taken root. She swiveled side to side, but it wouldn't give up its purchase.

"Peas and carrots!"

A chuckle sounded behind her.

Vivi bolted upright with a gasp and spun around.

Mr. Collier was regarding her with a crooked smile. His pale eyes were shot through with red, and his face looked puffy. "My apologies, Lady Vivian. I didn't intend to startle you."

"Mr. Collier." She swiped her forehead with the back of her hand "I-I wasn't expecting you."

"Nor would I expect you to." His grin widened as he extracted a handkerchief from his pocket and approached her. "You have a smudge on your face."

"Oh!" She reached out to accept his offering, but he didn't hand over the handkerchief. Instead, he stood too close and touched the cloth to her forehead.

"Allow me to assist, Lady Vivian." His nearness made her fidgety inside, and she stepped away from him.

"Thank you, sir. I am certain the smudge is gone now."

"My pleasure, my lady." He tucked the handkerchief back into his waistcoat. "May I inquire into what you are doing in the garden?"

A relevant inquiry, she supposed. Nevertheless, as foolishness rarely sufficed as a reasonable excuse in her experience, she was at a loss.

"There was a weed." She looked down at her dirty hands. "I saw a weed."

He must think her a ridiculous young woman. And his opinion might not trouble her under different circumstances, but everything she did now reflected on Luke.

"How interesting," Mr. Collier muttered. "Do you enjoy gardening?"

Vivi's gaze snapped to his.

He smiled in return. "My grandmother has an aptitude for growing plants."

"I enjoy being outside."

"Riverton Manor boasts impressive flower gardens. Perhaps you would like to visit sometime." He took another step toward her, and her heart began drumming in her ears.

She tried to ease away from him without her efforts appearing obvious. "Riverton sounds lovely, sir."

His eyelids drooped lazily as he allowed his gaze to roam over her. "I would consider it an honor if you paid us a visit. Grandmother enjoys having guests. She keeps a decent town house in Mayfair, as well. Of course, she is too frail to travel now, so I stay there during the Season to ensure it is well cared for in her absence. You should see the interior. It is something to behold."

Vivi stood up straighter. "I'm uncertain what you take me for, sir, but I do not call upon unmarried gentlemen, whether at their town houses or otherwise. Now, if you will excuse me, I shall be going."

When she tried to sweep past him, he captured her arm. "Forgive me, Lady Vivian. I didn't mean to imply anything untoward."

Mr. Collier may appear harmless with his ready smiles, but she had seen him deep in his cups last night. She was also aware of the company he kept. A man like him could ruin her within the blink of his bloodshot eyes.

Her gaze landed on his hand holding her, and he released her. Shrugging sheepishly, he stepped back. "I have done it again, haven't I? I am hopeless around ladies. I never know the correct thing to say, and I unfailingly make a cake of myself."

His embarrassment stirred her sympathy. She knew all about feeling lost when it came to interacting with the opposite gender. "We may have more in common than you know, Mr. Collier."

"Oh?" His thin brows arched up. "How so?"

"I, too, often find myself looking like a fool."

He laughed. It was a nice sound, like he had practiced until he'd honed the perfect expression of merriment. "I look like a fool, do I?"

Her stomach pitched. "No, I didn't mean—"

His smile widened. "Please, give it no more thought. I appreciate your attempts to make me feel less awkward. You are a kind young woman."

"Thank you, sir." She looked beyond his shoulder toward the path leading back to the stable yard. "I

hope you won't take offense, but I would like to avoid
being discovered alone in your company."

"None taken." Mr. Collier stepped aside, another
chuckle rumbling from his chest.

She scooted past him and hurried to put distance
between them. She glanced back once more to reassure herself he wasn't following before she turned the
corner and barreled into a hard chest; her face smashed
into a dusty cravat.

"Oh!" She stumbled backward, but strong fingers
closed around her shoulders and saved her from
tumbling to the ground.

A slight crease appeared on Luke's forehead. "*Here*
you are. Your maid is worried sick. I wish you
wouldn't wander off alone. What if someone else had
come upon you?"

She tossed another quick look over her shoulder,
fearful Mr. Collier would come around the corner
any moment, and Luke would know she hadn't
been alone.

"Forgive me. It won't happen again." She linked
arms and tried to drag him in the opposite direction,
which was not an easy task, a lady moving a mountain.

He slanted a smile at her as he allowed her to draw
him back toward the coaching yard. "No harm has
been done."

She exhaled, but her relief was premature.

Luke stopped and captured her hands. "Where are
your gloves?" His frown deepened when he flipped
her palms up. "Perhaps a better question is why are
your hands covered with dirt?"

She pulled from his grasp, a light sweat blanketing

her body, and took a deep, fortifying breath. This wouldn't be the first time she had incited a gentleman to raise his voice.

"I saw a weed."

"A weed?" A note of laughter rang in his voice, easing her concern.

"Several, actually. In the garden behind the inn. It has been horribly neglected."

"I see." He scratched the dark shadow on his jaw. "And your gloves?"

Her heart skipped a beat. "I—they are still in the garden." She held up a finger. "Wait here while I retrieve them."

"Don't be silly. I will retrieve them on your behalf."

If Luke sought out her gloves, he would discover Mr. Collier. "No!"

She stepped into his path. He came up short. He took a step to the left to go around her, but she countered his move.

"Vivian, what are you doing? Allow me to pass."

As he tried once more to go by, she darted in front of him. "Wait! You can't leave me. I—I'm feeling faint."

"Faint?" Luke's eyes narrowed. "You appear fine."

"No, no. I am not." She swayed on her feet to lend believability to her performance. "I might swoon." She considered holding a hand to her forehead, but it seemed too melodramatic by half.

He grabbed her around the waist, his hands hot through the fabric of her travel dress. Her throat stopped working properly, and her head swam. She might very well faint right here in his arms.

He leaned forward until they were eye to eye. Her

lids drifted to half-mast and her breath escaped her in shallow puffs.

"I would venture you have never swooned in your life, Vivian Worth."

His smug certainty shattered the spell, and she shoved her palms against his chest, breaking from his hold. "How could you know such a thing? Why, I might swoon twice a day for all you know."

"Because you, my darling, aren't faint of heart."

She huffed. When he phrased it that way, it sounded complimentary. Yet he was also calling her a liar. Her knees should buckle just to spite him, but they had a mind of their own and held steadfast.

He slipped past her, his long strides carrying him around the side of the building.

Vivian scrambled after him. "Wait! I can explain."

She clamped her lips together as she entered the clearing. Collier was gone.

"Here they are." Luke scooped up her gloves. Spinning on his heel, he strode toward her. The firm set to his jaw and his advance made her back up a step. He didn't stop until he stood right in front of her, much too close. Heat rolled off him and made her skin feel prickly.

"Vivian." His voice was a husky whisper.

Her knees knocked. Now was a fine time for them to decide to cooperate. "Yes?"

"What is it you wish to explain?"

She shook her head, willing her legs to stop quivering. "It was nothing."

Taking her hand and turning it palm up, he drew circles on her skin with his thumb. His eyes darkened as he leaned even closer; his lips parted. "Your gloves, my lady." His warm breath brushed across her ear.

She turned her face toward him, wanting nothing more than to touch her lips to his. He jerked back, his brow furrowed. His blue gaze roved over her then he shook his head as if dislodging a thought.

Perhaps a desire.

Blast it all! He wanted to kiss her, too. She could feel it. She held his gaze boldly, daring him to claim what he wanted.

He pressed the gloves into her hand. "We should go. Our party awaits us."

Her nostrils flared as he retreated. He had done it again. Made her think he was going to kiss her and then walked away.

No, that wasn't true! He had made her *hope* for his kiss.

"Why do you do that? Why do you refuse to kiss me?" The words flew from her before she could exercise restraint.

He faltered in his step and turned back toward her. He opened and closed his mouth several times before any sound escaped. "Did you truly ask why I refuse to kiss you?"

Yes, she *had* just humiliated herself beyond the pale. Patrice always said Vivi needed to learn when to hold her tongue, but she had never mastered the skill. In truth, she rarely practiced it at all.

"I…" She grasped fistfuls of her skirts and contemplated running away.

Luke lunged and caught her around the waist. "You will never run from me again, Vivian. I want an answer."

"You—you heard me the first time, Your Grace. You already know the answer."

He wrapped her in his arms, holding her tightly. "God help me, but I know nothing when you are close." His breath whispered across her lips and then his mouth came down on hers.

Vivi jumped. His mouth, soft and plump, played over hers and coaxed her to participate in her first kiss. Never had she expected a man to possess such luxurious lips.

The rigidness in her back began to melt away, and she dissolved against his uncompromising chest. His kiss elicited warm waves down her body, ending their travel in a quaking of limbs. She mimicked his movements as best she could, but she was half a heartbeat behind him. When his tongue skimmed the crease of her lips, she gasped and he swept inside her mouth.

A soft groan vibrated in his chest, beneath her palm where her fingers had tangled with his shirt. And by God, she wouldn't release him for all the gold at the end of the rainbow. Not now when she was embarking on the most invigorating adventure she could have ever imagined.

Luke pulled her closer, deepened their kiss. She tossed her arms around his neck and held tightly, smiling against his lips.

His hands cupped her bottom and lifted until she teetered on the tips of her toes. Something hard pressed against her belly, distracting her from his delicious kisses. Before she could wiggle her hand between them to see what it was, he set her away from him.

"Don't." His eyes burned with black fire, and his chest heaved with each labored breath.

Her stomach flipped. "What did I do?"

He squeezed his eyes together and ran a hand through his black curls. When he looked at her again, the darkness in his eyes had receded. Holding out her gloves, he forced a smile, a tightening at the corners of his lips. "It was nothing, Vivian. Shall we?"

It was nothing?

She puckered her lips and shoved her hand into her glove. Their kiss hadn't been nothing to her. And as sure as the sun would rise tomorrow, it had affected him too.

Refusing his arm, she stalked toward the stable yard. Luke followed at a less harried pace. Her chaperones were standing beside the carriage when Vivi pushed through the gate, their expressions giving away nothing at her state of disarray and agitation as she approached. She caught Winnie's eye, but her maid looked down quickly, uncommonly interested in the dirt beneath her boots.

Vivi came to a quick stop. Lord Andrew's horse had been fitted with a sidesaddle. Luke came up beside his brother. Her gaze darted between them.

Luke rubbed the back of his neck. Pink colored his face from cheek to cheek and across the bridge of his nose. "Drew is tired of riding. Would you care to join me?"

She brushed her hands over her skirts and lifted her chin. If she were wise, she would politely decline and nurse her wounds in privacy.

"A ride sounds lovely, thank you."

Thirteen

HELLFIRE AND DAMN!

Luke slanted a glance at Vivian. She rode with a straight back, her lips so tightly pressed together they might have been sewn shut.

What the hell had he been thinking to kiss her?

Oh, hell. He hadn't just kissed her; he had been close to ravishing her. How he had mustered the willpower to set her away, he didn't know.

He could still feel the curve and weight of her bottom cupped in his palm. Curling his fingers into a fist, he pressed his hand firmly against his thigh, battling with the voice inside him insisting it didn't matter that he had taken liberties. Vivian was his, given freely by her brother. The twisted reasoning held great appeal, but the selfish part of him must be held in check. He was a better man than her brother. He had offered her a choice, and he couldn't snatch it away. He had given his word to help her find a husband, but thoughts of surrendering her to another man were like an insidious poison, making his insides writhe.

Good God. He didn't know what to do. Several

options presented themselves: He could pretend nothing had happened, which seemed an ill-advised course given Vivian's peevish reaction earlier.

He could apologize for taking liberties and promise to be more considerate in the future. A vow he didn't wish to make, because the memory of her sweet taste was already making him hard again.

Or… A slow grin spread across his face. He could admit how much he had enjoyed kissing her and reveal all the ribald things he wished to do to her.

His smile slipped. No, that wouldn't do at all, would it?

He cleared his throat, uncertain what he would say next. "I fear I forgot myself earlier, Lady Vivian. I beg your forgiveness for my coarse treatment."

She turned toward him, her eyes expanding a fraction before she regained control of her composure. Stone-faced, she returned her attention to the rutted lane. "Of course, Your Grace."

Her curt forgiveness sucked the life from him. Well, what had he expected? He hadn't wanted her wrath. Or worse, tears. But he desired something more from her than a cool dismissal.

He opened his mouth then snapped it closed again. *Devil take it.* He didn't know what he wanted. His thoughts and feelings were as indistinguishable as the ingredients in Cook's fruit-and-nut cake. And he didn't know if he cared to explore what any of them were: fruit, nuts, *or* feelings.

"Are you as skilled in riding sidesaddle as you are astride?" he asked at last. "I wouldn't wish for you to take a tumble. From the horse, I mean."

Vivian frowned. "What else *could* you mean, Your Grace?"

His throat shrunk two sizes too small. "I— There is no other meaning. Do you intend to answer my question?"

"It seems a bit late for worry, wouldn't you agree?"

Luke's brow lifted. "Is it?"

Now that they had kissed, perhaps she would hold him accountable for his behavior and insist upon marriage.

"If I were unsafe," she said, her tone hassled, "it would be obvious by now, wouldn't you agree? I have already mounted and ridden a good hour."

All this talk of tumbling, mounting, and riding was not accomplishing what he'd intended. He wanted to forget about his urges to have her beneath him.

"Let's see a demonstration of your skill." He squeezed the reins tightly and cursed under his breath. "Your *equestrienne* skill, that is."

She cocked her head, her frown lines deepening. "Yes, I took your meaning the first time, Your Grace."

Good Lord, her innocence made him feel like the worst of lechers. Every thought he had bordered on vulgar.

"What type of demonstration do you propose?" she asked.

"We mustn't stay to the road. Let's explore the terrain."

"All right." An animated spark flashed in her eyes, her formal manner melting away. How he admired her fire. Vivian was typically game for most anything.

Of course, there was no true danger to her, or any surprise for him as to what lay over the next hill. They had entered one of his lesser properties where they would stay the night. Perhaps two. He no longer felt any urgency to reach Irvine Castle, for various reasons. Most notably, he wished to keep Vivian out of reach of those debauchees, Brookhaven and Collier.

Having either man in close proximity to her made Luke want to break something. When he hadn't been able to decide earlier between an arm, leg, or neck, he determined the best choice would be to lose the men.

The lesser-traveled road also made it possible to free Vivian from the boredom that must have been plaguing her in the carriage. She wasn't any more accustomed to being confined than he, which was another reason to postpone the inevitable arrival at Irvine Castle. Once they arrived and husband hunting began, she would be under much scrutiny.

"Wait here a moment." He rode back to the carriage and signaled to Drew that he and Vivian would reconvene with them at Twinspur Cottage. Then he led Vivian toward the glen.

The canopy of leaves blocked the strong afternoon sunlight, casting everything in muted color. Tension drained from him as he breathed in the earthy scents: soil, leaf mold, and fallen logs. The fragrance was primitive, the simplest building blocks of life, and free from pretention.

Vivian and her horse plodded along behind. She kept her silence as the forest absorbed them, closing them off from the world at large. The ground slanted downward toward a brook, the soft trickle barely audible in the midst of the horses' hooves crunching leaves.

Upon reaching the shallow waters, he urged Thor

to walk upstream. Glancing over his shoulder, he noted with satisfaction Vivian didn't pause before guiding her horse into the water. She glanced up at the tangled limbs above them, and he turned back with a smile.

"Searching for good climbing trees, my lady?"

"Hmm."

Her brief acknowledgment stung. He had thought she might let go of her reticence if they were alone. She had proven to be forthright in their past encounters, but he couldn't fault her for her cold response. Perhaps she was as confused as he was; likely more so given their kiss had been her first.

Oh, she may have received a stolen kiss on the cheek or a fervent squeeze to her hand, but her inexperience had been clear in her hesitant lips. Her eagerness, however, made up for a lack of skill. Luke liked that he had been her first. Vivian's naivety would require her introduction to many pleasures. Would her eagerness extend to the bedchamber? The air in his lungs seemed heavier all of a sudden, and he swiped a hand across his forehead, his body hot beyond reason.

"Luke? Back at the inn…"

A big grin split his face. He hadn't expected her to leave the situation alone. It wasn't in her nature.

"Was I horrible? At kissing?"

Luke's merriment disappeared. "What makes you think you were horrible?"

She didn't answer, but he could almost feel daggers at his back. His question was genuine, but perhaps unfair. She had no notion of how aroused he had been with the soft mounds of her breasts pressed against him and the taste of her on his tongue. She would have discovered soon enough, if he had allowed her exploration.

He led Thor from the water and up the gentle incline.

"You were far from horrible. I expect with more practice you will excel at kissing just as you have with most everything you've undertaken."

"Oh." Her small intake of breath made him smile.

Perhaps her thoughts were also back to their kiss and future interludes. He awaited her next impertinent question with eagerness, but she disappointed him. She didn't speak again as their horses continued on their own path.

Ahead, green pastures peeked through the trees. They would catch their first glimpse of the house nesting in the valley once they cleared the forest. "We are almost to our next lodgings for the evening."

"So early? We've barely traveled any distance today."

"We are under no time constraints. Besides, since we are this close, I should check on my tenants."

"Where are we?"

"Twinspur Cottage." As Luke rode out of the glen, he squinted against the brighter light. He waited for her to join him. "We spent summers here as children."

Vivian looked beyond his shoulder, her eyes widening. "*That* is your summer home?"

Luke tried to view it as she might upon seeing it for the first time. In comparison to the family home in Essex or Irvine Castle, the house was small, but with ten bedchambers, the term *cottage* was misleading.

"It was our summer home when I was a boy." It had been nine years since he'd visited the property, but everything was still fresh in his mind. He didn't wish to think on it, though. He'd had enough time for thinking when lying flat on his back.

"I imagine we can find all kinds of unladylike pursuits to fill your time," he said.

Vivian regarded him with her quicksilver gaze as if she could see inside him, past the jovial façade and teasing.

He glanced toward the house, locating the window to the chambers where he had spent most of his last days here. His mother had known how torturous it would have been for him to gaze out at the lake and remain stuck behind glass. She'd had his sick room moved to the north side of the house.

"Luke, is something troubling you?"

He banished those dark memories to the corner of his mind. "I spent some unhappy time here once, but I'd rather not think on it."

"Must we stay if the cottage brings you bad memories? Couldn't we take rooms at an inn?"

His disquiet faded as he met her compassionate gaze. Vivian would enjoy Twinspur as he once had when he was a lad. "There's a lake stocked with fish, and we'll have our privacy if you would like to ride astride."

"But what about your family?"

"Lana and Drew? They are the least proper of the entire clan. You have no reason to worry about offending either of them."

A true smile lit her eyes. "How long will we stay?"

His misgivings about staying at Twinspur melted away. Perhaps with Vivian to distract him, he could tolerate his time at his old prison.

"I should think we would be here three days at least

for me to adequately address any tenant needs. Would you like to come along when I call on them?"

"I—" She tipped her head to the side and studied him. "Are you certain you're a duke?"

Although her question was asked in jest, it cut to his heart. He knew he was different from other noblemen in his position. If she only knew to what extent, she would no longer think his differences were an asset.

He flashed a false smile. "What's the matter, Vivian? Am I not stuffy enough for you?"

"You're the perfect amount of stuffy to suit *me*, Your Grace. Not one ounce."

Her response sent a wave of warmth flowing over him and a real smile pushed its way out.

Fourteen

LUKE STUDIED THE CHESSBOARD, INTENT UPON ANNI-hilating his brother. Drew was clever and had a head for games, but chess was like war and Luke had always had a taste for battle. Unfortunately, his birthright meant he could only engage in battles of wit rather than on the field.

His brother had been accommodating, agreeing to keep him company when the ladies retired a few hours earlier, but the game was doing nothing for Luke's restlessness. His leg bounced up and down as if it had a mind of its own, and he fought against another wave of jitteriness that made him want to run. He hated being at Twinspur Cottage again.

He plopped his knight into position and tried to focus on his victory. In two more plays, Drew's king would be trapped.

His brother leaned back in his chair, sipped his scotch, and made no attempt at a move.

"It's your turn," Luke snapped.

With a smirk, Drew pushed his king into the line of fire.

"You can't move there. The game will be over."

Drew shrugged and hauled himself from the chair. "I'm running low on scotch."

As his brother sauntered to the sideboard, Luke snatched up the king. "I hate it when you stop trying."

"But you like winning, and I've grown bored. Now we are both satisfied." He turned his back as he pulled the stopper from the bottle of liquor. "I'm more interested in uncovering what happened between you and Lady Vivian today."

Luke's shoulders tensed. "I don't know your meaning."

His brother shot a chiding look over his shoulder before returning to his task. The silence in the library crackled. The glug, glug of scotch as Drew poured was as loud as gunshots.

Luke bolted from his seat and took his glass with him to the opened window. A weak breeze barely stirred the sticky air. Fall would be upon them shortly; it shouldn't be this blasted hot after sundown. Captain Pendry was waiting to hear if Luke still wanted to be part of the expedition, but Luke didn't know what to tell him. Vivian had him tangled in knots.

He drained his drink, trying to grasp hold of his thoughts as they whipped around in his head. A lone frog croaked somewhere close, his voice deep and mournful.

"Have you ever thought you knew where you were going only to feel completely lost moments later?" Luke asked without shifting his gaze from the darkness beyond the window.

Drew snorted. "Is that a rhetorical question? I'm married. I have children."

"Point taken." A few years earlier, if anyone had predicted his rakehell brother would be married and blessed with children, Luke would have called the person a fool.

Drew joined him in gazing into the nothingness outside. "Don't get me wrong. I wouldn't have it any other way. Lana and the girls are my life, but I never thought this would be my future." His brother nodded toward the window. "Do you see something out there?"

Luke shook his head. Maybe there was nothing for him out there beyond England as he had believed, but how could his destiny be here? He was damaged and a lousy stand-in for his father.

"I should have died that day," he muttered.

"You didn't."

"But I *should* have. Did they ever tell you I wasn't breathing?"

He glanced at his brother. Drew was leaning against the window frame and frowning. "Our parents said it was a miracle."

Or a mistake.

It seemed Luke had been outmaneuvering fate for the last decade. He had the scars to prove it. What if fate had been waiting for him to care about something again so it could be snatched away?

Someone to care about.

Luke turned from the window with a heavy sigh. It wasn't like him to engage in fatalistic thinking. He lived each moment and tried not to contemplate the future anymore. It was too uncertain and subject to change without warning. Yet Vivian had triggered something inside him that hadn't been alive since his accident. Hope. A part of him couldn't stop wondering what life might be like with someone sharing it with him.

No, not *someone*. Her.

"You always were abysmal at chess," Luke accused his brother, ready to shift his focus.

"But I excel at the things that matter." Drew tapped his finger against his glass. "My bride is tucked in bed by now and I would like to join her, but if you need me to stay…"

"No, you go. I am not long for bed myself." But the thought of climbing the stairs where his former prison lay made his stomach roil.

Drew hesitated a moment before he nodded, his lips pressed into a thin line. He placed his glass on a side table then quit the study.

Luke should get some sleep, too. Tomorrow he would call on his steward, and he wanted to be well rested. His headaches were always worse when he was tired. Still, he lingered in the library.

Reaching the opened double glass doors, he walked out into the night. Moonlight shimmered off the lake, visible through the trees in the distance. He breathed in the fresh air, so unlike the heaviness that hung inside the house.

The lake called to him. Perhaps if he sat on the bank for a while, his mind and heart would settle. Even if he could come to a decision about the expedition, he might be able to rest tonight.

❧

Vivi had given up sleep an hour earlier and moved to the window seat in her chambers. She had lain in bed as long as she could, trying to push thoughts of Luke from her head without success. She had relived their kiss many times over after she had climbed under the sheets. Yet it was his troubled gaze as he had looked down at Twinspur Cottage that kept her awake.

A somber mood had descended over him when they stopped on the hill. He had tried to hide behind his smiles, but they had been hollow. Vivi had known him long enough now to tell the difference.

Since she had no right to intrude on his privacy, she hadn't questioned him further about what had happened to him here, but she was concerned. Luke seemed to be wrestling with past demons, and she wanted to be his champion. Perhaps she would muddle being his champion as badly as she was at courting him, but her desire was sincere.

Vivi tucked her knees up under her nightrail and leaned her forehead against the smooth window glass and wished it were cooler. The air was exceptionally hot this evening. If she were home, she might steal away for a swim.

A patch of white entered her line of sight, standing out against the black backdrop. It appeared to be a gentleman, and he moved with purpose toward the lake. She sat up straight and watched, curious. He disappeared among a clump of trees and did not reemerge.

It had to be Luke. He had been edgy at dinner—distracted and irritable—as if he couldn't tolerate being enclosed by the walls of the cottage. Vivi twined a strand of hair around her finger and debated the wisdom of going to him. She knew she should stay in her chambers and respect his need for solitude.

Besides, it would be unseemly for a young lady to seek out a gentleman without a chaperone, or even with a chaperone at this hour.

But what if he was alone because there was no one he could confide in? Her heart ached at the thought.

Swinging her legs over the side of the window seat, she grabbed the folded blanket at the other end of the padded bench and headed for the corridor. She listened at the door before easing it open. Finding no one stirring, she hurried toward the stairs and descended as quietly as possible before winding through the house. She found a set of doors facing the lakeside and slipped outside.

A breeze lifted loose strands of hair around her face and cooled her damp skin. She gingerly picked her way across a wide veranda, mentally scolding herself for forgetting her slippers.

The night sounds surrounded her as she stepped onto the grass. She paused, her stomach unsettled as if a tumultuous storm brewed inside her.

This is a bad idea. Turn around. Her body refused to obey, and she continued toward her ruin.

He was standing by the water's edge and gave no indication he heard her approach. She halted several feet away.

"Luke," she called tentatively.

He spun on his heel. "What are you doing outside?"

A wave of heat that had nothing to do with the summer air engulfed her. "I saw you from the window. I brought you a blanket so you don't have to sit on the grass." Instead of offering it to him, she held it close, realizing how ridiculous she sounded. "Do you want to be alone?"

"Does it matter?" There was a touch of humor to his voice.

"I'll go." She edged back toward the house but pointed at the blanket. "Would you like it, Your Grace?"

He closed the distance between them and took it from her arms. "Thank you. That was thoughtful. You don't have to go."

But she should. Instead, she helped him spread the blanket over the ground then sat with him, but she stayed as close to the edge as possible for propriety's sake. Vivi rolled her eyes. She had crossed that boundary long before now.

Luke lowered down beside her and sprawled on the blanket. He appeared unaffected by their proximity while she struggled to quiet each breath, fearing she sounded like a windstorm.

"Is the heat making it difficult to sleep?" he asked.

"Hmm." She didn't trust herself to speak.

He looked over at her. "Everything would have been easier for you if your brother had allowed you a Season."

She started at his unexpected comment. "Easier how?"

"There would be no need to engage in this pretense. It would have been easier to choose a suitable husband in London. Ashden left you no choice but to accept the gentleman he had selected when he should have allowed you a Season."

Vivi lowered her gaze. That wasn't completely true. She was to have her coming out before Mrs. Honeywell had called too early in the day and discovered her with the groom. She had tried to explain the situation to her brother when he arrived, but Ash had blistered her ears for being too tempting to Owen. Her brother had gotten it all wrong. The groom had been fond of her, but Vivi had been the one to dangle after the handsome, older servant. He had always treated her like a younger sister.

When Mrs. Honeywell had discovered them together in the stables, her hair mussed from spending the night in a stall, Vivi had already given up her ridiculous dreams of one day marrying the groom. Ladies didn't marry lowborn servants, Owen had told her. And he'd had a sweetheart in the village.

Nothing she'd said made a difference to her brother. Owen had lost his position, and she had become Ash's greatest disappointment.

He had never treated her unkindly before that day. He had been rather permissible when he'd taken on the onerous task of being her guardian. Their relationship had altered, however, after he wed Muriel.

"I don't mind that Ash chose on my behalf," she said. The alternative of life in a convent was no life at all.

"You don't mind having no choice in whom you marry?"

She shrugged. Did anyone really have a say? Her brother had married to save them from financial ruin. He had had no choice for himself, but he had chosen well for her. Perhaps it was her brother's way of apologizing for sending her away to live with Patrice. The only trouble she faced was in convincing Luke that they were well suited.

She hugged her knees and lightly rocked. "At some point, you have to trust what is meant to be will be."

He made a bitter sound at the back of his throat.

Biting down on her lip, she forced herself to stop talking. She was being selfish, thinking only of herself and how she would benefit from their union. Luke had said he didn't wish for a match between them, and she hadn't cared. Now she had goaded him into kissing her. What if he felt duty-bound to marry her?

He dropped back on the blanket with a heavy sigh. "How can you be certain everything works out for the best, Viv?"

"I didn't say things always work out for the best. Just that life happens no matter what we think or want."

She stretched out on her back, too, and stared into the dark sky. The same stars that had been there last night and the night before and the night before that winked down at her. Nothing much ever seemed to change in the heavens.

"I don't worry what the future holds because what-ever comes will come," she said. "I will find a way to cope."

They lay there in silence for a long time. The only sounds came from the night surrounding them.

"I heard you lost both parents in a carriage acci-dent," Luke said at last.

She nodded even though she knew he wouldn't see her. "I was seven."

Luke rolled toward her and propped up on his elbow. "I'm sorry. That is a lot for any child to bear."

Her throat grew tight. She barely remembered her parents, but she remembered the devastation and fear of what would happen to her and her brother. Luke must have experienced similar emotions with the loss of his father. Perhaps he felt these things more deeply since his family relied on him to care for them.

"I'm sorry about your father." She rolled to face him and held her hand out in invitation. He met her in the middle, their fingers curling together to form a link.

His eyes shimmered in the darkness.

"Luke, do you want to talk about what happened to you here?"

He rolled onto his back again and broke their contact, but then he surprised her by taking her hand again. "I had a fall. It didn't happen here, but at University. I went through a window of an upper floor." He grimaced. "Obviously, I survived, but I had injuries."

Is that how he had broken his nose? She wanted to trail her finger over the small bump, to soothe his past hurt, but she didn't dare.

"My parents brought me to Twinspur as soon as it was possible to move me. Mother thought it would be good for me to convalesce here since I had always loved the cottage."

And now he abhorred a place he had loved. Vivi blinked away the tears that filled her eyes. "How badly were you hurt?"

"I broke a leg, cracked most of my ribs, and fractured my pelvis. My head was bandaged, and I am told I was unconscious for two days. I was awake for the carriage ride here, though, and I had wished I wasn't. When we arrived, I had to lie in bed for weeks while my bones mended, flat on my back."

"That sounds horrible." Vivi squeezed his hand. How awful that would be for anyone, but especially for an active man like Luke.

"Just as I thought I was becoming well enough to attempt walking again, a fever came. I had developed a lung illness, but I survived that as well, as you can see."

She had never heard him be caustic. It didn't fit his nature.

"I'm glad you survived," she murmured.

He paused and turned his head to study her. They said nothing, as he seemed to be puzzling her out. He did that often, though she had no idea what he found complicated about her. She was just a lady who wanted what any other lady wanted: to be a wife and mother, and to make a home for those she loved.

He looked back toward the sky. "I'm uncertain what happened for the next few days, but I must have been out of my mind. Every time I woke, I couldn't move my arms or legs. It was like someone had tied me down. It was the worst—" A shiver raced through her, and his gaze snapped to her again. "I didn't mean to upset you."

"I'm not upset, at least not in the way you think. I can't believe all you went through. It's no wonder you are troubled by being here again."

He blew out a breath, stirring the dark curl on his forehead. "I don't want to be bothered by memories. It's ludicrous and weak. They can't hurt me."

"No, but they can bring back all those feelings you had at the time. It must have been scary to be that ill."

"I guess it was."

They lay there in silence a long time, holding hands

and gazing up at the sky. She didn't know what to say to ease his burden, so she said nothing.

"I almost died," he said, his voice merely a ragged whisper.

Vivi reached out to caress his whiskered jaw. She didn't care about propriety or foolishness any longer. She only wanted to give him comfort. "I am thankful you didn't."

He captured her hand and brought it to his lips, feathering a kiss over her sensitive skin. "So am I. Could I hold you, Viv? Just for a moment?"

Her heart gave a small leap of joy. She vowed to make this last more than a moment. She was well on her way to having him hold her for a lifetime.

When he opened his arms, she snuggled against him, his chest hard beneath her cheek. Her fingers picked at his linen shirt since she was unsure where to leave them. "I take it you haven't been back to Twinspur since you recovered. Perhaps it would help to make new memories."

He smoothed her hair from her face and kissed the top of her head. "This is a good beginning. Thank you for being here with me."

Fifteen

Vivi's mount pranced on the lane as she, Luke, and Lord Andrew neared the tenants' cottages. Her horse was a high-spirited mare likely made more rambunctious by Vivi's excitement. Father and Ash had kept her ignorant of their responsibilities and goings-on, so Luke's suggestion that she accompany them to visit the tenants provided more evidence he was unlike other noble gentlemen. She liked that about him.

She and Luke had stayed out talking until the first streaks of dawn had swept the sky. She had shared the happier times in her life when she had lived with her brother, and Luke had told her funny stories about growing up with his two brothers. For long intervals, they had simply lain there in silence, holding hands, and Vivi had held her breath, hoping he might kiss her again.

He hadn't.

The tenants' homes were nestled in a valley, snug and safe from nature. Thick clouds of gray smoke rolled into the air, and flames licked at large black cauldrons suspended above fires. Several women stood at wooden tubs, elbow deep in water, while others draped garments over bushes to dry. Most of the women stopped to stare as their party approached.

One of the older women snagged a child to whisper in his ear when he and his playmates ran by. The lad's laughter faded as he glanced their way, his eyes bulging. With a quick nod, he took off in the opposite direction, his bare feet kicking up dust.

Curious, the other children moved toward the lane as if to watch a parade. The boy's mother, or perhaps grandmother, wiped her hands on her apron and curtsied as they drew near. "Your Grace."

The other tenants followed her example now that Luke had been identified.

He dismounted and went to greet the woman. "Mrs. Ogden, how lovely to see you again. You remember my brother, Lord Andrew."

"Of course, Your Grace, although it has been a long time."

Lord Andrew flashed a dimpled grin. "I promise not to cause any mischief this time. Is George around? I should like to catch up."

The woman's cheeks flushed, and an affectionate light shone in her brown eyes. "You boys were always up to mischief, my lord. He'd like to see you, I'm sure. You will find him tending sheep."

"Thank you." He handed the basket he carried on Vivi's behalf to her then urged his horse along the lane.

Luke reached up to help Vivi dismount then tucked her hand into the hollow of his arm. "Mrs. Ogden, may I present my betrothed, Lady Vivian Worth, the Marquess of Ashden's sister."

"Greetings, milady." The woman lowered her head and bowed, but not before Vivi spotted a broad smile breaking across her face, nor did she miss the note of surprise in the woman's greeting.

Before Vivi could respond, a man appeared on the lane. His craggy face and graying hair spoke of his years, but his barrel chest and large arms could have belonged to a man half his age.

"Your Grace, is something amiss? I pray Lord Richard is well," the man said.

Luke's friendly smile didn't falter, but his bicep shifted beneath Vivi's fingers.

"He is well, Mr. Ogden, and residing at Shafer Hall. We will join my family in Northumberland in several days, but I wished to check on the properties at Twinspur before we continue our journey."

Mr. Ogden blotted the perspiration beading on his upper lip with a yellowed handkerchief. "Of course, Your Grace. We can speak in my cottage." He motioned to two older boys to tend the horses.

Luke patted Vivi's hand. "Mrs. Ogden, would you be kind enough to keep Lady Vivian occupied while I speak with your husband? She's a curious sort, so do not be surprised if she has several questions for you."

Vivi would have offered a smart retort if she didn't have several pairs of eyes glued to her at the moment. The teasing sparkle in Luke's blue eyes made her think he would have added "behave yourself" if they didn't have an audience.

"It's my pleasure, Your Grace," Mrs. Ogden said before turning to Vivi. "Would you like some tea, milady? I can put on the kettle."

"Thank you for the offer, but I would prefer to enjoy your company rather than have you waiting on me. I don't wish to keep you from your wash. Is there anything I can do to assist?"

The woman's warm smile returned. "No, milady."

She hadn't expected Mrs. Ogden to accept her help, but she wished she had something to do while she waited for Luke. Vivi found a stump and sat with the basket in her lap as the woman returned to her wash.

Mrs. Ogden watched her surreptitiously as she reached into the tub and extracted a garment to scrub against the washboard. It seemed Vivi wasn't the only curious one.

"Do you like living here, Mrs. Ogden?"

The woman blinked. "Uh…"

"The area is beautiful," Vivi added, "and the cottages seem to be in good repair."

"Aye, milady. Lord Richard is usually quick to respond to our requests."

Vivi tipped her head to the side. It made no sense that Luke's brother would see to the tenants' needs rather than Luke. "Why does Lord Richard respond to your requests?"

"I couldn't say, milady." Mrs. Ogden's attention fell to her task. When it became apparent she had nothing else to say, Vivi suppressed a sigh. Her gaze strayed to the other women, who looked away quickly. She would get no answers from them either. She would have to ask Luke about this later. Eventually, she settled on watching a group of children playing in the distance.

Upon returning her attentions to the women, she

discovered a young girl clinging to her mother's skirts and peeking at her. Vivi waved, and the little girl buried her face against her mother's legs.

"Mary tends to be shy, milady. Please forgive her."

"There's nothing to forgive. She is a clever girl. Why, if I didn't know myself, I wouldn't speak to me either. As a matter of fact, even though I *do* know me, I probably shouldn't talk to myself, but I just can't help it. I have so much to say."

The girl's mother chuckled, and the tense lines in her face faded.

"I am sure you have noticed, Mrs…?"

"Mrs. Turner, milady. And I apologize for laughing."

"Nonsense," Vivi said. "Everyone should laugh at least a hundred times a day for a healthy constitution."

Mary looked at her curiously, and Vivi made a silly face. The girl giggled.

Vivi tapped her fingers against the basket and mouthed "May I?" to Mary's mother. The woman nodded, her smile growing wider.

Vivi opened the top. "I almost forgot. Mrs. Dillingham, Twinspur's cook, prepared sugar biscuits for me to bring, but I am afraid they may not taste good. I really shouldn't hand out biscuits that haven't been tested by anyone."

Mary eased from behind her mother, but still held a fistful of her skirts.

Vivi made a show of pulling a sweet from the basket and waved it. "I wonder if anyone would be so kind as to taste one for me. Perhaps one of the other children—?"

"Me," Mary declared in a soft voice.

"Why, dear Mary, would you do me such a kindness? I don't know how to thank you."

Vivi waved the biscuit in the air again. The girl released her hold on her mother and wandered to Vivi's side to take the offering.

In a matter of two bites, she and Mary became bosom friends.

"Would it be acceptable for me to offer biscuits to the other children?" she asked the women.

They had stopped regarding her with wariness and smiled kindly. "Of course, milady."

"Mary, would you like to be my helper?"

When she agreed with an eager nod, Vivi took her small hand, and off they went to deliver their treats. The other children were much less shy and accepted the sweet gifts readily. They had many questions for her, some of which she wasn't sure how to answer, such as who she was.

No, she wasn't the duke's sister. She wasn't a princess either.

Yes, she did think His Grace was kind, and she agreed he appeared tall when he sat upon his horse.

She was fairly certain his dark hair did not make him a highwayman, no. But he would be an excellent one if he so chose, given his skill with firearms.

Once the children had exhausted their curiosity, an older boy asked if she would like to play tag. Vivi accepted his invitation with a curtsy, and cried foul when he declared she was It. She set the basket aside and chased after the darlings, laughing at their delighted squeals.

⌇

Luke shook hands with Mr. Ogden, his steward, at the conclusion of the man's detailed description of the tenants' living conditions. He had been relieved when his man had chosen to provide a verbal accounting instead of handing over a book for him to read.

"You may expect digging to begin on the new well as soon as possible, Mr. Ogden. I will summon a surveyor at once to determine the best location."

"Thank you, Your Grace."

"In the meantime, you may draw water from the well at Twinspur. No one is to use the other. Close it off today."

The steward bobbed his head. "Yes, sir."

Luke didn't understand his brother's delay in seeing to the project. The well was running dry, and the remaining water might be contaminated, given the five cases of stomach ailments. He was grateful the outbreak did not appear to be cholera. In all instances, the tenants recovered, but he didn't want to take any more risks. There was no telling how the illness would affect a young child or elder.

How many other needs had gone unmet this past year? Richard had been assisting Father with overseeing the lands for ages, and he had stepped into their sire's shoes upon his death, managing their wealth and settling accounts when Luke hadn't seized control. Luke had been caring for his mother and sisters at the family home, but now he realized the inadequacy of his excuse. He had neglected many other people who relied on him. He may have trusted his brother to manage everything, but Luke should have been more engaged in the welfare of his tenants.

As he and Mr. Ogden left the cottage, he spotted Drew and George, their childhood playmate, with George's mother. Vivian, however, was missing. He scanned the area, his heart skipping a beat when she wasn't within sight, before he chided himself for behaving like a nervous grandmother. Vivian may have a tendency to get into trouble, but there was no danger here.

"Where has Lady Vivian hied off to?" he asked as he approached.

One of the women pointed down the lane. "She and the children were last seen walking that way, Your Grace."

Luke checked his watch. "We had best retrieve her. Mrs. Dillingham is planning luncheon, and if memory serves, she likes everything to run on a precise schedule."

He was eager to tell Vivian about his conversation with Mr. Ogden. It was the first time he'd felt competent in a long while.

Luke had been a good student before his accident and taken his abilities for granted. His later struggles in the classroom had shaken him; his concentration had vanished. Everything seemed to rile his temper at that time, too, and he'd wound up in several rounds of fisticuffs. It was no telling how many fights he would have fought if his brother, Richard, hadn't informed their father of his troubles.

Luke had been summoned home. His father hadn't wanted to believe his difficulties were real, and he'd pushed Luke to prove that he could still do what would be required of him. He failed the tasks time and again, growing more devastated each time his father looked at him in despair. Eventually, his father sent him to the continent for his grand tour. He thought Luke would find himself again, but a year later, Luke knew the truth. He had regained his concentration and his rages disappeared, but he would never be the same. Nevertheless, today had gone well. He wanted to celebrate his small victory with Vivian, even if she wouldn't understand the significance.

Drew and George fell into step with Luke on the lane as he went in search of Vivian. As they neared the fifth cottage, a loud screech made his heart spasm. "Vivian?"

He broke into a run and rounded the house, but came up short.

For the love of God.

Vivian was on her hands and knees, her head wedged under a back porch. Half the children were also on the ground, peering beneath the structure. A chit ran by, chasing a boy twice her size. When she tossed a limp worm at the boy, he let loose a high-pitched scream. Drew and George caught up to Luke and froze. Vivian's derriere wiggled as she lowered to her elbows and tried to crawl farther under the porch.

"It's all right, little one. No one is going to hurt you," she cooed.

One of the boys lowered to his belly, too. "He's right there, Lady Vivian. You almost have him."

"I see him, Matthew."

George Ogden gaped, his cheeks as red as if he had been slapped.

Luke crossed his arms and glared. "That's the future Duchess of Foxhaven you are ogling, George."

"Oh!" He whirled around, his back to her. "Pardon me, Your Grace."

Luke raised an eyebrow at Drew. "You may not look either."

His brother's smile just widened, dimples piercing his cheeks. He slanted his head to the side. "She bears a striking resemblance to Mother, wouldn't you agree?"

"No!" Luke punched his arm.

"Ow!" Drew laughed and rubbed a hand over his arm. "In behavior, I mean. What did you think I meant?"

Luke just shook his head, his eyes rolled toward the sky.

"Lord Andrew is correct, Your Grace," George piped up. "The duchess never had any qualms about getting her hands dirty either."

"I have him," Vivian called then wriggled her way back out and sat on her haunches. She held a trembling puppy at arm's length, looked him up and down, and then cradled him against her chest. The children scooted closer to reverently touch the pup.

"All is well," she said in a soothing voice. And just like that, Luke knew she'd had *him* from the moment he had discovered her in the spring. She was part of his destiny.

The best part.

But after his noble talk of offering her choices, he couldn't break their agreement and demand she honor her brother's promise.

He would just have to make certain she chose him.

Sixteen

VIVI SUPPRESSED A SIGH AS SHE DROPPED HER LINE BACK into the water, willing to try once more for a nibble. Not that she would know what one felt like, since this was her first time fishing. The two hours she and Luke had been at the water's edge this afternoon had yielded nothing. She clamped her lips together when the urge to ask him again if the lake was truly stocked with fish bubbled up in the back of her throat.

How much longer would this pointless activity go on?

Even the sun seemed to be giving up. Yet, as it sank on the horizon, the earth absorbing it, Luke continued with a determined set to his jaw.

She shifted her weight. Her toes were screaming to be freed from her boots. Unable to stand it any longer, she plopped to the grass and tugged at her laces. "Are you—?"

"Yes, Vivian. The lake is well stocked."

"That wasn't what I was going to ask."

He glanced her way, a twinkle lighting his blue eyes. "Wasn't it?"

"No." Well, it was, but he needn't be presumptuous. After freeing her feet from her boots and stockings, she pulled her knees up and rested her forearms across them. "An afternoon of fishing sounded more stimulating than it has proven to be."

"It's only fun if you catch something, and today has been slow."

What a talent he had for understatement.

Luke sat beside her on the bank, leaving his line trailing in the water. His heat warmed her side. At least there was some reward to the activity, time alone with Luke. She wanted nothing more than to lay her head against his shoulder and savor his nearness as she had two nights ago.

She didn't do it, though.

While picking at the grass, she counted the faint ripples around his fishing line as it drifted in the wind. She had very little experience with men, and Lana's instruction on how to entice a gentleman left Vivi with doubts as to her ability to ever be like other women.

She had felt foolish practicing smoldering looks in the mirror that morning. Instead of appearing tempting, she had only managed to look confused, like she couldn't remember if she had left the lamp burning in the library.

"Will we resume our journey tomorrow as planned?" she asked, hoping for at least one more day to work on charming Luke, if she even possessed the ability.

"Mother is expecting us. I promised we wouldn't be delayed for long."

So much for extra time.

She breathed in deeply, savoring the smell of

sunbaked earth. A soft breeze lifted wisps of hair that had slipped from her knot and carried the promise of a cooler evening. The glass-like lake reflected shades of orange and pink from the setting sun. She didn't want to leave Twinspur for more than one reason.

"It's peaceful here," she said.

His shoulder touched hers. A brush so soft she couldn't determine if the contact was purposeful or not. "Do you think you would like to summer at the cottage?"

Her heart bolted at his unexpected question. She glanced at him from the corner of her eye, not wishing to reveal her hope that his question held some significance. "I am certain I could tolerate it if I must," she teased, attempting to sound normal and unaffected. "Did you have fun here as a boy?"

An easy smile spread across his lips. "I did. It's the perfect place for children. Richard, Drew, and I would head outside as soon as the sun rose. There were many things to keep us occupied: fishing, swimming, sword fighting with large sticks." He pointed to a crescent scar at his temple. "Richard once split my head with a well-aimed blow. Father took him to task for it, but it could have as easily been the other way around."

She turned toward him fully, reminded of Mrs. Ogden's statement about Lord Richard. "Why has your brother been the one responding to the steward's requests? Yesterday Mrs. Ogden said Lord Richard has been good about responding to most of their needs."

An almost unnoticeable tic of his eyebrow alerted her that she might have tread where she was not welcome. "He acted as our father's representative when he was alive, so naturally Richard assumed the role upon his death."

Vivi studied Luke's face for clues as to how he viewed his brother claiming what should have fallen to him. As always, he hid his feelings well behind a mask of contentment.

"At dinner last night, you spoke enthusiastically about your conversation with Mr. Ogden," she said, "and the prospect of making improvements to the village aside from the new well."

Luke's eagerness had surprised her. The projects he had mentioned paled in comparison to discovering a new continent, but he had seemed equally as excited by doing something that would improve his tenants' lives. She had fallen for him a little more in that moment.

"The well was something they needed months ago, but Richard denied the request," he said. "I intend to speak with him when we reach the castle. I have come to accept it may be time to relieve him of some responsibilities, but I'm uncertain how he will take the news."

Vivi tried to hold back a smile. He was talking about a future in England. She didn't know yet if she would be part of it, but it felt like a small victory all the same.

"I'm sure your brother will understand." It was an absurd reply. She knew nothing about Lord Richard, but if he was anything like Luke or Lord Andrew, he couldn't be a bad man.

Luke nodded thoughtfully. "I will still require his assistance in some matters. Now, shall we discuss something more pleasant on our last evening at Twinspur Cottage?"

"Agreed." From anyone else, it would have sounded liked a reprimand for prying, but Luke's tone was conversational.

"In light of your suggestion that I attempt to make new memories, I have requested Mrs. Dillingham pack a supper for us."

"Just you and me?"

"Aha!" He hopped up and jerked on the fishing pole. When he lifted the line from the water, there was a fish on the other end, thrashing its tail. He tossed a playful look over his shoulder. "I'm sorry, Vivian. I was talking to this fellow, but would you like to join us?"

Her cheeks heated even though she knew he was teasing her. She didn't wish to assign more meaning to his invitation than he had intended. "Not if that poor fellow is to be our dinner. He's tiny. Couldn't you do any better, Your Grace?"

"At least I caught a fish, and I have shown you there are indeed fish in the lake."

She shrugged one shoulder. "I suppose I must grant you that much."

He waved her over then reached for the line to bring the fish closer. "Since you're unimpressed with my catch, let's release him. I'll show you how to remove the hook."

She moved to his side to watch. "May I touch him before you set him free?"

"If you wish." He gripped the fish so his hand held down the top fin and wiggled the hook from the fish's lip. Once the creature was freed, he held it out to her.

She ran her finger over its slick, iridescent scales. "He is pretty up close, isn't he?"

"I believe you are the only lady in England capable of finding beauty in such an unlikely place." Luke's grin widened as he returned the fish to the water's edge and let him go. "I like that quality."

She had that expanding sensation in her chest again, like her heart had swollen ten times its normal size. At a loss for words, she joined him at the waterline and squatted to rinse her hands as he was doing. She stood and, overcome by a rush of mischief, flicked droplets at him.

Still kneeling, Luke lifted a brow and flashed a wicked grin. She backed up a step, but not fast enough. He smacked the water with his hand and aimed a stream at her. The shock of cold water against her bodice made her gasp.

"Luke!"

Her nipples tightened and jutted through her thin muslin gown. Crossing her arms, she spun away from him. "You are evil," she accused, laughing in spite of her embarrassment.

"You started it, water sprite." He came up behind her, wrapped his arms around her waist, and nuzzled her ear. "And I always play to win," he whispered.

His hot breath on her neck sent delicious pulses to her core and made her breasts tingle.

In the distance, she spotted servants coming their way with baskets. She stepped from his embrace and spun back toward the water. She kept her back to the young girls as they delivered their meal.

"Offer my thanks to Mrs. Dillingham," he said, "and see that we are not disturbed again this evening."

"Yes, Your Grace." Vivi imagined the girls offering

a rushed curtsy before dashing back to the house, eager to share what they had witnessed.

Heaviness settled in her chest, overriding her earlier lightheartedness. She had known she shouldn't be alone with Luke, but she hadn't sent for a chaperone when he had extended the invitation. In truth, she had practically run him down in her eagerness to escape the cottage. Every decision she made seemed fraught with recklessness. It had always been that way for her. She didn't understand the reason Luke hadn't yet noticed she wasn't like other proper young ladies. Yet he must see her as she really was eventually. She dreaded arriving at Irvine Castle, where he would compare her to the other young ladies in attendance. How would she win his heart then?

Maybe she should let go of her ridiculous plan. She had made no real progress since they had departed from Brighthurst. He may have kissed her once, but that hardly meant a proposal was close at hand.

Luke slipped up behind her again and touched her shoulder. "Is everything all right, Viv? I didn't mean to embarrass you."

His gentle concern filled her heart to overflowing. Lord help her, but she didn't have it in her to give up. Not with Luke. She turned, threw her arms around him, and buried her face against his neck. His skin was fragrant, robust and woodsy, as if he had bathed in water scented with clover.

He embraced her tightly, and she wilted against him as his hands traveled her back in slow caresses that made her long for more. Even though she feared never being capable of becoming the type of lady his position required, she couldn't let him go. She needed him.

"I'm so sorry," she said softly.

❧

Luke's heart was battering against his ribs. He tried to work out Vivian's mumblings as she snuggled against him, her lips playing over his neck. He might have asked her to repeat herself, but that would mean she must pull away to be heard, and he liked her where she was.

He wanted to kiss her, but even in the fading light, someone might spy them from an upper floor of the cottage. After dusk, he could safely kiss away whatever worries were plaguing her without the chance of embarrassing her again.

It might be unfair to begin his courtship of her before she had met other potential suitors, but he didn't care. If having her alone allowed him an advantage over other would-be suitors, he would take it. As he had admitted a moment ago, he was playing to win, and Vivian was a prize worth winning.

She would want for nothing as his wife, including the freedom to be herself. No other gentleman could pose a better offer. This knowledge alone eased his conscience somewhat for breaking his promise to help her make another match and binding her to him.

Reluctantly, he eased her from his arms and captured her hand. "Shall we see what Mrs. Dillingham has prepared for us?"

She nodded, uncommonly reserved.

He led her to the blanket the kitchen maids had

spread over the grass and helped her lower herself onto it. At his request, Mrs. Dillingham had prepared a simple meal of cold meat sandwiches, fruit, and Vivian's favorite, chocolate biscuits.

He hesitated when he spotted the jug of lemonade sitting on the ground. He had asked for casual, but perhaps this was too unrefined. Most courtships began with hothouse flowers and strolls through the park, not a meal better suited for peasants. But an extravagant dinner would have meant having footmen present, and he wanted Vivian alone their last night together.

He removed the stopper from the jug, poured lemonade into a glass, and held it out to her.

Her arched brows lifted and she teased him with a smile. "No wine tonight, Your Grace?"

"None for you," he said with a wink. "I'm unprepared for further inquiries about the gap between my teeth."

Her face flushed bright red, but she laughed. "I shall never live that down, I suppose."

"Never."

Nor would he forget discovering her in the spring or sharing the most amusing meal with her wearing that ridiculous wig or her attempting to milk a cow. Every moment spent with Vivian became a happy memory. And in truth, he needed that in his life.

By the time they had finished their meal, twilight had settled over his land. "Soon everything will be different for us."

Her eyes appeared large and luminous in the fading light. "How—" She cleared her throat. "How so?"

"I may have to behave like a stuffy old duke when everyone is looking. But I'm encouraged that you will know I am pretending."

She laughed softly. "And I must behave myself."

He reached for her hand and squeezed it. "Only when someone is watching, but I'll know what no one else does. Behind your polite words and charming smiles hides an adventuress. My kindred spirit."

"Truly?" she murmured.

"Truly." He climbed to his feet then helped her to stand. "What do you think about one last swim before we have to put on our masks?"

"Oh, I don't— I'm not sure we should."

"I promise not to look," he coaxed. Not touching was harder to promise.

In the dark, he couldn't read her expression, but he knew her well enough to know she was working her bottom lip and fighting against the urge to give in.

"It's dark, Viv, and I know how you love the water. This will be our last chance to just be ourselves. Please, don't make me swim alone."

She blew out a noisy breath and he knew he had won. "You are a bad influence, Your Grace."

Seventeen

A CHILL CHASED DOWN VIVI'S BACK WHEN LUKE GENTLY turned her away to unfasten her gown. She attempted to will her rapid heartbeat to slow, but it thundered on.

He slid her still-damp gown from her shoulders. "Raise your arms, darling."

Although it appeared she had won, he had yet to say he wanted to marry her. A voice inside her screamed for her to come to her senses. Surely he would recover his soon enough and realize he'd made a mistake.

He brushed a kiss against her shoulder. "Have you changed your mind, Viv?"

Heavens knew she should raise a fuss and play the put-upon lady, but she wanted to stay with him.

She hesitated, then lifted her arms. The removal of her petticoats followed her gown and fell away from her body, landing in a heap around her feet. Luke would take the honorable path if they were discovered together, she reassured herself. It was what gentlemen of noble birth did in those circumstances. At least the gallant ones. Nevertheless, she didn't want to win him that way. Did he desire a match between them?

When Luke's fingers moved to the laces of her corset, she twisted around and planted a hand against his chest.

Her throat refused to work properly. "If someone finds us…" Her voice sounded tight and thin.

He swept a lock of hair behind her ear. "No one will bother us. But if they do, I promise to accept responsibility."

"I'm aware of the risks. I can't let you…"

"So am I. And I am prepared to accept them." His hand made soothing passes from her shoulder to her waist and back again. When she couldn't find the correct words to respond, he sighed. "It's all right, Vivian. I understand. I'll help you dress then escort you back to the house."

He bent to retrieve her gown, but she urged him to stand.

"I don't want to leave you," she whispered.

His quiet laugh came out on a breath and stirred a strand of hair at her cheek. "I don't want you to go either."

When he hugged her, she snuggled against him and savored the feel of him surrounding her. Longing pulled at her heart, threatening to steal it from her and leave her empty inside. She held him tighter and cursed her weakness.

She thought she might be falling in love with him. She groped for words to free her from her stupor. "Wh-what would you tell someone if they found us together?"

He released her. Even in the dark, she knew he smiled. Amusement rang in his voice. "I would tell them what we do is none of their concern. After all, we are betrothed."

"But it is a pretense, a lie." She couldn't make light of the situation as he did. She needed a promise. Before she could escape back to the house, he captured her hand.

"It wouldn't have to be a lie." He drew circles on her wrist with his thumb, lulling her. "All it takes is two signatures on the marriage settlement, and we could become husband and wife. Would you sign it when your brother sent it, Viv?"

Tears welled in her eyes and she blinked them away. His words almost sounded like a real proposal.

"My brother has already signed it. You don't need my signature."

"I would want it. Your consent is most important. I'll dictate a letter to your brother at once to request the marriage settlement. Then I will arrange to have the banns cried. Or perhaps I can send Drew for a special license."

When he would have kept talking, she placed her fingers over his mouth. She sensed his frown more than saw it.

"Do you *want* to marry me?" she asked.

He mumbled something she couldn't make out.

"What?"

Grasping her hand, he pulled it away from his mouth. "Didn't I just say I wanted to marry you?"

"No!" He'd been discussing a business arrangement, not declaring his love. "Was that your idea of a proposal?"

Luke scrubbed a hand over his jaw. "Damn. I should have gotten down on one knee." He knelt at her feet and captured her hand. "Vivian Worth, would you do me the honor of becoming my wife?"

A lock of hair was falling down over his eye and

driving her mad. She swept it aside and cupped his cheek. "Is this truly what you want, Luke? This isn't because you feel obligated after kissing me?"

"I don't feel obligated. Do you?"

She shook her head.

"I know I promised to assist you in making another match, but I can't surrender you to another man. If you wish to hold me to my word—"

"No!" She dropped her hand from his face. "I want *you*."

"And I want you, Vivian. It's settled between us now." He stood and placed a soft kiss on her lips, then patted her bottom. "Allow me to untie your laces, love. This may be our only chance to swim together."

She turned her back to him, her heart sprinting. Without her corset holding her prisoner, she was able to draw in a deep breath, and she laughed. Who knew her clumsy attempts at courting him would actually be successful?

He gave her a nudge toward the lake. "I will join you in a moment."

She crossed her arms over her chest, suddenly shy about being scantily clad. "You won't peek?"

He chuckled. "Not today, but if I can't look, neither can you."

The water lapped at her calves as she walked into the lake, cooling her feverish skin. Reaching deeper water, she sank down to her neck. There was a splash and Luke emerged from the lake a short distance away. She couldn't determine what articles of clothing he had removed, but the thought of him in half-dress made her insides quiver.

He shook his head and water droplets hit her hot cheeks. "Come. Show me you can do more than nearly drown."

Her back stiffened, her nervousness forgotten. "I told you, I *know* how to swim."

"So you say," he teased and splashed her. "Prove it, water sprite."

"You—oh, I *will* prove it." And afterward, she would serve him a huge slice of humble pie. He could stand to learn a thing or two about humility. "I challenge you to a race," she blurted.

"Hardly seems right for me to beat a lady." He laughed, goading her.

"I wouldn't celebrate a victory yet, Your Grace."

When they'd still had daylight, Vivi had noted a small island a decent distance from shore. She gathered the hem of her chemise and tied the two ends in a knot between her legs. "The first one to reach the island wins."

"I assume you are aware of what prize I will demand for my victory."

Her stomach lurched. "Yes, well. You aren't going to win, so *I* will be the one claiming the prize."

His teeth flashed white in the moonlight. "Either way is satisfactory to me. On your mark, my lady."

Luke moved even with her, placating her pride some. At least he wasn't allowing her a lead. Perhaps she was unbalanced to believe she could compete with a man of his strength, but she could boast less body mass, which had to work to her advantage.

"Go!" she yelled and dove under the water. When she broke the surface, she kicked like a child in a full-blown tantrum. Her long strokes set a quick and steady rhythm. Luke kept pace with her. She tried to ignore his proximity and concentrated on executing flawless movements. When he pulled ahead, she pushed harder to keep the lead from widening. Her lungs were burning, but she refused to quit. If he beat her, then so be it, but she would never hand over the victory to him.

He reached shallower water around the island a moment before her and tried to stand, but she grabbed the seat of his drawers and pulled as hard as she could. He lost his footing and fell face down. She scrambled to get her footing on the slick lake bottom and raced for the island.

"You little devil!" He snagged her around the waist before she went more than a step and hauled her back. She twisted in his hold, trying to break loose, but her legs tangled with his and she fell on top of him. His head went under, and when he resurfaced, sputtering, he trapped her against his chest. She struggled, determined to be victorious, but she couldn't break free.

Giving up, she stilled, her hand resting between their bodies as she sprawled on top of him. His heartbeat matched her erratic tempo and they were panting.

"Fine," she laughed. "You win."

He sat up and settled her on his lap facing him. His arm around her lower back kept her from escaping, but she no longer knew if she cared to be free.

"You are a worthy competitor."

She warmed in response to his praise. "I told you," she grumbled, but she couldn't hold back her pleased smile. "Next time I *will* beat you."

"I look forward to next time." He brushed his thumb across her cheek in a gentle arc. "May I claim my prize now?"

Her heart skipped. "A kiss?"

Luke's fingers cradled her neck and he urged her forward until they were lip to lip with barely a breath between them. "Yes."

"I had forgotten you collected winnings in...*kisses*," she said on an exhale.

"Only from beautiful women who challenge me." His smile was but a brief flash before his mouth came down on hers, hot and captivating. She could think of nothing besides the feel of his lips coaxing her to surrender to her deepest wishes. She wanted him, too. For the rest of her life.

When their kiss ended, she stared beyond his shoulder to the dark outline of the cottage in the distance. She counted the lighted windows in an attempt to calm her racing pulse. She fiddled with the wet curls lying against his collar. "What do you think Lana and Lord Andrew are doing this evening?"

"I can't say I care."

She risked looking at him again. "Will they be searching for us?"

Her hair had lost its pins and hung around her shoulders. He pushed her hair behind her back and massaged her neck. "I doubt they will notice we are missing."

"They do seem engrossed with each other at times, which make them less than ideal chaperones." She closed her eyes as he kneaded a particularly tense spot at the base of her head.

His lips touched her temple and lingered. "I had

assumed you wouldn't want someone monitoring you every moment. Are you unhappy I chose them?"

"No. I don't know. Maybe." If she had more diligent chaperones, she wouldn't be in this predicament, wondering if she should give in to temptation or begin to act like a lady and insist they return to the house. She pulled back to see Luke's face, but it remained in shadow. "Did you know they would allow me more freedom?"

"I had a suspicion. Drew has never been one to adhere to propriety, and he reserves judgment in most instances." He eased her from his lap. His shirt was plastered to his body, and his muscles shifted beneath the saturated linen. "Let's rest on the island."

When he stood and moved toward land, his drawers molded to his bottom and thighs.

She must have made a noise, because he glanced over his shoulder. "You promised not to peek."

"Sorry." She closed her eyes. She hadn't meant to look, but curiosity was a dangerous attribute. Very dangerous. And hard to ignore. She stole another glance and sucked in a sharp breath when she discovered he was still watching her.

She wagged a finger toward the far shoreline. "Maybe I should swim back."

"Come here," he said with a laugh and extended his hand to help her up.

She hesitated but could think of no reason to refuse him that didn't make her feel foolish. A brief rest couldn't hurt. It wasn't until she was out of the water that she realized her chemise was still tied in a knot, exposing her legs.

Luke led her to an old tree trunk that had washed ashore and urged her to sit down beside him. They sat in silence, staring at the moonlight shimmering on the glistening, black water.

He smoothed a finger over the fleshy part of her thigh. "You have strong legs."

"You aren't supposed to be looking either," she chided with as much conviction as she could marshal, which wasn't nearly as much as she should have.

"Then remove the temptation."

When he reached between her legs to loosen the knot, she started. His head brushed her breast as he sat up again, sending a rush of heat throughout her body.

"You may cover your legs now if you wish," he said when she remained frozen.

She snapped out of her trance and wiggled side to side, tugging at her chemise to cover her bare limbs. Settling beside him, she allowed her gaze to travel along the contours of his legs then quickly jerked it back to the water. It was difficult to keep her promise not to look when she had never seen a man in his state of undress, nor did she expect to ever see another one as spectacularly made as him.

She lifted her head and her breath left her. Luke was studying her with gleaming eyes as black as onyx. A corner of her mouth turned up. So much for promises. Her curiosity chased away any shyness as she allowed her gaze to roam over his masculine form. He was leaner than most gentlemen, strong and svelte, but she didn't mind.

"You look beautiful," Luke said, "just like the first

time I saw you. All I have been able to think of since that day at the coaching inn is kissing you again."

"Just kissing me?" she managed to eke out.

"Vivian," he said on a groan and reached for her.

Eighteen

LUKE SAVORED HER SWEET KISS, ADMONISHING HIMSELF to remain a gentleman. Perhaps he had rushed his court-ship this evening, but he hadn't wanted to reach Irvine Castle without having her bound to him. Nothing would be official until the marriage settlement was signed, but a promise between them eased his concerns about losing her. He would try to be what she deserved.

Guilt still plagued him when it came to his brother. Richard had given up his youth to work with their father. Luke knew it should have been him, but he'd been too much of a daredevil, too bored to be cooped up in the study all day going over ledgers. Only now with Vivian was he able to see how his desire to run from a life that had felt wrong led to an even greater sense of imprisonment.

A life devoid of a future or lasting connections.

A life of solitude.

A life without love.

When she shivered, he wrapped his arm around her shoulders and helped her to her feet. "You're cold. We should go back to the house."

"No! I'm not." She shrugged him off.

A shocked laugh burst from his lips. "I knew you were difficult from the start, but will this streak of defiance follow us into our marriage?"

Her impish chuckle carried on the night air. "Very likely. Do you want to retract your offer?"

"Never." As Drew had noted, she was much like their mother in temperament and audacity. Luke had no worry that he could grow to love Vivian just as his father had adored his mother.

"Well, then. If I'm to be your wife"—she adopted a tone much like her brother's when he had been discussing the terms of the marital contract—"you may kiss me as often as you like. I don't want to wait for banns to be cried or a silly special license."

"I see." A ridiculous grin threatened to make an appearance, but he held it back. "I suppose you would appreciate a similar promise from me?"

"That does seem fair, Your Grace."

"Yes, it does." He hauled her into his arms again and kissed her like he'd wanted to from the moment she had arrived for dinner wearing that ridiculous headdress. He teased her lips apart with the tip of his tongue and slowly, sensually swept inside her mouth. He would never get enough of her taste or the softness of her lips. With a sigh, she wiggled even closer. Her breasts flattened against him. He wanted to taste her there, too.

He broke the kiss before he crossed a boundary then hugged her to him. "Is there anything else you would like to offer your future husband?" He tried to speak with humor, but his voice had grown hoarse.

She laid her head against his shoulder; her quick puffs of breath tickled his neck. Her fingers twined with the hair at his nape, creating pleasurable shivers along his spine. He was hard and ached for her.

"You may have all of me, Your Grace, although I cannot promise you will always like everything. What more do you have to offer me?"

Even though her question rang with playful innocence, it aroused him.

"I'm afraid you may not like everything about me either, but it's yours as well."

She lifted her head and met his gaze. Something in her posture indicated a shift. She had lost the lighthearted air she'd had. "I'll try not to be a disappointment to you, Luke. I promise."

"You could never disappoint me."

❧

"But—" Vivi's protest was swallowed up by his kiss. When his mouth moved against hers, she forgot everything. Her awareness was only of him and his effect on her.

The sound of her heart in her ears.

His scent and heat surrounding her.

A faint trace of tart lemonade lingering on his lips.

Egads. And something was digging into her belly again. She reached between them to adjust whatever object he kept in his pocket. A loud hiss slipped from his lips.

She froze with Luke in her hand. No wonder he had stopped her in the stable yard. Dear Lord, she wanted to bury her head in the sand. *Now* she had done the most humiliating thing of her life. Her fingers refused to work properly, and they tightened around him instead of letting him go.

"Careful," he said, his breath coming out in heavy pants.

"Am I hurting you?"

"God, no."

She tipped her head to the side and studied his expression in the scant moonlight. Touching him there seemed to be the opposite of painful. She tentatively tested her observation and squeezed. His body gave a small jerk against her palm.

"Vivian." His tone held a note of warning.

Curiosity overrode her initial embarrassment. "What does it do to you when I touch your... your...?" She raised her eyebrows in question.

"Some ladies refer to it as my manhood."

Manhood? She giggled partly from nerves and definitely from discomfort with the thought of other ladies having held him this intimately. "I don't want to call it what other ladies have. Supply me with another term."

He leaned his forehead against hers and gulped. His breath feathered over her cheeks. "Call it my cock."

She repeated the word in her head before she dared to speak it aloud. Her fingers curled tighter around him to gauge his size, and he groaned softly.

"Vivian." He spoke her name, not as a warning this time, but with reverence.

"What does it do when I hold your cock?"

He slipped his hand into her wet hair, his finger splayed to cradle her head, and he kissed her until she forgot her question. *Almost.* Gently tugging her hair, he angled her neck to expose her throat and placed his lips on her sensitive skin. His tongue swept over the hollow of her collarbone then slowly licked up her neck and captured her earlobe. Chills raced through her body with searing heat following in its path.

This was the most daring and exhilarating game she had ever played, and like Luke, she played to win. "What...does it...do to you?" she repeated, uncertain if she would be able to focus on his answer even if he gave one.

"It drives me to madness." He trailed kisses along her jawline and over her cheekbone. His moist lips touched her eyelid and lingered. "Your touch makes me want to behave in ungentlemanly ways. Unless you wish to learn the meaning of ungentlemanly, you should release me."

She was certain Lana's husband was ungentlemanly with her, and her friend never complained. Perhaps Vivian did want to know the meaning. She squeezed him again.

"Vivian Worth, if you continue down this path, I'll have a hell of a time stopping."

Her fingers kneaded him, and he closed his eyes on a sigh. "I don't think I want to stop," she murmured, "and neither do you."

"No, I don't."

Covering her breast with his palm, he rubbed a circle over her nipple. His fingers closed on the peak and lightly pinched. A pleasing jolt raced through her and ended with a pulse between her legs.

She gasped.

"*That's* what it feels like, minx."

"And it is wonderful. You definitely don't want me to stop."

He chuckled. "Fine, you win, but I plan to touch you, too."

Lowering to the ground, he coaxed her into straddling him and then kissed her deeply. He captured her breast again and tweaked it until her nipple stood taut. Luke ceased his ministrations long enough to slip the strap of her chemise off her shoulder and bare her breast. This time when he touched her, the sensation was intensified. Cupping both breasts, he rubbed his thumbs over the tips until she began to feel damp between her legs and the urge to squirm became harder to ignore.

She rocked her hips forward to ease the pressure building in her core. He grinned.

"What?" she asked breathlessly. "Did I...do something wrong?" The way he held her gaze and smiled like he knew some secret had her slowly withdrawing, but he wrapped one arm around her back and halted her retreat.

"You're perfect, Vivian. Exactly as I imagined." Hauling her closer, he nipped her bottom lip and gently sucked it into his mouth.

He had imagined touching her bare breast? And kissing her like this? The smoldering embers inside her burst into flame and filled her with a burning need she didn't fully understand. She wanted to be closer. She wanted to feel his skin against hers, their arms and legs intertwined.

Cradling his head, she kissed him back, welcoming each sweep of his tongue. She became bolder as their kiss grew more passionate, first licking his lips before venturing farther when he parted them. He groaned into her mouth when she thrust her tongue into the recesses as he had done to her.

He broke their kiss and pulled back to stare at her, his chest rising and falling rapidly with each harsh breath. "I can't take you like this."

In her hazy state, he sounded far away. His scent surrounded her, and his body heat made her blood flow like lava through her veins.

"How?" she uttered.

He kissed her forehead. "It's your first time. I won't take your innocence in the dirt. And we should be married first."

She blinked. He was making no sense. Her body was in a state of distress, and she could barely stand it another minute. Weeks would be torture. "I think I might die if I must wait."

Luke laughed. "I thought only men felt that way."

"Please, I—" She wiggled and flattened her breasts against his chest.

"Vivian, I can't. I gave your brother my word I would see you safely to Irvine Castle." Even as he argued with her, his hand skimmed her waist and found her breast again. "Deflowering you would be a breach of promise."

He rolled her nipple between his fingers, giving no hint that he planned to stop, no matter what he said. Her head rolled back, a silent prayer of thanks on her lips.

"I won't tell him. We barely speak anymore," she said, only halfway teasing.

"Pity, that. But"—he trailed hot kisses down her

neck and along her collarbone, speaking between pecks—"a promise is a promise."

She swallowed her growl of frustration. He was right, of course. A promise should not be broken.

He bestowed a wicked smile. "Bringing you pleasure isn't the same as deflowering you, however."

When his mouth closed over her nipple, she gasped. His tongue teased it until it was hard like a pebble. A strong pulse beat between her legs with each draw from his lips.

She moaned.

Burying her fingers in his hair, she held him at her breast, never wanting the exquisite sensations to end.

She reveled in the novelty and could have easily forgotten about exploring his body, but now that she understood the true meaning of pleasure, she wanted to share it with him.

Vivi worked her hand into his drawers and ran her fingers up and down his flesh in amazement. "It's soft!"

He released a strangled laugh. "That isn't a compliment."

"Why not? It's true." She had never felt anything like it. Neither velvet nor silk nor satin could adequately compare to the softness of his skin. She explored the ridge and rounded tip carefully.

He grabbed her hand to still her movements. "Someday soon I'll show you how to please me. Tonight is just for you."

Before she could debate the matter, he laid her down and stretched out beside her. He returned his attention to her breasts. His hand skated along her inner thigh, stopping every few inches to knead her flesh. She stirred restlessly, anticipating his touch between her legs. Part of her was horrified by her desire to have his fingers down there. But another, more lustful part had been awakened and demanded satisfaction.

The first pass of his fingers brought her hips off the ground. The sensation was intense and unfamiliar. By the third and fourth sweep, she began to melt beneath his touch.

His tongue flicked across her nipple before his lips closed over it. Each gentle tug on her breast and caress of her flesh filled her with affection until she thought she might burst from the warmth of it expanding in her chest.

She cupped his face and stroked his dark hair, wishing she had the words to express what stirred within her heart. Luke lifted his gaze to hers, his tongue still lovingly circling her bud.

"Kiss me," she murmured.

He shifted his body to cover her mouth with his. His full lips were exquisite, soft and moist. They pulled even more from her, feelings she didn't know how to handle, so she hugged them tightly inside.

A sensual fog surrounded her, making it hard to think. To breathe.

To do anything except revel in the sensations created within her. A pressure built in her lower abdomen with every stroke of Luke's fingers, growing until she was filled with nothing but the thought of him.

His scent. His heat. His taste.

She moaned softly, her back arching.

"Yes," he whispered, his breath grazing her ear. "Surrender to it."

The pleasure had no more room to expand, and it burst from her in a gasping cry again and again. She was carried on the moment, weightless and at Luke's mercy, but he held her tenderly. Grounded her to the earth still. And even as she slowly came back, he held her and stroked the hair from her eyes. He kissed her cheeks and brushed his lips across hers.

"Has your curiosity been satisfied, my love?"

She sighed contentedly and stretched. "Partly."

He laughed and nuzzled her neck. "That will have to be enough for now."

"For tonight," she agreed.

He rose to his elbow. "Until we have received the marriage contract. A man can only practice so much restraint."

She smirked. "Good to know."

"Behave yourself, Vivian." He tried to look stern, but the corners of his lips kept curving up.

"I *am* behaving." At least for the rest of the night. She wouldn't promise anything for the future, because if she had another opportunity to be this close with him, she wasn't going to let it pass her by.

Nineteen

Luke's brother gently jostled his wife awake when the carriage passed through the gates of Irvine Castle. "We've arrived, Lana."

The oppressive, graying walls cast the carriage in shadow. Luke didn't look forward to a confrontation with his brother, but it was overdue.

Vivian clasped his hand and smiled reassuringly, righting his world once again. He squeezed her hand before climbing from the carriage then turned to assist her down the steps rather than entrusting a footman with the task.

Drew and Lana walked arm in arm to their carriage to retrieve the children. Servants were lining up outside, waiting to greet them. It wasn't his entire staff, since many were still needed to tend to his mother's guests.

He slanted a glance at Vivian on his arm. She was nibbling her bottom lip. "There are so many," she whispered.

Compared to the small staff at Brighthurst, he supposed the prospect of becoming mistress of the castle could be daunting. Perhaps he could postpone his business with Richard for a few days until she had grown accustomed to life at the castle.

This would be her first encounter with the *ton*, also, which could intimidate even the bravest of hearts. Yet he couldn't spend every moment with her. He could just picture his mother's scandalized look when he followed the ladies into the parlor after dinner rather than staying behind to entertain the gentlemen.

Luke went through the motions of allowing his staff to be presented, introduced Vivian to the butler and head housekeeper, then escorted her inside where Drew and Lana stood in the foyer.

His younger sister, Liz, came barreling down the stairway with her twin, Katie, on her heels. "The babies are here!"

"I want one, too," Katie called out as her sister reached the bottom step before her.

Drew laughed. "Not until you're much older, Kitten."

"Agreed," Luke said. "You must be at least thirty first."

Liz rolled her eyes at both of them. "That is much too old, and you know it."

Mother followed the young girls down the stairs at a more dignified pace, a censorious frown in place. "Elizabeth and Katherine, do recall you are ladies and not a herd of cattle set loose in the castle."

"Yes, Mama," Katie responded dutifully, but neither girl slowed her pace as they dashed across the foyer to each claim one of Drew's daughters.

At sixteen, Luke's youngest sisters were still all arms and spindly legs. They likely couldn't help clambering like cattle.

Cousin Johanna passed his mother on the curved

staircase, her skirts lifted high enough to reveal a flash
of ankle. "Your Grace, you have arrived at last."

"Miss Truax," he said, returning Johanna's eager
greeting. "I hope today finds you well."

Mother swept past her with a broad grin. "And
this must be Lady Vivian. How lovely she is." Before
Vivian could respond, his mother embraced her.
"Welcome to Irvine, my dear. Luke's letter was full of
praise for you."

Johanna glanced between his mother and him.
He could guess at the questions running through her
mind. What had happened to his plan to sever the
agreement with Ashden?

Mother bestowed the same enthusiastic greeting
on Lana, even though the two had been parted for a
couple of weeks only. Tension drained from Luke's
shoulders as he watched her interactions. His mother
was beginning to behave more like her old self. Of
course, she would likely never fully recover from the
loss of his father, but she was emerging from the cloud
of sadness that had been surrounding her.

She kissed Drew's children before Liz and Katie
could whisk them away to the nursery then motioned
for everyone else to follow her.

"Let's retire to the drawing room." She didn't wait
for a reply before turning on her heel and heading
toward the stairs.

Vivian fell in step with Lana as his sister-in-law
began to list the activities they would enjoy at the
house party and the ladies Vivian must meet. Drew
trailed behind them at a leisurely pace, allowing the
women to enjoy their camaraderie.

Johanna, however, seemed frozen in the foyer. She stared at Luke with large, round eyes. Her lips parted then she pressed them tightly together, a white ring forming around them. She never questioned him now that he was the duke, no matter how freely they may have spoken in the past. Her deference made him too aware of his rank.

Vivian was the only woman who seemed to see him and not his title.

"Lady Vivian was different than I expected," he said by way of explanation.

The wounded look in Johanna's eyes before she lowered them caused him a stab of remorse. Before he had left for Brighthurst House, he had spoken at length with her about his plans. In the past few months, she'd proved a wise advisor in dealing with his family. Perhaps he should have written to Johanna, too, but he expected his mother would have informed her that he was arriving with his betrothed.

He offered his arm to his cousin. "Shall we join the others? I will explain everything later. It's complicated." Only it wasn't really. Falling in love with Vivian had been easy.

Johanna's mouth curved up slightly. "Of course, Your Grace."

He returned her smile, and they climbed the stairs in silence. Outside the doorway of the drawing room, he drew her to a stop. "Miss Truax, may I ask a favor?"

"Anything."

"This is Lady Vivian's first time in society, and she may be a little anxious. You know how treacherous the waters can be."

Her chin hitched up a notch. "Very treacherous, and I have managed to survive despite the odds stacked against me."

The daughter of a baron, Johanna possessed the grace of a noble lady but no fortune or future prospects. Three years earlier, she had come to live with his family after being turned out by her father's heir. Luke's mother had been more than happy to take her kinswoman on as her companion, and Johanna's sharp wit and genuine gratitude had endeared her to the family.

"You are a force to be reckoned with," Luke agreed. "I have always admired your mettle."

Her easy smile reappeared briefly.

"You and Lady Vivian are alike in that way," he added, "but she lacks your experience. I wonder if you would watch out for her while I'm occupied this afternoon. I will rest easier knowing she has an ally. Perhaps the two of you could walk in the gardens and become better acquainted."

A muscle at her jaw twitched beneath her pale skin. "You would like us to become better acquainted? Perhaps to become bosom friends and share confidences?"

Luke held his amusement in check. He had never seen his cousin appear so serious, as if the Crown were sending her on a mission rather than his suggesting a pleasant stroll. "I suppose I am. Do you mind?"

"Of course not. I will do whatever is necessary to assist you."

He patted her shoulder. "You have my gratitude. Come, I'll make introductions."

Twenty

Luke had a difficult task ahead of him. Reviewing the estate accounts and reading through all correspondence received since their father's death would be excruciating. He ignored the pinch at his temple. This was something he couldn't avoid any longer.

If Richard had neglected to act upon Mr. Ogden's reports of a drying well, there could be other problems requiring immediate attention. Luke didn't blame his brother as much as he blamed himself. At least Richard had been trying, while he had turned his back on everything.

His brother swept into Luke's study and skidded to a stop when he spotted him behind the massive desk. "You wished to speak with me?"

Luke rose from his seat and rounded the desk to clap his brother affectionately on the back. Richard stood stiffly with the ledgers in his arms and didn't attempt to reciprocate.

"It has been too long, Rich. You are looking well."

It was a lie. His brother looked like hell with bags

under his eyes and his face thinner than when Luke had last seen him.

Richard's dark eyes narrowed. "It has been almost a year. Phoebe and I had begun to wonder if we would ever see you again."

Richard's wife probably didn't care if she ever saw Luke again if he was responsible for his brother's haggard appearance.

"You knew of my whereabouts."

The sharp angles of his brother's face stood out more when he was angered. "I saw no reason to drag Phoebe and my boys away from the comforts of home to chase after you."

You saw no reason to give up control. Luke took a deep breath. He wasn't here to feud with his brother.

"I hope Phoebe and my nephews are well." He spoke quietly, sincerely.

"They are healthy," Richard said with a sniff. "I doubt you would recognize the boys now. They have grown tremendously."

Luke ignored his brother's insinuation. He couldn't fall into old patterns today by resurrecting past grievances. There was too much to sort out.

He swept an arm toward one of the chairs in front of his desk. "Please have a seat. Would you like a drink?"

"I'll have a brandy." Richard lowered onto the chair, laid the books across his lap, and tugged at his sleeves.

"I've had it stocked with scotch as well. For Drew." Luke sauntered to the sideboard and poured two fingers of brandy into cut crystal glasses, then carried one to his brother. "Perhaps later the three of us can enjoy a nightcap."

"Just like old times, eh?" Richard sipped his drink, his glare fixed on Luke.

Luke smiled to hide his irritation. His brother was spoiling for a fight, but he wouldn't oblige. "I wish there were old times to recall, but I cannot change the past."

"Why did you summon me? I have important matters that require my attention today."

Luke leaned against the desk, crossing his legs in front of him. He nodded toward the books. "I want to review the accounts, and I will need all correspondence from the last year no later than tomorrow."

Richard drained his drink, his face turning red. "Do you think I have done something wrong?"

Luke held up a hand when Richard shot from his chair in a bluster. "No, but *I* have. You kept our family afloat, and for your devotion, I will always be grateful. But it's time for me to live up to my responsibilities. It was unfair to lay the burden at your feet."

His brother blinked, apparently at a loss for words. What could he say when Luke spoke the truth? Richard looked down at the empty glass in his hand, absently tipping it back and forth.

Luke gently took it from him. "When was the last time you had a good night's sleep?"

"I don't know." His brother raked his fingers through his dark hair and blew out a noisy breath. "A long time ago. Phoebe has been scolding me for burning the midnight oil, but there's too much to do."

Now Luke was certain Phoebe wanted nothing to do with him. "Tonight you will retire with your wife. No more late-night work."

Richard raised his wary gaze. "And who is going to guard the coffers if I stop working into the night?"

His brother had been guarding them a little too closely in Luke's estimation, but he would never criticize Richard's efforts. "It is my responsibility. I will see to our family's welfare now."

"For how long? Until you leave on your foolish expedition and get yourself killed?"

"I have sent word to Captain Pendry. He is to proceed without me since I am to be married soon."

Richard's eyes widened.

"Don't look so surprised. I intend to wed Lady Vivian, the young woman Father chose on my behalf."

"But I *am* surprised, or more accurately, shocked." A sharp laugh burst from him. "Egads. This must be a dream. Have I fallen asleep at the desk again?"

"Perhaps." Luke reached out and pinched him.

His brother slapped his hand away. "What the hell, you blasted bugger?"

"There. We have our answer," Luke said with a chuckle. "You are awake and as foul-mouthed as ever."

"Sod off." Richard moved behind the desk, ducking his head as if attempting to hide his smile. "I have filed every letter already answered." He tugged open a drawer, extracted a stack of papers, and dropped them on the desktop. "These still require an answer. Many are from members of the House. I didn't know how to respond, so I haven't."

Luke rubbed his temple and contemplated the stack. He may have underestimated the amount of time it would take him to address what required his attention. He met his brother's questioning glance across the desk. "Let's review the accounts first. Then you will be free to enjoy the house party."

Richard's gaze locked on Luke's fingers at his head. Luke snatched his hand away. "I'll help you as long as you need me," his brother said.

"Thank you. I won't take up any more of your time than necessary."

His brother scooped up the ledgers and correspondence then moved to the table where they could spread out. Luke poured another drink for both of them before joining him.

His brother had opened the book and was flipping through the pages. Pointing, he looked up. "This is where I took over."

Luke studied his brother rather than the numbers. He looked younger already, as though a great burden had been lifted.

"Drew said you never wanted to be duke," Luke said. "Was he correct?"

Richard simply stared back for a long time until Luke began to wonder if he would answer. "I prayed every night for your safe return." His eyes misted over and he looked away, clearing his throat.

How could Luke have ever thought his brother wanted to usurp him? His own throat felt scratchy. He coughed into his fist and nodded toward the ledger. "So this was your first entry?"

"That is the amount received for the sale of wool from Marshfield. Why don't I read you what I have recorded?"

Luke leaned back in his chair, the pressure in his head easing. He listened to his brother rattle off their expenditures and gains, along with his thoughts on the potential for the Marshfeld estate to turn a hefty profit next year if they added to the flock.

At one time, he and Richard had been inseparable and equally put out with their youngest brother, who always wanted to be part of their fun. Luke didn't know if they could ever recapture the closeness they had shared as lads, but he would be content if everything could be like this. Living in peace with one another and working cooperatively.

"I don't know if I can ever make up for abandoning you, but I promise to do right by our family from now on."

"I will hold you to it," Richard said without looking up from the scribbled notes in the margins. "You know I will."

❧

Vivi had eagerly accepted Miss Truax's invitation to join her for a walk through the gardens, happy for an excuse to escape the duchess's drawing room.

She had been cautious not to make any missteps in the Duchess of Foxhaven's presence, even though Her Grace seemed like a kind lady. Vivi didn't want to provide Luke's mother with any reason to object to their union. A walk outside allowed her to drop her guard a little.

Dressed in her best walking gown and armed with a parasol, she meandered along the twisting path through the phlox, matching Miss Truax's snail's pace.

"Luke tells me you are the duchess's cousin. How wonderful that you were available to support her this past year."

Miss Truax slanted a look at her. "You should refer

to him as His Grace. It is unbecoming to refer to him by his Christian name."

"Oh! Yes, I just thought…" She trailed off when the woman lifted a harsh eyebrow. Luke had assured her Miss Truax would become her friend, but Vivi feared they were getting off to a tenuous start.

Miss Truax stopped and faced her with a strained smile. "Forgive me, my lady. I did not intend to sound cross. I am simply trying to do as His Grace wishes."

"What are his wishes?"

"To train you to be a duchess, of course. You have never been in society, am I correct?"

Vivi nodded; her insides were tying themselves into tight little knots. What was the lady insinuating?

"With your inexperience, you are likely to make a blunder. His Grace doesn't want to be embarrassed, so I have agreed to coach you."

Coach her? Why did that make her think of bits and harnesses? "I see."

Miss Truax crossed her arms. "Lady Vivian, have you any idea who Foxhaven is? He is in line for the throne."

Vivi snorted. Luke was as likely to inherit the crown as she was, and she almost told her companion so, but the other lady's severe frown gave her pause.

"You must take these matters seriously," Miss Truax chided. "How can you expect to become a proper wife when you are mocking His Grace?"

"I'm not mocking him."

The lady wrinkled her nose. "And you are not exhibiting respect for his station either. You want to bring him honor, do you not?"

Vivi nodded sharply once. She didn't care for the

other woman's tone or condescending manner, but if Luke thought she needed Miss Truax's help…

She swallowed hard, trying to view her circumstances with logic rather than being hurt by his doubts in her.

"Very good," Miss Truax said. "Perhaps we should start with you telling me about yourself. We wouldn't want any skeletons from your past making an appearance and embarrassing His Grace." Her eyebrows rose higher, and her smile looked suspiciously like a smirk. "The first thing everyone will want to know is the reason your brother did not allow you a Season. After all, you are becoming a bit long in the tooth for husband hunting."

Vivi's jaw dropped. She was hardly close to being placed on the shelf. "Uh…I'm not sure I take your meaning."

But she did. All too well. If Miss Truax had already ascertained something in her past had kept her brother from presenting her to society, how long would it take for others to draw the same conclusion?

Two gentlemen rounded a curve headed in their direction. It was Lord Brookhaven and Mr. Collier, minus their female traveling partner. Vivi never thought she would be happy to see either man again, but what a boon to run into them at this moment.

She waved and called out to them.

"Do you know those gentlemen?" Miss Truax asked.

"I called them by name, did I not?"

The lady huffed but said nothing more.

Mr. Collier's grin widened as the men approached. "Lady Vivian, how lovely to see you at Irvine Castle at last."

"It is lovely to be here at last," she lied. She would give anything to be back at Twinspur Cottage with only Luke, Lord Andrew, and Lana to keep her company. "Allow me to introduce you to my companion. Gentlemen, I'm pleased to present Miss Truax, cousin to the Duchess of Foxhaven. Miss Truax, Lord Brookhaven and Mr. Collier."

The viscount tipped his hat then leaned his weight on his walking stick.

Mr. Collier captured the young woman's hand and placed a kiss on her knuckles. "How charming to make your acquaintance, Miss Truax. Perhaps we could accompany you on your stroll."

Vivi was wise enough not to accept invitations from gentlemen she barely knew, but Miss Truax had apparently skipped her lessons on that topic. She accepted Mr. Collier's arm and began down the path with him.

Lord Brookhaven winced.

"We were just returning to the castle," Vivi said. "We are expected."

"Are we?" Miss Truax threw over her shoulder.

The viscount saved her from having to answer. "We were returning to the castle as well. I promise we will see you safely inside, my lady."

"Thank you, my lord."

Vivi couldn't explain the reason his promise felt reassuring. Perhaps because he wasn't deep into his cups this afternoon and he had a kind light to his eyes. She fell into step with him behind Miss Truax and Mr. Collier.

Mr. Collier cut a fine figure in his buckskins and

jacket. His bulging calves reminded her of Luke's glorious body and the way he had touched her their last night at the cottage. How she would love to steal away for another assignation, but Luke had warned her that he wouldn't have much leisure time until he had a handle on the books.

Vivi tipped her head to the side, intrigued by the movement of Mr. Collier's calves as he sauntered along the path. There was an odd shifting back and forth like a clock pendulum. She opened her mouth to ask Lord Brookhaven if he thought the gentleman padded his calves, but snapped it shut again.

Sweet strawberry jam. Maybe she did require a keeper.

Mr. Collier glanced over his shoulder as if sensing he was being watched. She looked away quickly. He stopped and spun around with a wide grin. He had nice teeth and full lips that were better suited for a lady. For that matter, his lushly curled eyelashes combined with his rosy cheeks made him much too pretty for a man. She might think him handsome if his smile ever reached his pale blue eyes.

"I am told there will be dancing this evening. Perhaps you ladies will allow me to sign your dance cards."

Miss Truax pursed her lips and glanced between Mr. Collier and Vivi.

Lord Brookhaven gestured to the path with his stick. "The ladies are expected, Mr. Collier. Let's not detain them."

The gentleman laughed and offered his escort to Miss Truax again.

Vivi didn't see what he found humorous. He was an odd fellow to be sure.

She breathed a sigh of relief when they emerged from the gardens.

"How lovely to see you again, my lord. Mr. Collier." Vivi's smile didn't reach her eyes either. "Miss Truax, thank you for the kind invitation to join you this afternoon. Now, if you will excuse me, I should begin preparations to attend dinner this evening."

She dashed for the house without waiting for a reply. When she passed into the darker interior of the castle, light footsteps sounded on the stone floor behind her.

"Lady Vivian, please wait."

She bit back a curse. It was Miss Truax. Vivi stopped and tried to appear patient when she turned to face the woman. "Yes, Miss Truax? How may I help you?"

Miss Truax slumped over, resting her hands on her knees, breathing heavily. "Mr. Collier," she said, panting hard.

"What about him?"

"H–how do…you…know him?"

Vivi crossed her arms. "His Grace introduced us the first night of our journey. He and Lord Brookhaven joined our party for dinner."

Miss Truax frowned. "Oh."

"Why do you ask how I know him?"

"I thought—"

When she didn't finish speaking, Vivi waved for her to continue. "Tell me what you thought, Miss Truax, so I may put your mind at ease before I retire to my chambers."

The lady straightened, having caught her breath.

"Lady Vivian, I am sorry for my harsh words earlier. The Forests have been through a trying time this past year."

Miss Truax held a hand out to her in offering. "Please understand I only want to save them from further heartache. Mr. Collier seems to hold you in high esteem. If you return his regard, you shouldn't allow Luke to believe your affections are his to win."

Vivi's smile was tight. "*His Grace* is well aware of where my affections lie."

"Of course." Her hand dropped by her side. "Others may wonder too, my lady, if they see you in Mr. Collier's company. This family does not need any more problems. They are good people."

"Thank you for your concern, Miss Truax. I can assure you I have no intentions of causing any trouble." Vivi wheeled around and marched for the staircase.

Miss Truax's words repeated in her head all the way to her chambers. When she closed the door, she leaned against it with a defeated sigh.

How long would it be before she embarrassed Luke and made his family a source of ridicule? It hadn't taken long at all when she had moved in with her cousin. The village had already been gossiping about her unladylike behaviors long before Mrs. Honeywell spread the rumor about her being ruined. Her past actions had probably made the gossip easier to believe.

Luke's family didn't need any more problems, and that was all Vivi had been most of her life.

One giant problem.

Twenty-one

Vivi's heartbeat sped up as Luke offered his escort to the ballroom. Her mood had improved upon seeing him this evening. They had spent a pleasant dinner engaging in conversation with his brother Richard and Richard's wife, Phoebe. Vivi had been relieved to discover Miss Truax had been placed far away from her at the table. Unfortunately, she had still been too close. Vivi had remained too aware of the other woman's presence throughout the meal.

Every glimpse of the auburn-haired lady had reminded her that she needed to secure a moment alone with Luke. It seemed wise to address the issue of Miss Truax now before Vivi lost her temper with the woman. If Luke believed she required more instruction on how to be a lady, she must eliminate his doubts. He was her new beginning, and she had no intentions of becoming an object of ridicule again. Her past was behind her and she had a glorious future ahead.

"You look beautiful tonight," he murmured as they reentered the ballroom. "Yellow suits you."

"It's called daffodil, Your Grace."

He gave her a covert wink. "Thank you for giving me the proper respect when you correct me, Lady Vivian."

Heat rushed into her cheeks. Perhaps she had over-stepped her bounds in past encounters, but she didn't understand the reason he entrusted Miss Truax with bringing it to her attention. "I didn't mean to be contrary."

"Are you ever anything else, dearest?" He gave her hand an affectionate squeeze and directed her toward a corner of the ballroom away from the crowd. "We haven't long to talk before someone will demand our attention."

His attention, he meant. Although Vivi had received many curious stares, no one aside from Luke's family had spoken to her. Their betrothal hadn't been announced, but she had heard snatches of whispers when she had entered the retiring room earlier. The young lady and her mother conversing in the corner of the retiring room apparently hadn't given up hope of snaring the Duke of Foxhaven yet, even if it appeared he might be spoken for now.

Luke's hip brushed against Vivi's, making her blood simmer.

"How was your walk with Miss Truax?"

Vivi suppressed a grimace. She had hoped he wouldn't ask until they were alone. "The gardens are beautiful."

If he found her answer evasive, he didn't press her further. "Tomorrow you should explore the maze. I will ask Gabby to show you."

She perked up at the mention of a different companion. She had briefly met Lady Gabrielle, another of Luke's sisters, when the ladies retired to the drawing room after dinner. Gabby was a beautiful young woman with ebony hair like Luke and his mother. More importantly, she was friendly and didn't act like a dour old aunt.

Speaking of dour, Miss Truax was staring daggers at them from across the room. Perhaps the woman thought it inappropriate for Vivi to linger in a corner with Luke. Never mind that she was correct and Vivi's behavior might be construed as loose.

She flicked open her fan and used it as a shield against prying eyes. "Would it be possible to speak with you later in private?"

He didn't even look her way, giving the appearance of scanning the crowd of guests. "You may speak, but I would rather ravish you."

"Your Grace," she hissed and waved the fan in an attempt to cool her face before anyone noticed her blushing.

The corner of his mouth twitched, the only chink in his armor. "Tomorrow I'll take you for a ride."

Lord Brookhaven approached to claim the dance she had promised him. Luke smiled benevolently at the viscount, then bid her good evening. He moved on to speak with a group of gentlemen clustered at the edge of the dance floor.

Vivi tried not to watch him as he made his way from guest to guest, but it was nearly impossible. He fit into the ballroom as easily as he did a saddle; his movements were fluid and graceful. Reaching a lone gentleman leaning against the far wall, Luke stood with his feet planted wide, demanding his space. He was a stunning sight.

Vivi tore her gaze away long enough to smile politely at her dance partner, but Lord Brookhaven's attention was directed elsewhere, so she resumed ogling her intended. She noticed a lady to his left was admiring him as well. And another. Then another. Her mouth felt dry. He had command of the room and his pick of ladies, all of whom likely knew more than she did about how to be charming.

Perhaps she would be wise to bite her tongue when it came to Miss Truax's tutoring and follow Luke's wishes. She suppressed the urge to roll her eyes.

There was a good chance she would have a sore tongue before this house party was over.

"It was a pleasant surprise coming upon you and Miss Truax in the gardens today," Lord Brookhaven said.

"Yes, it was delightful," she lied.

Vivi had no objections to Lord Brookhaven—he proved to be a considerate and gentlemanly sort when he wasn't intoxicated—but she was less fond of Miss Truax and Mr. Collier.

His grin widened. "Splendid. I had feared we had made a nuisance of ourselves."

"Not at all." Luke continued his path around the ballroom.

"Perhaps we could take another turn about the grounds tomorrow," Lord Brookhaven said. "With a proper chaperone of course."

Vivi snapped to attention. "Oh! I–I'm afraid I must beg off, my lord. I have a prior commitment." Specifically to Luke.

"No, no. I understand." His gaze fixed on something toward the sidelines. Vivi turned to see what accounted for his forlorn stare and discovered Miss Truax chatting with Luke's sister, Lady Gabrielle. "Do you think Miss Truax would welcome an invitation?" he asked.

Her spine softened and she lowered her guard. "I imagine any unattached lady would welcome your company, my lord."

❧

Luke barely had gotten two words out of Lord Brookhaven since he had stopped to talk with the viscount in a corner. "I wanted to thank you for sending Mrs. Price back to London," he said.

Brookhaven's eyes flicked his direction briefly before traveling back toward the dance floor. "Mrs. Price was Jonathan Collier's guest. I should have sent him back as well." He nodded once in the direction of the dancers.

Luke looked up to find Collier circling Johanna, their palms pressed together as they danced the minuet. It wasn't unusual for her to participate in whatever festivities his mother enjoyed, and Johanna was fond of dancing. He didn't understand Brookhaven's objections to Collier partnering with her. "Explain yourself."

Brookhaven hooked a finger inside his cravat and tugged. "The young woman is your relation, is she not?"

"Miss Truax is my mother's cousin and companion."

"I have no desire to cross you, Your Grace. You must know I have little in common with Mr. Collier, despite our years of acquaintance."

Luke nailed him with a glare. "If you have something to say, speak up."

Brookhaven checked the area then stepped closer to Luke. "He has a proclivity for innocents," he mumbled.

"I beg your pardon?"

"He may have identified your kinswoman as fair game seeing as how she is not strictly under your protection."

"She is under my roof and therefore protected." His voice came out low and gravelly, similar to the warning growl of a dog. Johanna was his mother's source of comfort, and he wouldn't see his mother suffer any more than she already had.

As the dance drew to a close, he stalked across the ballroom to intercept Collier when it appeared he might lead Johanna outside onto the veranda. Collier's smile thinned when faced with Luke's glower.

"It was an honor, Miss Truax," Collier said. "Perhaps you will save a spot on your dance card tomorrow evening."

He offered a token bow to Johanna. It was an empty gesture of respect from a man who would see her ruined. Luke had heard tales of Collier's conquests, but he hadn't known whether the rumors were true, until now. If Collier's friend had no faith in him, Luke had no qualms about believing the worst about the man.

Once Collier left, Luke offered Johanna his arm. "Let's take refreshment, shall we?"

She appeared flushed, splotchy red places appearing on her neck and chest like a patchwork quilt. He narrowed his eyes. "Did Mr. Collier say something inappropriate to you? He will have to answer to me if he did."

Her hand fluttered to her chest. "No, Your Grace."

They walked toward the refreshment room in silence, and he retrieved a glass of lemonade for her. After she drained her drink, they took up position at the threshold of an empty alcove. They remained within sight of everyone and he maintained a respectable distance between them.

"I want you to steer clear of Jonathan Collier. He is bad seed."

Her eyebrows lifted. "How so? He seems like an honorable man."

"Appearances can be deceiving, Miss Truax. Please, do as I command and avoid him. I wouldn't want any harm to come to you."

The tightness around her mouth melted away. "Of course, I will heed your warnings, Your Grace. You know best."

"Your compliance is appreciated." *Obedient and amiable.* He smiled, fondly recalling the words Vivian's brother had used to describe her. "I haven't had a chance to thank you for entertaining Lady Vivian today. She said the two of you had a pleasant walk in the gardens."

"She did?" When he slanted a look at Johanna, she twittered. "Yes, we did. It was a very pleasant afternoon, even if Mr. Collier joined us without an invitation."

Luke's frown returned. Now he had no doubts about Collier's intentions to woo Johanna. He would caution Vivian when he claimed the next waltz and request that she keep Johanna close for the duration of the house party. There was safety in numbers, and he would see his household protected. Perhaps he would even assign a footman to accompany them outside of the castle.

"Promise you will be careful of Mr. Collier," he said to his cousin.

Johanna nodded, her eyes wide. "I will do whatever you command of me. Anything at all, Your Grace."

He didn't know what had gotten into her, but Johanna's fawning was beginning to make him uncomfortable. With a gentle push at her elbow, he directed her back toward the crowd. "Perhaps you would be kind enough to see that Mother is having a good time."

"It would be my pleasure."

Of course it would.

❧

Luke stoked the fire in the grate to keep the chill in his study at bay. If he intended to take Vivian for a ride tomorrow, he needed to attend to the some of the correspondence on his desk. The authors of the letters had been kept waiting long enough for a response.

He shouldn't have suggested he wanted to make love to her when she'd asked to speak with him. It was not well done of him. Nevertheless, he had and he did. He wanted her with an intensity that made him feel as if pieces had been ripped from him, vital parts that he didn't know how to live without, and only she could put him together again.

He remained adamant he would not take her innocence until they had signed the marital contract, but in reality, every romantic encounter chipped away at her naivety. A greedy part of him liked that she would come to his bed with some experience, and therefore no fear.

Desire, thick and hot, surged through his veins.

As he replaced the poker, a light knock sounded at the door. The door eased open and Johanna's anxious face filled the crack. "Is everything all right?"

His desire receded quickly, and he waved her inside before someone discovered her. She slipped into his study, closed the door, and leaned against it. Her tongue darted across her lips.

"I saw the light burning underneath the door on my way to the kitchens. Your mother couldn't sleep so I've requested chamomile tea for her."

He came forward, prepared to go comfort his mother as he had in those first few months after his father's death. "How is she now? Did she have another bad dream?"

Johanna shook her head and halted his exit. "It's nothing like that, Your Grace. There was a lot of excitement today with your arrival. She is having difficulty settling in. The dreams appear to have stopped troubling her."

She sauntered into his space as she had done on many occasions.

"I'm glad to hear that is the case," he said and swept a hand toward the desk where the pile of letters lay. "I will be sorting through my correspondence awhile longer, but it's late. You should get some rest."

She drew up short, her lips turning down. "Very well. I'll leave you to your work. But before I go, I would like to thank you again for warning me about Mr. Collier."

"I felt it was my duty." He returned to his desk, hoping she would take her leave. He had no desire to be rude, but it was highly improper for her to be in his study at this hour.

Johanna looked down at her hands, pink splotches appearing on her neck again. "Luke, may I ask what danger he poses? I realize it may be none of my concern…"

He didn't agree. It was her concern since an association with Collier could bring her harm. He didn't believe in hiding the truth to protect the fairer gender's sensibilities. How else were they to know of the dangers around them?

"It has come to my attention Mr. Collier has no honor. He is a threat to unsuspecting young ladies, and he should be avoided."

She blanched. "I see. Well then, I won't go near him again."

"Very good. I will rest easier tonight knowing you are aware of the danger and plan to avoid him."

Her face brightened again. "I should go so you can get back to your work." She made a quick curtsy and left his study as quietly as she had entered.

Luke glanced at the mantel clock. It was two o'clock. He couldn't procrastinate any longer. He sat in his chair and picked up the first piece of post. Perhaps he could do this without any pain if he read it in small portions. And his reward would be time with Vivian. He didn't require more motivation than that to begin his arduous task.

Twenty-two

VIVI HID IN THE SHADOWS, HER HEART TRYING TO burst from her chest. There had been much more activity in the corridors after dark than she ever would have guessed. Did everyone have a case of insomnia this evening? She had no idea how she would explain being out of her chambers if anyone discovered her.

She considered turning back, but she had made her way to the wing where Luke's study rested without crossing paths with anyone. Besides, she was almost there. A strip of light pushed under his door down the corridor. In a dozen steps, she would be safe.

Vivi crept from her hiding spot and hurried toward his study, but the door swung open. Frantic, she searched for a place to hide. She brushed against heavy material—curtains—and batted them aside to slip behind them.

Light footsteps padded her way. Perhaps those of a female servant? When the woman passed, Vivi peeked but the passerby was nothing but a shadow moving quickly down the corridor.

Several moments passed before she determined no

one else was stirring. Fearful of making too much noise, she rushed for Luke's study and crept inside without knocking.

Luke was behind his desk, his face a strained mask of concentration. He seemed unaware he wasn't alone. Indecisiveness held her in place; the raised panel of the door dug into her shoulder blades.

Lying in bed moments earlier, worries had whipped around in her head until her entire body had grown stiff with tension. Sleep was too far off to see it. She'd thought she might find peace if she could question Luke about the reason he had enlisted Miss Truax to tutor her. In truth, she felt like an intruder.

"Damn," he said through clenched teeth and dropped the letter on the desk.

Vivi trembled, certain he knew she had invaded his study and was angry, but he closed his eyes and squeezed the bridge of his nose. A soft groan sounded deep in his throat.

"What is wrong?" she murmured.

His head snapped up. "Johanna—" Whatever he was going to say was forgotten. His eyes expanded and his mouth fell open.

"I'm sorry for intruding."

He crossed his arms and leaned back in his chair. There was no spark of amusement in his gaze this time. "Vivian, what are you doing out of your chambers?"

"I wanted to see you. I shouldn't have come."

"No, you shouldn't have."

If she could back her way through the solid door, she would be gone already. She'd rarely seen him angry, and the sharp edge to his voice was unsettling.

"But you are here now, and I won't have you putting yourself at risk again by sending you back to your chambers unescorted. Come here."

She hesitated, her heart slamming against her ribs, but then entreated her legs to obey. She stood before his desk with her hands clutched at her waist.

His cold stare melted and his mouth softened. "Don't look so dire, darling. I'm not the headmaster about to take you to task for an infraction. I would like you on this side of my desk, if you please."

Her misgivings lessened as he held out his hand in invitation. She rounded the desk and allowed him to draw her onto his lap. He wrapped her in his arms and nuzzled her cheek.

"I missed you," he said. "I'm unhappy you stole from your chambers without an escort, but I am pleased to see you."

Vivi slipped her fingers around his nape. "Peas and carrots! What happened to your neck? It feels like granite."

"Don't." He reached to extract her hand but closed his eyes and sighed when she kneaded a knot she found at the base of his head.

"Do you suffer headaches, too? My poor cousin has battled them for years." Vivi hopped up from his lap and went behind his chair. Placing her hands on his shoulders, she squeezed.

He groaned under his breath.

"Patrice's pain usually comes when she frets. It is uncanny how predictable her headaches have become."

"I'm not fretting."

Vivi made a noncommittal sound and pressed harder

against another knotted muscle she discovered. "I wouldn't blame you if you were a tad anxious. That pile of post looks rather daunting."

"I'm not anxious," he snapped.

"Very well. Let's call you surly instead." She pushed her thumb along a ridge where his shoulder met neck.

He groaned again and sank against the seat. "Is that what you do for your cousin?"

"It seems to help her. How are you feeling?"

"Better." He sounded surprised. "Where did you learn to do this?"

She faltered in her movement then pressed even harder. She wanted to forget Owen, but he had been a major influence in her life; it seemed impossible to banish him from her memory without forgetting the good parts, too. "When my horse had an injury, one of our grooms allowed me to watch as he made a poultice and rubbed it into Romie's sore leg. It helped him tremendously, so I thought it should work as well for people."

"Clever." He caught her hand and brought it to his lips.

Triumph swelled within her. He was hers at last. Every caress, loving kiss, and soft endearment told her it was so.

She returned to the warmth of his embrace, leaned her head on his shoulder, and rested her hand on his chest. "Do you know what brings on your head pain?"

His body twitched beneath her fingers. "It just comes."

She pulled back to look into his eyes. A dusky shadow had begun to form on his jaw and created a pleasant roughness against her palm when she caressed his cheek. He met her gaze for a second then looked away.

"What is wrong, my love? I can see something is bothering you."

He grabbed her hand, encircling her wrist with his thumb and forefinger. A thousand emotions flashed in his blue eyes, every one of them troubling. Eventually, he released a weary breath. "I suppose you will find out at some point. It is best you know now."

She sat up straighter and frowned. What horrible confession was he about to make, for his stricken expression left her with no doubt he had a terrible secret?

"I haven't been able to read since the accident."

"That cannot be true. You penned a note to me at Brighthurst."

He shook his head. "No, I don't mean I am illiterate. Reading brings on my headaches. A short missive is manageable."

"Oh." Vivi didn't see how this revelation was horrible in the least, aside from the discomfort he experienced. Still, that should be easy enough to avoid. "Then I recommend you don't read."

He laughed, but his usual cheerfulness was missing. "Do you see the pile of correspondence requiring my attention? This is the result of not reading. How am I to fulfill my duties when I can't perform the most basic functions?"

She nibbled her bottom lip. Perhaps he had a point, but there must be some way to manage. "I could rub your neck every day if need be. I don't mind."

"Am I to smuggle you into the House of Lords under my cloak?" He flashed a real smile for the first time since she had entered his study. "Why does that thought bring me immense pleasure?"

Her belly flopped when her mind drifted to what she would find under his cloak. She cleared her throat. "I saw a woman leaving your study. Was it Miss Truax?"

His smile faded and he rubbed the back of his neck. "It's not what it seems."

"I'm not sure what it seems. Miss Truax was here, so I assume you spoke." Vivi was more than curious to know what the other woman had to say. Had she told him about their exchange in the garden?

He released a long sigh. "We spoke of my mother. I think she is improving each day."

This good news did not explain the deep lines between his brows.

"Is that all?" Her voice quivered.

"Not exactly." He opened his arms. "Come here."

She laid her cheek against his chest. His heartbeat echoed in her ear.

He kissed the top of her head and hugged her closer. "I became concerned about Miss Truax this evening when I saw her waltzing with Jonathan Collier. I warned her away from him."

She drew back. "Why? What has he done?"

"It's nothing you must worry about. Mr. Collier isn't likely to bother you after our talk at the inn, unless he wishes to have a ball put in his chest."

His stern frown startled her. She didn't know if she could live with being the cause of another person's injury or death. Nor could she imagine Luke being able to live with himself.

"You could never shoot a man for my sake," she said, making light of his assertion.

He tipped her chin up, his intense eyes holding her entranced. "I could and I would if anyone tried to hurt you. Have you any idea how precious you are to me?"

When he kissed her, she could taste promise. His ardent conviction shook her. How had he come to feel so strongly for her in their short time together? It was true *she* had fallen in love with *him*, but Luke was more to her than she could ever be to him. He was her path to freedom. All she could ever become to him was a dutiful wife, one who never embarrassed him or cast a shadow on his reputation. And she wasn't even certain she could be that for him.

If he wanted her to accept Miss Truax's assistance, she wouldn't defy him.

She broke their kiss, but he took the opportunity to nibble on her earlobe. "I don't want to let you down, Luke."

He brushed her hair from her eyes and cradled her head. His thumb drew circles on her neck and sent a shiver down her spine. "You are incapable of letting me down, Viv."

His eyes bore into hers, as if he could see inside her.

"B-but I could. It wouldn't be my intention, but that would hardly matter. I don't want to cause trouble for you or your family."

"Then don't." His mouth on hers silenced her.

If only everything was that simple. As his lips moved over hers, she tried to hold on to her thoughts, the things she wanted to say to him, but her head felt foggy and soon she had to let it go. *Only for a moment.* For now she just wanted to drink in his kisses and breathe in his scent.

He parted her lips and flicked his tongue into her mouth. His teasing made her want him even more, and she pressed her body closer to his. He stood with a moan and cupped her bottom, dragging her against him. His hardness no longer surprised her or sparked her curiosity. She knew what she would find in his breeches and how touching him could bring him pleasure. What she didn't know was if she could carry him over the edge as he had done to her at the lake.

The image of him writhing in ecstasy with a bit of coaxing from her fingers made her heart hammer. She burned with the desire to pleasure *him* this time.

Creating a space between their bodies, she eased her hand down his rippled stomach and burrowed beneath his waistband. The tips of her fingers brushed the rounded head of his cock, and he grunted.

She looked up into midnight blue eyes and held his gaze, daring him to stop her, then circled him with her fingers. His black lashes fluttered closed and his nostrils flared. Emboldened, she explored the length of him, noting the husky groan deep within his chest. "Do you like when I touch you this way?"

His Adam's apple jerked. "Yes."

She smiled, but when he grabbed her hand to still it, she sighed. "What am I doing wrong?"

His eyes flew open and he blinked as if trying to bring her into focus. "Nothing."

"Then why are you stopping me?" She stroked him again and was rewarded with a sharp hiss. He liked her touch as much as she enjoyed touching him, but he stopped her again, pulling her hand from his breeches.

"This is still new for you. I can't allow you to do such things."

"Even if I want to?"

He laughed softly, but she wasn't joking. He had escorted her into a world of unimaginable bliss their last time alone. Didn't men feel everything the way women did? "I want to make you feel good, too."

His grip around her wrist tightened when she tried to wiggle her hand free. "You are… Viv, I can't—"

He most certainly could if he wanted. "Fine." Hooking her other hand around his neck, she pulled him toward her for another kiss. She would share this experience with him whether he thought he could allow it or not. Shrinking violets had delicate sensibilities. Vivi was no shrinking violet.

The meeting of their lips ignited a fire in her belly. His fingers slid into her hair, and he slanted her head to delve his tongue deep into her mouth. Brandy lent his breath a fiery, sweet scent that was both familiar and exotic. Their tongues engaged in a sensual dance until she bumped against the edge of his desk.

He shoved the letters aside then lifted her. She landed on the surface, her backside smarting a little from the impact. She forgot about any momentary discomfort when his fingers stole inside her wrapper and tweaked her nipple. She gasped and pulled back a fraction. Their lips hovered together as they shared a shaky breath.

There were many things she wanted to say to him. *You excite me. I love your touch. Your kiss. You.*

The words flowed from her, though they remained unspoken. They had to be in her ardent gaze. Her caress.

"Yes," he whispered and captured her mouth again.

Luke's grip on his control was slippery. He could easily devour Vivian on his desk then have her again and again. On the Aubusson. The settee. Against the wall. He could carry her up to his bed and make love to her there as well.

And yet, he couldn't.

She was his intended, promised to him but not his. He had been a fool to refuse to honor the betrothal promise. Vivian was everything he never knew he wanted. He should have married her a year ago. But he hadn't and Vivian would not carry his child before they had pledged their devotion in front of witnesses.

Sliding his hand up her calf, he squeezed the soft flesh below her knee. She had divine legs, firm and well formed. Hitching her knee up, he laid her out on his desk in one swift move. It was possessive and bold, and completely inappropriate for a husband to demand of his wife, but Vivian stared back at him with eyes like mercury. Her chest rose and fell in rapid pants. Her hair fanned out on the oak surface, almost the same warm color as the wood grain.

Vivian would be more than a wife to him. She would become his lover. No, she *was* his lover.

And she was ready for more. He was the only one holding back.

He eased the hem of her dressing gown up her thighs and pulled her to the edge of the desk. When she had dressed to leave her room, she hadn't donned drawers.

He hooked his foot around the leg of a chair and dragged it forward. "I wish my business was half as inspiring as you."

When he sat in the chair, she lifted to her elbows. Her arched brows migrated together.

He grinned. "Trust me."

She opened her mouth but snapped it shut when he pushed her knees up and gently parted her legs. He placed a kiss on her inner thigh then licked her soft skin. She stiffened, her eyes giant orbs staring at him in alarm.

"Trust me, Vivian. I won't hurt you."

"What are you going to do?" she whispered.

He dipped a finger inside her then rubbed it over her swollen flesh. Her eyelids grew heavy as he stroked her, and she rested her head back against the desk.

"That's better, sweetheart." He kissed her other thigh and she let go even more, her knees falling out to her sides. "I'm going to taste you, and you will like it."

As he trailed kisses up her quivering thigh and touched her most intimately, she clenched her legs, cradling his head. He licked her, slowly, languorously. And he did it again. With each pass of his tongue, she melted against the desk.

He cupped her hips and kneaded her pert bottom while his mouth suckled and circled her apex. Her breathy sighs transformed into moans. Her husky voice washed over him and made him even harder. He wanted to feel her hand wrapped around him again. He wanted to teach her how to bring him to completion, but a gentleman would never ask that of his intended.

She writhed on the desk, so close to her climax, but she shocked him by sitting up and gently pushing him away.

"Is something wrong?"

"No." She caressed his jaw. Her eyes held that curious glint he often saw there. She leaned forward to kiss him tenderly, not releasing his face when she drew back. "I was wondering what you tasted."

He stifled a groan. "And?"

"It's different, but not bad."

"No," he agreed. "I like it. Shall I continue?"

She shook her head. "Luke, please let me touch you. You can trust me, too."

Her honeyed lashes fluttered, her hair had tumbled around her shoulders, and she nibbled on her swollen bottom lip. His heart skipped. God, how he adored her. He couldn't deny her anything she wanted, and he counted himself fortunate that she wanted him.

He nodded reluctantly. "You may do as you wish."

Lifting her from the desk, he carried her to the settee and sat with her on his lap. She wiggled around until she was on her knees straddling him. She unfastened the front fall of his breeches. Her slender fingers circled and stroked him. He jumped and she jerked her hand back. Her wide eyes were filled with uncertainty.

"It's all right," he said then tried to kiss away her worries.

Her moist, warm skin touched him and he swallowed a groan. He wanted to be inside her. He moved against her, sliding along her slick flesh, fighting the urge to plunge deep. Taking her hand, he curled her fingers around him again and moved her hand up and down his length. She allowed him to guide her until she learned the rhythm and hold he preferred then he gave up control.

Every caress erased the day's worries until all he could think of was her. Her flushed cheeks, parted lips, and seductive gaze held him in a suspended state he never wanted to leave. Yet he wanted her hovering there with him.

He swept his fingers between her thighs, stroking over her hardened pearl. She gasped and stopped moving for several heartbeats. Her breath came out in shallow rasps as he continued to coax her toward completion.

Pressing her hips forward, she made contact with him again. He hissed through clenched teeth. How easy it would be to end this torture and make her his, but he held back. Her hand began its pleasant teasing again, bringing him closer to coming just as he carried her toward her climax. Several more passes of her hand over his flesh and he surrendered. His eyes closed and he arched his back, his release hitting him hard. He moaned softly and laid his head against the seat back.

His fingers still played over her dewy skin. Vivian's nails penetrated his lawn shirt, holding fast to his shoulder as she too neared her release. She sucked in a sharp breath and held it a second before it burst from her on the most alluring sound. The cries of a woman in ecstasy made even more beautiful because it came from the woman he loved.

As their breathing slowed, he brushed the hair from her eyes and cradled her face between his palms. A thousand thoughts raced through his mind as he gazed into her silver-blue eyes.

How much she meant to him.

How blessed he was to have found her.

How grateful he was that she hadn't turned away from him when she learned of his weakness.

But the words that formed on his tongue seemed trite. There were no words to express the depth of his feelings for Vivian, so he told her the only way he knew how.

He kissed her again.

10 September 1818

Dear Duchess of Foxhaven,

I had the good fortune of making His Grace's acquaintance recently in Dunstable. Clearly, he is an honorable gentleman. Despite my close friendship with Lady Ashden, my conscience cannot allow me to hold my tongue when an upstanding member of the nobility is in danger of being duped. It gives me no pleasure to inform you, Madame, that your son's betrothed is a lady of loose morals. I have personal knowledge of her involvement with a servant once under the employ of Lady Vivian Ashden's cousin, Lady Brighthurst.

I would be happy to journey to Irvine Castle as a witness to the lady's immoral behavior and bear testimony. His Grace should not be held to a promise given without sufficient knowledge of his intended's reprehensible habits. I could set out for Northumberland immediately once your invitation arrives. I am certain we shall get on quite well once we have met.

Your humble servant,
Mrs. Virgil Honeywell

Twenty-three

LUKE ENTERED HIS MOTHER'S CHAMBERS WITH A mixture of elation after his night with Vivian and worry for his mother. He hadn't doubted Miss Truax's account of Mother's cause for insomnia, necessarily. He simply needed to see his mother for himself.

When Mother had found his father the morning after he had passed, it had shaken her badly. Father had slipped away sometime in the night after retiring to bed early with complaints of a stomachache. She had blamed herself for allowing him to sleep alone that evening, but there would have been nothing she could have done to save him. Likely she wouldn't have known anything was amiss, for the doctor had said he'd gone peacefully in his sleep. This did not stop Mother's haunted dreams from coming nightly for months.

On many occasions during their period of mourning, Luke had heard her crying and sacrificed sleep to sit with her until she had surrendered to slumber again. He truly hoped she was free from the horror and despair that had accompanied her dreams all those months as Johanna had claimed.

He found his mother at her desk, scribbling on a piece of foolscap. "Rearranging the seating for this evening, or are you making last-minute changes to the menu again?"

She grinned up at him and replaced her quill. "I'm afraid poor Mrs. Winchcombe would be beside herself if I altered dinner this late in the day. Where have you been hiding?"

"Not hiding. Richard and I have been reconciling the accounts and answering correspondence." He moved behind her to place a kiss on her dark hair. A few silver strands grew at her temples, but her face remained remarkably unlined for a lady her age.

She gestured toward the settee. "Please join me. Would you like refreshment? I could ring for tea."

"I should get back to my work soon. There's still much to sift through and arrangements to be made in Town if Lady Vivian and I are to take up residence at Talliah House after the honeymoon."

As he and his mother settled on the lavender sofa, she patted his hand. Her eyes shone with tears, her emotions still fragile under the surface. "Your father would be proud."

He shrugged, uncomfortable with her assertion. Luke had yet to do much to make his father proud of him, but he wouldn't turn his back on his duties again. "Perhaps you and my sisters would like to join us in Town come spring."

They hadn't spoken of his mother rejoining London society yet, but his sister, Gabby, should return next Season to continue husband hunting.

His mother nodded slowly and dabbed at her tears with a handkerchief. "Perhaps."

That seemed the most he would receive from her at the moment, so he didn't pursue the topic.

She shifted toward him and pursed her lips, a worry line appearing between her brows.

"What is troubling you, Mother? Did you ask Miss Truax to keep it secret that you had another of your dreams last night?"

She made a dismissive sound. "Nothing like that. I am beyond such things now. You have enough demands on your time that you shouldn't spend it fretting over me. It's just that I received an annoying letter in the post this morning from a lady I have never met. A Mrs. Honeywell from Dunstable. She claims to know Lady Vivian."

The busybody from the church picnic? His jaw tightened. "And what does she want?"

"I assume what most ladies desire, an elevation in social status. I believe she is hoping for an invitation to the castle. She insinuated we would get on well together." His mother stood and retreated to her desk to pull a letter from the neat stack at the edge. She waved it as she carried it back to the settee. "Lord knows why Mrs. Honeywell thinks threatening my future daughter-in-law will further her cause."

"She threatened Vivian?" Luke snatched the letter when his mother held it out to him and scanned the contents. He felt sick to his stomach. The woman was insinuating Vivian had taken another man to her bed. Vivian hadn't even known how to kiss properly their first time. He crumbled the letter into a ball. "It is a lie."

"Of course it is. Your father was not a foolish man. He suspected something was amiss when Lady Vivian's brother approached him about a union between our families."

Luke recoiled. "Father had her investigated?"

"He did what any father would do, and it is a good thing he did. Otherwise, this Mrs. Honeywell might have convinced us Lady Vivian is not as she seems."

"What did Father learn?"

His mother crossed her arms and fixed him with a challenging stare. "As Mrs. Honeywell suggested, Lady Vivian was discovered in the stables with a groom in a state of dishabille. Further inquires by your father's hired man suggested Lady Vivian might have been judged unfairly. Her activities were perhaps a bit unorthodox, but certainly nothing immoral was uncovered. Your father confronted Ashden about the rumors, and he was satisfied her brother was telling the truth about her remaining an innocent."

"I still can't believe Father sent a man to uncover Vivian's secrets."

"Really, darling, why would you think poorly of your father for trying to protect his family's honor? You always were too harsh with him."

She was right, of course.

"I have many regrets when it comes to Father. If I could undo them, I would. I fear I haven't done right by any of you. Not like he would have done."

She held her hand out and he took it. "You were there for your sisters and me when we needed you most. I don't know how I would have survived those first months without your comforting presence."

"But I could have been tending to business, too. Instead, I shifted my burden onto Richard's shoulders."

She sighed. "I'm your mother, Luke. I could defend you forever, but it is true you could have done more. Is there anything to be gained from castigating yourself now? Leave the past where it belongs. It's hard to see where you're going if you are always looking back." She squeezed his hand then released him. "I should let you return to your tasks."

He stood and assisted her to her feet. Moving with delicate grace, she left the settee and returned to her writing desk to pick up her quill. A soft smile graced her lips as she extracted another sheet of foolscap from the stack.

"After meeting Lady Vivian, I must agree with your father," she said. "He knew the moment her brother provided a true representation of the lady's nature that she would make the perfect wife for you."

Luke's heart skipped. Had his father really known him so well? It certainly appeared to be the case. And Luke had been a complete arse with his father. Nevertheless, his mother was correct. He needed to look ahead, and in the future he imagined for himself and Vivian, she would not be the victim of false rumors.

"About Mrs. Honeywell…" he said. "I have a mind to ride straight through to Dunstable and set her straight."

His mother looked up from her writing. "I know how to deal with Mrs. Honeywell and her kind. Allow me to take care of the situation."

The hard glint in her dark eyes told him Mrs. Honeywell would be handled well indeed.

He nodded once. "Mother, please don't mention this to Vivian. I don't want to embarrass her. When she is ready, she will tell me about the incident."

"Agreed. I shan't mention it to anyone."

He kissed his mother's cheek and left her to finish the correspondence while he went in search of Richard. His brother had offered to read some of the letters still scattered atop Luke's desk, and Luke had set his pride aside and accepted. He descended the stairs with a secret smile as he recalled the cause of his disorderly study.

Vivian had graciously released him from his promise to take her riding today since he hadn't accomplished near enough with her interruption last night. He had arranged for a groom to accompany her and enlisted Johanna to keep her company. He hoped this would keep both women out of trouble. Although Vivian and Johanna didn't seem to get on as well as he had expected, they seemed amiable toward each other. Perhaps a friendship would grow over time.

Now more than ever, Vivian would require a strong ally in London if Mrs. Honeywell's gossip had reached anyone else. Johanna would be a valuable friend to have. She had shown exceptional skill at taking others to task when needed. No one who crossed the lady escaped without receiving blistered ears.

Luke chuckled. Yes, Vivian would have no trouble with Johanna by her side.

❧

Vivi, tired of waiting in the foyer for Miss Truax to make an appearance, swept out the double doors of the castle and headed toward the stables. It was vexing to learn Luke had requested the lady accompany her on a ride when she had hoped for a less critical companion. Miss Truax's tardiness only added to her disgruntlement. To keep another person waiting twenty minutes with no word was beyond rude, although perhaps Miss Truax deemed her undeserving of common courtesy.

She tried to shake off her irritation as she stalked to the stables. It wouldn't do to remain in a foul mood when she sat her mount unless she wished to risk her neck. Horses were sensitive creatures. Besides, she didn't wish to spend her first day exploring the fields of Irvine Castle in a fit of pique.

When the stables came into view, she forgot about her irritation with Miss Truax. Never had Vivi seen anything as stunning. Irvine stables could easily house thirty horses. Her breath quickened as she passed into the darkened belly of the building and recognized the heady aroma of fresh hay and horseflesh.

She scanned the area, searching for the groom assigned to escort her.

"Is anyone here?" she called out.

Her inquiry was met with the soft snort of a horse and a swish of a tail from one of the closer stalls. She strolled down the aisle, craning her neck to peer inside each stall as she passed. The first two were empty, but the next held one of the finest horses in England. It was pure white and surely belonged to one of the ladies of the house.

The horse shook out its mane, preening for her benefit, no doubt, and pushed its nose against the opening in the stall gate. Vivi moved closer to stroke the horse's nose.

"My, but you are a beauty. And just look at your lovely eyelashes. I'm positively jealous."

A noise at the stable doors drew her attention. The figure of a man stood silhouetted in the entry.

"At last, someone arrives. I am Lady Vivian. Do you know if my mount has been readied?"

The man froze, poised as if to spin on his heel and dash away.

"Hold there." She stepped forward, her hand raised in greeting. "You need only point me in the appropriate direction. Unless you are the groom assigned to accompany Miss Truax and me."

He squared his shoulders and walked toward her. His deliberate footsteps struck the stable floors in an angry staccato.

Dear Heavens. Had she said something wrong? She began to back away until he moved into a shaft of light and his features were revealed.

"Owen?"

Her former groom's glower could have reduced even the bravest of hearts to a quivering mess. Yet she knew Owen well. He was a harmless sort.

His golden brown eyes maintained their warmth, although his anger might account for the glow somewhat.

He had every right to be infuriated with her. She had caused him to lose his position and necessitated his move from Dunstable. After Mrs. Honeywell had spread the gossip around the village, no self-respecting family would hire him.

"My lady," he said through clenched teeth.

"What are you doing at Irvine Castle? Are you employed by the duke?" It seemed too coincidental by half.

He stopped a foot in front of her. "Nay. I've a decent position with the dowager Countess of Stanwood, thanks to your cousin. Lady Brighthurst made certain I left with a letter of reference."

"Oh?"

This was a much better outcome for his life than she had imagined. Why hadn't Patrice told her Owen hadn't been turned out without a reference?

She looked him up and down, unable to determine anything from his clothing. He dressed just as he had when he was a groom in her cousin's stables. Even though he had crow's feet and a weathered face now, she could still see the handsome youth he had been.

"What is your position?" she asked.

His frown deepened, and she realized she had been ogling him.

"Pardon me," she mumbled and shifted her gaze to the ground.

"I'm an outrider."

Her head popped up. "Truly? How marvelous. Do you often travel with the countess? I can't imagine how exciting it must be to see the countryside from high on your perch."

He narrowed his eyes. "Forgive me, my lady, but I should steer clear of you. Wouldn't want you to cry foul again."

"Cry foul?"

He tried to slip past her, but she halted him with a hand on his arm.

He recoiled.

"I never said a word, Owen. What is your meaning?"

"We can't speak in the open if you refuse to let me go," he whispered harshly.

Looking both directions and apparently determining all was clear, he grasped her elbow and pulled her into an empty stall. She almost laughed at his absurd solution. This was what had gotten them into trouble from the start.

His manner was too bold for a servant, but she had always considered him a friend. She could never take him to task for his presumptuous behavior. In truth, as a young girl she had thought they would marry and had told him as much. He had chucked her on the chin good-naturedly and said he would never marry a knobby-kneed twig like her. His comment had hurt her tender feelings, but later he had offered to help her climb the big oak tree she'd been pestering him about. She had forgiven him at once and renewed her determination to win his regard.

It wasn't until two years later she had come to realize the truth. A lady of noble birth couldn't marry a servant.

He closed the stall door behind them and whirled on her. "You told your brother I compromised you."

"I did not! I told him nothing of the sort. He believed Mrs. Honeywell over me."

Owen's jaw hardened. "Do you swear it, Lady Vivian? Did you think we would be forced to marry if your brother thought—?"

"Heavens no! And I didn't want to marry you anymore. I was just a girl when I said those things." She covered her forehead with her palm and grimaced. All this time he'd thought she had lied about him? This was even worse than anything she had imagined. "How could you believe I would do anything so foolish?"

A corner of his mouth kicked up, providing a glimpse of the young man she had once known and admired. No doubt he was recalling several foolish things she had attempted in her younger years.

"Hold your tongue, Owen Randal." She dropped her hand to her side. "So we are clear, life hasn't been easy on me either."

His brow arched slightly, but he said nothing.

"I speak the truth. Once Mrs. Honeywell told everyone in the village about what she had seen, I became an outcast. I no longer received invitations, and my dearest friends were forbidden from associating with me."

She blinked away the tears blurring her vision. Why cry now? The moment had passed. Yet a vague worry gnawed at her. The past had a way of reappearing, and Owen was proof.

"I never meant to cause trouble for either of us," she said. "Nevertheless, I did and I'm deeply sorry."

His expression softened and he pulled a dingy handkerchief from his pocket then held it out to her.

She waved it away. "I am all right now. It has passed."

He tucked it back in his pocket. "I shouldn't have allowed you to stay in the stables when you should have been abed. I'm as much at fault, if not more."

"I only blame myself." Her reunion with Owen pulled her from the fantasy she had weaved together last night.

This was exactly the type of situation Miss Truax

had reference when she had spoken of skeletons. What if news of her tarnished reputation came in the form of whispered speculation in the ballroom? Maybe it would come as a veiled comment over dinner. Did it really matter how Luke learned of her misstep? He had a right to know the type of woman he had pledged to marry. It wasn't too late to rescind his offer.

"Owen, I'm to be married to the Duke of Foxhaven. I must tell him what has occurred. He may wish to speak to you to verify my claim."

Owen's eyes flew wide open. "No! Please, milady. If the duke questions me, Lady Stanwood will hear about it. I cannot be turned out again."

"Lady Stanwood would never have to know."

He backed away from her and bumped into the stall. "My fellow servants would know if I was summoned to speak with His Grace, and they would feel it was their duty to inform her."

"I shouldn't keep secrets from my future husband." Especially when it had pained him last night to tell her of his difficulties.

"Please, milady. You could wait to tell him. Lady Stanwood plans to return to her country house at the end of the week. Once we have left, you could tell him whatever you like."

Vivi's stomach churned with uncertainty. Anything could happen in three days, and she could miss the chance to tell Luke her version of the incident. "I don't know…"

Owen rushed forward to take her hands in his. "I beg of you to wait. There is someone—" His voice broke; his Adam's apple bobbed.

"Oh." Warmth flowed over her and filled her heart with happiness on his behalf. "Someone waits for you at home."

He nodded. "Her name is Mary."

Vivi nibbled her bottom lip and pulled her hands from his grasp. She shouldn't make him any promises. Her loyalty should be to Luke first and foremost, but she had nearly ruined Owen's life. She couldn't tear it apart again.

"If your lady extends her stay beyond the week, my promise no longer counts. I will speak with the duke."

Laughter sounded outside of the stables, and Owen jumped back. He waved her out of the stall and snatched a pitchfork leaning against the wall. Turning his back, he set to work as if he was a castle groom.

Vivi walked toward the stable doors, and two figures appeared.

"Lady Vivian, there you are." Miss Truax's incensed tone set her teeth on edge. "I searched everywhere for you."

"Not everywhere," Vivi said breezily, "or you would have located me sooner."

The gentleman at her side laughed and came forward, his features suddenly identifiable in the light. "The lady has a valid point, Miss Truax."

Vivi made fists at her side. Whatever was the woman thinking bringing him along? "Mr. Collier, what a surprise."

"Pleasant, I hope." He peered beyond her shoulder. "Where were you just now? I thought I heard you speaking to someone."

"I was." She notched her chin up to distract from

the nervous quiver in her voice. "This beautiful white mare. She is a lovely conversationalist."

His eyes narrowed as his smile widened. "Is she now?"

"Better than some." Her barb was directed at him, but he didn't seem to notice.

"Your horses are waiting for you behind the stables. I ran into Miss Truax returning from my morning ride and offered my escort."

"How kind, sir."

Miss Truax smiled at him as she reached Vivi's side. "Exceptionally kind, Mr. Collier. I enjoyed our discourse."

Her tone dripped with meaning, and Vivi could only conclude the conversation had bordered on salacious. She expected no better from the scoundrel.

He gave a small bow. "Please, don't allow me to keep you from your ride."

"We shan't. Good day, sir." Vivi linked arms with Miss Truax and tugged her quickly toward the opened doorway at the other end of the stables. The woman must be touched in the head. Luke had warned her against associating with Mr. Collier, and yet here she had arrived on his arm.

Vivi chanced a quick glance over her shoulder to discover Mr. Collier standing outside the stall where Owen pretended to work. He stared at the servant with a grim smile.

Her stomach pitched and she thought for a moment she might become ill.

Miss Truax frowned. "Are you unwell, Lady Vivian?"

"Perhaps." She considered offering an excuse and escaping to her chambers, but she had a few words for her companion once they were clear of Mr. Collier's unwelcome company.

Once they walked their horses down the well-worn trail with a groom trailing behind them on horseback, Vivi broke the silence. "You would do well to heed His Grace's warnings about Mr. Collier."

"Surely Foxhaven doesn't know Mr. Collier as well as he believes. He is a charming gentleman."

"Charm is often used to distract from one's true purpose."

Miss Truax tsked. "You judge the man too harshly. I assure you he only has the most honorable intentions."

Vivi said no more. The lady was deluded. Without a dowry, Mr. Collier could want only one thing from her, but Vivi was too kind to point out anything so obvious.

Perhaps she should inform Luke of Miss Truax's carelessness. She suppressed a sigh. That would be hypocritical of her given all the times she had been careless.

"You would be wise to proceed with caution, Miss Truax."

"I am always deliberate in my actions. You needn't fear on my behalf."

For Vivian,
A rare flower for a rare beauty.
Forever yours,
L

Twenty-four

VIVI BRUSHED HER FINGERS OVER THE SPECKLED, WAXY petals of the orchid and blew out a long breath. Given time to stew over her encounter with Owen, she had come to realize holding on to Luke forever was going to be impossible. Sorrow began to swell within her heart, filling her chest with a despairing ache.

She had wanted to run away from her past, but today only proved there was no escape. No matter where she went, her mistake would shroud everything in ugliness. Luke might marry her before he learned the truth, but how could he do anything but hate her later for lying to him?

Under normal circumstances, if word of her ruin became common knowledge, she would be marked as loose and excluded from most respectable gatherings. Losing her innocence to a servant, however, would see her banned from every ballroom in London. She would be a pariah, and she would take Luke's family down with her.

That she remained unspoiled mattered not. She had been found in a state of disarray in Owen's company.

As her brother had reminded her when he'd ranted until she thought he might pass out from the exertion, gossips were eager to believe and spread rumors. Another's ruin was a form of entertainment for the perpetually bored. Innocence didn't matter. And Vivi's reckless behavior would reflect as badly on him and Muriel as it did on her. Lady Ashden had been beside herself and took to bed upon hearing the tale.

She had become a liability to her brother and sister-in-law, and now she was putting Luke's family at risk. She must tell him the truth and offer to speak with her brother if that was still his wish. Her throat ached at the idea of him accepting.

Yet, he must if he cared for his family. He couldn't bring her into the fold, noble birth aside, not if he wanted the best for his sisters.

One rotten apple spoils the whole bushel.

Tears welled in her eyes and she swiped them away. She would go to the convent quietly this time. Even if her brother agreed to allow her to reside at Brighthurst House, she couldn't return. Patrice finally had a chance for happiness with her far away and out of mind. In Dunstable, Vivi would always be considered a fallen woman and a constant reminder that Patrice bore relations who rendered her unsuitable for the position of vicar's wife. She couldn't ask her cousin to give up a life with Vicar Ramsey, especially now that Vivi knew what it was like to love another person.

She placed Luke's note on the dressing table and prepared to summon her maid to dress her for the evening's entertainments. Charades, the duchess had announced with much enthusiasm when they had taken tea earlier.

Vivi's heart ached anew. She could love Luke's family very much if she were to marry him. With only three days left to bask in the warmth of belonging someplace, she shoved her worries to a corner of her mind. She would make memories tonight that she could recall in the lonely days ahead.

A soft knock sounded at her door before it eased open. Luke slipped into her chambers then turned the lock.

"Your Grace, what are you doing?"

His gaze paused on the pot of orchids before settling on her. His blue eyes sparkled like sapphires and he grinned, the gap between his teeth showing. How she would miss the small imperfections that seemed so perfect on him. She grew misty-eyed again.

"Vivian?" His merriment vanished as he came forward to wrap her in his arms. "What's wrong?"

A burning ball clogged her throat and prevented her from speaking. *Molasses.* Must she cry now? As if acknowledging their existence was the same as permission to come, more tears sprang to her eyes.

He touched his thumb to her cheek when they began to slide down her cheeks. "Am I responsible for your tears?"

"No." She choked on a sob. "Not directly."

Luke gathered her against him. "Shh. Whatever it is cannot be so bad as to warrant tears. Please, don't cry."

His words, which were likely meant to soothe her, had the opposite effect. Great hiccupping sounds burst from her.

Vivi was an ugly crier. She always had been. And if she kept up this nonsense, her nose would turn bright red and start running.

Luke snuggled her closer, tucking her head under his chin. "There, there, love."

Those words of comfort had always struck her as odd. What did they mean? There, there what?

There, there. You're making a fool of yourself. There, there. You're behaving like a silly girl.

"I'll soil your shirt," she croaked. When she tried to wriggle free, he held her firmly in place.

"I care nothing for my shirt. I'd as soon take it off." He slanted a teasing look down at her. "What do you say?"

She laughed despite her misery. How unfair to be so close to being loved by this man and know she was losing him.

You only have yourself to blame.

She backed out of his embrace. "I should ready myself for the evening festivities."

"Soon." He scooped her up into his arms and carried her to the bed, laying her on the counterpane.

"Luke, I will be late if I don't—"

"I won't keep you long."

His words were like a dagger between her ribs and stole her breath.

He joined her on the bed and propped up on his elbow beside her. His fingers trailed down her cheek and over her lips. There was a question in his gaze, a furrow between his brows.

"Why were you crying?"

She swallowed hard lest she start bawling again. "I don't know."

"Did you and Miss Truax have a quarrel today?"

"No." She snorted. Miss Truax was the last person on her mind, and she was more likely to cheer if they were to become estranged. "I became overwrought for a moment. I'm better now."

The line on his forehead deepened and his darkened eyes bore into her. "You know you may tell me anything."

Did he know something already? Looking away, she wiped her sweaty palms against the counterpane. "I know."

He captured her chin and made her look at him again. "Do you, Vivian? Do you trust me enough?"

"Of-of course, I do." She forced a smile to ease his worries, but her lips trembled. He placed his gently against hers. Could he taste her lie?

If he did, he gave no indication. He parted her lips and touched the tip of his tongue to hers. They shared one breath, their life forces in harmony, before their mouths came together fully. He buried his fingers into her hair and kissed her deeply.

Her will to hold on to him flickered to life. Each drink from his lips fed her desperation. Perhaps he would understand. Maybe he would come to forgive her, given time.

She surrendered to self-deception just as she did to his kiss.

Eventually, he drew back and brushed her hair behind her ear. "As much as I love kissing you, this isn't the reason I came to see you."

She stomach dropped. "Oh?"

"The marriage contract arrived by messenger this

afternoon. I've arranged for Mother and my brother to witness our signatures on the morrow. Richard will be available at noon."

"So soon?" She could barely swallow around the lump in her throat again.

Signing the contract without first informing Luke of the risks associated with marrying her made her feel dirty. It was true some women lied about their virtue. Gentlemen occasionally lied about their worth, too. And anyone could pretend to be amiable when they were more often cantankerous or claim a love for poetry when they found it a waste of time. Nevertheless, Vivi had never considered becoming one of those people.

Luke's neutral mask fell back into place. "Are you having second thoughts?"

"No! Heavens, no!" At least not about him.

"Then we shall convene tomorrow at noon in my study." He tapped the end of her nose with his finger. "Don't be late, water sprite, or I will be cross."

"But shouldn't we wait? For just a little while? Patrice would want to know, and it would only take a few days for a letter to reach Brighthurst."

A muscle shifted at his jaw. "Vivian, what is truly concerning you? Your cousin knew we planned to marry. You will have time to inform her before we speak our vows. Has something happened to cause you doubt?"

"No! Nothing." *Double molasses!* She couldn't cost Owen his livelihood again. "I will be there," she murmured.

"And you must be on time."

"You are beginning to sound more and more like a stuffy old duke."

He graced her with his heart-stopping grin. "Become accustomed to it, love. You will have a lifetime of dealing with me."

She hoped that was true.

◦◦◦

Luke had never been one to look forward to social gatherings with enthusiasm, but he had arrived for dinner as eagerly as a boy awakening on Christmas morn. Vivian made him feel alive and grounded in a way nothing ever had.

He tried not to think on their earlier exchange. Her reluctance to sign the agreement could be nothing more than a case of nerves. Her response didn't mean she had lost confidence in him. He had been repeating this all afternoon, but the words had little effect on the underlying sense of dread lurking in the shadows.

Her warm hand closed around his arm reassuringly. Perhaps he should whisk her away from the dull game of charades and discover a way to reassure her. With too many people to witness their exit, however, they were stuck.

Mr. Shaw was reenacting *King Lear*, although if Luke didn't know his mother always included the work in any game of charades she organized, he would have been as lost as everyone else.

"Don't just stand there with your eyes closed," Lord Flockton huffed, his full cheeks a shiny red. "Act it out, man."

"I *am*." Mr. Shaw squeezed his eyes tighter. "Can't you see I'm blind?"

"No talking," Lady Connick called out then swung her head side to side until she located Luke's mother. "He cannot talk, can he, Your Grace? He should be disqualified."

Mr. Shaw's eyes popped open. "Disqualified! But I was defending my honor. Lord Flockton said I was doing nothing when clearly I was acting out blindness."

His mother smiled graciously, a lively sparkle in her eyes. "Lady Connick is correct, I'm afraid. There is no talking in charades, but I shall allow it this once. Perhaps you should provide another clue, Mr. Shaw."

He nodded then pursed his lips as if deep in thought before slapping his hands over his eyes.

"Let me guess," Luke's brother Drew said with an amused drawl. "You're blind."

"Yes." Mr. Shaw flashed a broad smile. "And I wear a crown."

"He's talking again," Lady Connick complained.

Luke chuckled as he checked his watch. Mr. Shaw had been torturing his mother's guests for a good seven minutes. Any longer and there might be a riot. He snapped his watch closed and slipped it back into his waistcoat pocket. "Is it *King Lear*?"

"Bravo, Your Grace." Mr. Shaw tossed his hands in the air in a gesture that communicated his frustration with everyone else's lack of intelligence. "At least *someone* knows his literature."

Mr. Shaw looked down his nose at Lord Flockton before making his way back to his seat. Lord Flockton grumbled something Luke couldn't make out over the loud clapping of the other guests. Their good humor was restored with Mr. Shaw offstage.

Luke's mother looked to him. "It is your turn now."

He glanced down at Vivian. Her face was turned up toward him in expectation, the color high in her cheeks from laughter and her lips plump, inviting. His body began to stir as he imagined the possibilities of what he could do with her if they were alone. He cleared his throat. "Perhaps Lady Vivian will stand in for me."

She drew back. "Me?"

"What a marvelous choice," his mother said and motioned to Vivian. "Come, my lady."

"Unless you're afraid you can't compete with Mr. Shaw's performance," Luke said under his breath.

Vivian raised an eyebrow at him before walking forward as regal as a queen. His intended was apparently powerless to back down from any challenge. This quality would serve her well in the days to come. His mother's shoes wouldn't be any easier to fill than his father's were, but Vivian would give her best efforts.

She leaned down so Mother could whisper in her ear then she glanced up with an enigmatic smile. She took position and when Mother gave the mark, Vivian launched into a lively rendition of a brawl.

Some of the ladies gasped and looked to his mother to gauge her reaction. Mother shifted to the edge of her seat, a broad grin in place. Their looks of horror gave way to tentative smiles, and murmurs traveled around the room.

"She is exceptionally good," Lady Eldridge said to her sister who was sitting at her elbow.

Her sister nodded vigorously. "The best all evening."

"Is it *Beowulf*?" a gentleman called out from behind Luke.

Mother shook her head. "Guess again."

After the fight and pretending to have been run through with a sword, Vivian lowered to one knee and folded her hands over her heart as if beseeching someone.

Lady Connick twittered. "Why, it's a story of love."

Vivian pointed at her encouragingly. Luke again knew the answer, but he was too enchanted by her performance to end her turn.

Hopping up, she spun around to play the role of the second person. Her face took on the soft glow of a love-struck lady as she batted her eyes and pretended to lean over a railing, extending her fingers toward her admirer below. Her gaze, however, strayed toward him. They locked eyes; his heart sped up.

Whispers flittered around the circle, and curious glances were cast his direction. His entire life Luke had been trained to hide his emotions behind a placid mask. Not tonight.

A slow grin eased across his face.

Vivian extended her hand in invitation. "Perhaps His Grace would assist me?"

Going to her side would declare his intentions as clearly as a formal announcement. There would be no more speculation about their intentions or need to hide his regard. The *ton* forgave much when a love match was made.

"*Romeo and Juliet*," a high-pitched voice blurted out as he took a step forward.

Luke halted and searched the blur of faces around him, his sight landing on Johanna. Mr. Collier was by her side studying him shrewdly.

"I believe the answer is *Romeo and Juliet*," she repeated. "Well done, Lady Vivian."

His mother stood. "Yes, well done."

She applauded and her guests joined in. The spell between Vivian and him was broken, and he donned his mask again.

Mr. Collier whispered something in Johanna's ear and she blushed.

Luke gritted his teeth. The gentleman was becoming a nuisance in his household.

He made his way toward his mother's companion while fixing Collier with a feral glare that should have the coward turning tail. Just as Luke expected, the gentleman made a hasty departure before he reached them.

He offered Johanna his arm. "Take a turn about the room with me."

"As you wish, Your Grace."

Satisfied Mother was occupying Vivian and she was safe, he led Johanna around the perimeter of the room. "Was Mr. Collier bothering you? I shall order his departure on the morrow if he is making a pest of himself."

"He's harmless." Her fingers twitched on his arm. She was lying, but he couldn't accuse her outright. Perhaps she was already caught up in Collier's web of seduction. Luke couldn't allow her to be destroyed by the man. She was as much Luke's responsibility as his mother and sisters.

They stopped a fair distance away from the other guests so he could speak in confidence. "The man is far from harmless when given opportunity. I don't wish you to speak with him again. Do I make myself clear?"

She blinked up at him, her eyes widening. "I—I believe I understand."

"See that you follow my wishes on the matter. I shan't have this conversation again, Miss Truax."

Her cheeks flushed and she smiled. "I wouldn't dream of displeasing you. Forgive me, Your Grace."

He grunted in satisfaction. The matter was settled then. Now he could turn his attention to more pleasing topics. He spotted Vivian across the room chatting with Lady Eldridge and, from the looks of it, charming the prestigious matron.

"She is marvelous, is she not?" he said.

Johanna followed his line of sight and frowned. "If I may be frank, the lady plays you for a fool."

"What the devil do you mean? Plays me how?"

She inclined her head to indicate they should move to the terrace. He signaled his consent and allowed her to proceed ahead of him by several seconds. No one appeared to be watching as he too slipped outside. He found Johanna at the far end of the terrace, hidden in darkness.

"I didn't want to tell you in this manner," she said.

"Tell me what?" Her stalling only served to claw at his insides, and he hated it.

"You asked if Mr. Collier was making a pest of himself. He was not. He made a discovery today, and he wasn't sure if he should tell you."

"Why come to you?"

She reached out to caress his arm. "We've enjoyed a close friendship, have we not?"

Luke pulled back from her touch. She likely meant it as a comforting gesture, as she had done on occasion in the months after his father's death, but there was something different about her hand on his arm tonight.

"You were a compassionate friend when I needed one," he agreed. "And I will always be grateful to you. But—"

"That's the reason I cannot allow you to become a cuckold."

"A cuckold?" His temper flared. "You've insulted my intended *and* me. This conversation is over."

"Please, allow me to explain. When I came down to the foyer to meet Lady Vivian so we might walk to the stables together, I found she had already gone."

He halted halfway to the door and spun back toward Johanna. "Alone?"

"She hadn't even taken an escort."

Luke's fingers curled into fists. What had Vivian been thinking to leave the house without protection? Especially after he had warned her.

"I can only assume from Mr. Collier's report she stole away to meet with a former...um...*lover*," she finished on a whisper. "Mr. Collier suspected something untoward when he spotted the groom inside a stall where Lady Vivian had been standing when we entered the stables. It was clear he was not a castle servant when he didn't know anything about the horses housed at Irvine stables. After some pressure from Mr. Collier, the man revealed he was a former groom under Lady Brighthurst's employ. It seems he was asked to leave, and when Mr. Collier inquired into the reason, the man began to behave oddly. Mr. Collier asked what Lady Vivian had to do with him leaving and the man nearly ran him over escaping from the stall."

Luke clenched his jaw to keep from yelling at her for repeating such nonsense. "That is speculation on Mr. Collier's part, and I should call him out for spreading vile rumors about Lady Vivian."

Johanna's hands landed on her hips. "You cannot be that foolish, Luke. There is something suspicious about her. Why was she never given a Season? Why was she found alone today with a former Brighthurst servant? At least demand answers from her."

"Say nothing of this to anyone else."

"You must know I would protect your honor at any cost."

His honor? "Lady Vivian hasn't dishonored me."

"But how can you—?"

"She has done nothing wrong," he said on a growl. "And I won't have rumors spread about the future duchess, particularly by those who wish to stay under my roof."

Johanna emitted a small squeak and turned from him.

Instantly, he regretted striking out at her. She was acting as a true friend by bringing this to him, and he repaid her with surliness and threats.

He placed a hand on her shoulder. "Forgive me. I am grateful for your concern, but I know Lady Vivian. She is innocent of any wrongdoing."

Did he know it with certainty? He had accepted Vivian's halting kisses as proof of her inexperience, but perhaps he had simply taken her by surprise when he'd kissed her at the coaching inn. In further encounters, she had behaved boldly for a virgin.

Yet she was bold in everything she did. She ran three-legged races, challenged him to swimming competitions, and jumped horses over fences. He couldn't use the quality he most admired as a basis to judge her purity. Did it even matter?

He gritted his teeth, hating the thought of her lying with another man, but even if it were true, Vivian was still the woman he had fallen in love with at Twinspur Cottage.

"We should return before it's discovered we are missing. Please allow me to see you safely inside."

Johanna complied with his request, but stopped outside the door and clutched his arm. "I only want the best for you. Have I ever done anything to make you doubt my regard?"

He pressed his lips tightly together. In truth, she had been a loyal and compassionate friend these past months. He had no reason to doubt her intentions, but Johanna didn't know Vivian like he did.

She also hadn't known how lost he had been since his father's death, a rudderless ship traveling away from his destiny. His future had never lain beyond the horizon. It was here in England as protector and provider for the people he loved most. Vivian had shown him the truth of his heart's longings. He wanted a family and roots. Not to tie him down, but to nurture his growth, to make him stronger.

"You have always been a steadfast friend," he said. "I would never question your sincerity."

"Thank you." Her grip relaxed. "I'd never wish to see you come to harm. I would sooner die."

He smiled and patted her hand, trying to break free of her hold without hurting her feelings. "I wouldn't ask you to put yourself in peril on my account, but I'm grateful for your devotion. There are other ways you could serve me, however."

"H-how? You need only ask and I'll grant your wish."

Her intensity caused uneasiness to churn in his gut. Gently, he removed her hand from his forearm. "I would ask you to befriend Lady Vivian as you have me. She will need a loyal companion by her side if Collier spreads his lies to anyone else."

Her head lowered and she said nothing for a long time while she plucked at her glove. Each movement propelled him toward an awkward awareness of something he didn't want to acknowledge.

"I have promised to do anything for you," she said, not looking up, "and you make a request on Lady Vivian's behalf."

His gaze narrowed in on her slumped posture and her fingers picking at her glove again. *Damnation*. Did Johanna fancy herself in love with him?

She was beyond the age when most ladies married, but she seemed to hold fast to the romantic notions of youth. Luke blamed the gothic novels she favored. And he cursed his great-uncle again for leaving her without a dowry. She likely would have enjoyed becoming a wife and mother.

But not his wife. He had never thought of her in that

light. She was family, like a sister and never anything more. He had been sure her regard was similar.

He suppressed a sigh, uncertain how to proceed while allowing her to maintain her dignity. He chose the coward's path and pretended to notice nothing out of the ordinary.

"Lady Vivian is my intended," he said softly. "I am compelled to see to her happiness. This is the reason I make a request on her behalf."

Johanna glanced up, her head tilted at an angle while she studied him. "You are promised to each other, and you are a man of your word."

"I am."

She nodded slowly as if allowing the truth to sink in. "I believe I understand now, Your Grace. And I will do whatever I can to assist you."

Tension drained from his shoulders and he offered her an easy smile. He hadn't wanted to hurt her by spurning her. It was a relief to be spared the difficult task. "You have a generous heart, cousin, and you will be rewarded for your service."

She curtsied then opened the glass door to slip inside.

He waited several minutes before he went inside, too. He needed to speak with Vivian at once. They were no longer at Brighthurst House where she could wander away without an escort. He didn't relish the thought of taking her to task, but she must understand she couldn't run about at will.

His heart softened the moment he spied her among a group of ladies eagerly vying for her attention. Vivian listened with a bright spark in her eyes, and she laughed like only she could, by fully giving over to the act. The ladies responded with beaming smiles of their own.

His resolve faltered. She appeared so happy, and she clearly had been accepted into the fold. She deserved a night to celebrate her victory. Tomorrow would be soon enough for him to gently scold her.

Collier was standing a short distance from Vivian and her newfound friends, watching him with keen eyes. He smirked, and a fresh wave of anger swept over Luke. Warning the man against spreading lies about his intended needn't wait another minute.

Luke stalked toward him. "Join me in my study, Mr. Collier. We have matters to discuss."

Collier shrugged. "I can't imagine what, but as you wish, Your Grace."

The other man kept Luke at a distance as they wound through the stone corridor then up the curved staircase. Silence reigned over the deserted areas of the castle except for the sharp echo of their footsteps.

A fire burned in the hearth inside his study, and he used the flame to light the candles of a candelabra before carrying it to a side table. Collier hung back at the door.

"Come inside."

"Perhaps you should tell me what this is about first."

Luke made his way to the sideboard and poured two glasses of brandy. "Let's be civilized about this, shall we? Share a drink with me while we discuss our business."

He rounded the settee, took a seat, and held one of the glasses out for Collier. The man rolled his shoulders then sauntered across the room to accept. He took a swig of his drink then lowered into a chair.

"Miss Truax informs me you are spreading lies about Lady Vivian, and I want it to stop."

"I confided in Miss Truax only. That hardly warrants an accusation of spreading lies." Collier studied Luke over the rim of his glass as he downed his brandy. "I didn't say anything that was untrue."

Luke's fingers tightened around his glass. "You insinuated something untoward happened between my betrothed and a former employee. I won't allow an insult such as that to go unanswered."

Collier laughed. "Would you call me out? Little good that would do after everyone has heard your wife-to-be is a trollop. There will still be whispers."

Luke slammed his glass against the side table. "If you so much as utter her name to anyone, I'll—"

"You'll what? Beat me bloody and humiliate me in front of my friends?" Collier jumped to his feet and flung his arms wide. "Will you make me a laughingstock again and a whipping boy for every hot-tempered jackass with a gift for violence?"

That day came back to Luke in rapid flashes. It was after his return to Oxford. Often in those first weeks back a blinding anger had possessed him. It was unreasonable and demanded vengeance on anyone unfortunate enough to step into its path. Luke's blood had boiled and seared his veins as it pulsed through his body, triggered by anything. Or nothing. He most regretted those days when he had lacked command over himself, but he couldn't change the past.

"I offer you my deepest apology, Collier. Something came over me that day and I was as powerless to stop it as you."

Collier's eyes flamed black with hatred. "Do you think an apology will appease me? I want you to pay for what you did."

"Then make *me* pay. Not her. If you want to humiliate anyone, it should be me and only me. Vivian is innocent."

Collier bore his teeth. "I will hit you where it most hurts. You will receive no mercy from me, just as you showed me none."

Luke rose from the settee and towered over the other man. "Tomorrow at first light, I want you gone. If you dare to speak of Lady Vivian to anyone, I *will* beat you bloody. And I won't have any regrets this time."

He brushed past Collier but turned back at the doorway. "See yourself out."

Twenty-five

VIVI WOKE THE NEXT MORNING WITH HER SPIRITS renewed. After a successful evening in the company of the duchess's guests, she was more hopeful about convincing Luke she could be an asset to him. The ladies had been kind and gracious, and seemed to like her.

Because they don't know the truth about you. She shut out the damning voice and tried to retain her cheerful mood.

Her maid entered her chambers balancing a tray laden with food. "Today is something of a celebration in the kitchens," Winnie said as she placed the hand-painted tray on the table.

A slender vase held a single red poppy. Vivi gently plucked the flower from its container to admire the delicate petals then replaced it with a sigh. "A celebration. How so?"

"Everyone is talking about your betrothal." Winnie buzzed around her, shaking out the napkin and placing it across her lap then bustled to the wardrobe and flung the doors open. "I have a special gown in mind for your audience with the duke."

Vivi swiveled in her chair to peer at her maid. "How do they know about our meeting?"

"How do servants know about anything, milady?" She laughed and selected a pale blue gown. "This color draws notice to your eyes."

She crossed to the bed to lay out the garment and continued her animated chatter. "The duke's man of business was present when His Grace received the marriage settlement your brother sent. And the duchess's maid overheard His Grace requesting her presence to witness the signing."

"What a lot of gossips there are at Irvine Castle. I must watch my step from this moment forward."

Winnie chuckled. "You have nothing to fear, milady. Everyone is pleased the duke has chosen you. The cook says she never thought His Grace would claim his seat. She believes you are a good influence on him."

Vivi scowled. "I don't wish to hear any such talk about the duke. He is a good man and he will be an excellent leader."

"Aye, milady. That's exactly what I told the busy-body." Winnie whisked toward the chamber door with the gown draped over her arm. "I must press this before beginning your toilette. You should look your best today."

She was gone in a swish of fabric.

Vivi turned back to her poached eggs and picked up her silverware. A rolled-up piece of foolscap rolled out from under the edge of her plate. She smiled and set her fork aside. Had Luke hidden a message to her on her breakfast tray? He was full of surprises.

She unrolled the paper, momentarily confused by the unfamiliar script.

Lady Vivian, I must speak with you. Please meet me behind the stables at eleven. Your humble servant, O.

She stared at the message mutely. Owen's spelling and penmanship had improved a great deal since his departure from Brighthurst House. Vivi had taught several of the servants to read and write to help occupy her days, although she had only offered her services to Owen in an effort to get closer to him. What a silly girl she had been.

She dropped the note back on the tray and started on her breakfast again, her mood more somber now. No doubt word of her meeting with Luke had reached Owen, too, but he had no reason to fear for his position. She had already assured him that he was safe, and his lack of faith in her rubbed her the wrong way. Still, he had been through quite the ordeal because of her in Dunstable. She supposed she could understand his anxiety.

Perhaps there would be time to put his worries to rest before she met Luke and his family to sign the agreement. She quickly finished her meal and brushed her teeth before Winnie returned with her gown.

Once she was dressed and her maid had satisfied the need to fuss over her, Vivi smiled at her. "You may go now. I wish to read until it is time to meet with the duke."

"Of course, milady."

She adored her maid, but she didn't know if Winnie was a passive participant in the servant gossip mill or an instigator. And since Vivi had promised to protect Owen's secret, she must make every effort to keep her word.

When Winnie stopped to retrieve her tray, Vivi's heart leapt. She had forgotten to destroy Owen's note.

"Leave it. I didn't finish my chocolate."

Her maid lifted the cup and sniffed. "Wouldn't you prefer a fresh pot?"

"No, it's fine."

Winnie shrugged and left the tray undisturbed.

When she was certain her servant had cleared the corridor, Vivi donned a bonnet, grabbed a parasol, and then headed downstairs. There weren't many guests stirring yet at this hour, so she was spared the task of pretending she planned to walk in the gardens.

Outside, remnants of a morning mist hung on the air. She raised her parasol as a shield to hide from any curious onlookers who might be standing at their chamber windows and hurried toward the stables.

Upon reaching her destination, she closed her parasol and stole into the darker interior of the stables. She stalked down the aisle with the intent of granting a brief audience to Owen then returning to the castle with no one the wiser.

A phaeton stood beyond the opened doors at the far end of the stables, and a groom was tending to the horses. Otherwise the area was deserted. She opened her mouth to ask if the servant had seen Owen, but then thought better of it and snapped it closed. She was to be the lady of the manor soon. It wouldn't do to ask after Lady Stanwood's servant.

The groom glanced her way with a bemused smile.

"Pay me no mind," she said. "I'm here for a breath of fresh air."

"Fresh air, milady?"

Well, now that she had said it aloud, her explanation for being there did sound odd. No one in her right mind would traipse to the stables in search of fresh air.

She wagged a finger back toward the building. "Perhaps I should keep searching." Turning on her heel, she marched straight into another body. Her breath left her in an inelegant grunt. Two arms circled her and kept her from falling. Unlike the calm she had experienced in Luke's embrace, this gentleman's touch set off her internal alarm.

She looked up into a set of hard green eyes. "Mr. Collier, I didn't hear your approach."

He offered a charming smile likely designed to put her at ease. It had the opposite effect. "Lady Vivian, I didn't expect to find you alone in the stable yard."

She swallowed. His words rang with falsehood, but she couldn't call him a liar without insulting him. She pulled from his embrace and straightened her bonnet.

"I was just heading back to the castle. Good day, sir."

When she tried to sweep past him, he blocked her escape. "Do not tell me you came all this way for the air," he said under his breath.

She cringed. So he had overheard her exchange with the groom.

He leaned closer to her ear. "What is it that really brings you here, Lady Vivian? Are you meeting someone?"

"No!" She tried to infuse her protest with the appropriate amount of outrage, but she couldn't play the insulted lady easily. He had caught her in a lie. She knew it and so did he.

His smile resembled a leer now. "Splendid. Then

you are free to enjoy a carriage ride." He took her arm and dragged her toward the phaeton.

"I am not free, sir. Release me." She dug in her heels, but he was much stronger than her.

"Come now, Lady Vivian. Just a short jaunt. The countryside is beautiful."

He lifted her into the carriage as if she were a sack of grain tossed into a wagon. Before she could gather her senses, he was in the carriage too and shoving her down in the seat.

The groom released the horses and stepped toward the carriage. "Forgive me, sir, but I believe the lady wishes to be allowed to—"

Mr. Collier slapped the reins just as Vivi tried to stand. She tumbled back against the seat and might have fallen from the carriage if he hadn't grabbed a handful of her skirts and jerked her back. She caught a brief flash of the groom's shocked face as he was nearly run down.

"Sit before you fall," Mr. Collier said. "I don't mean to see any harm come to you."

The carriage sped out of the gates and turned onto a lane.

"Take me back at once."

His hand clamped on her leg and squeezed. "When our ride is over, you may go back."

His coat flapped in the wind, revealing a leather holster and pistol. Vivi's heart began to pound as heavily as the horses' hooves.

"Why are you armed?"

He slanted a grin in her direction before glancing back at the lane and urging the horses to go faster. "A firearm has persuasive powers, does it not? But I'm certain it will be unnecessary to use it."

Vivi still didn't understand, but she kept silent. The ground below was a blur and her fingers ached from gripping the seat to keep her position. His driving was going to kill them both.

"Slow down, Mr. Collier."

"Have faith, my lady. I'm a skilled driver."

She was tempted to crack him over the head with her parasol, but she wasn't certain she could catch the ribbons fast enough if he lost his hold. She eyed the gun against his side. Perhaps if she could get her fingers around the handle without him noticing…

"Why invite me for a ride? Certainly there are several ladies who would be honored to receive your attentions."

"Perhaps they have already received my attentions." He winked. "Calm yourself, my dear. You will enjoy our time together."

She didn't care for the sound of that. There was no chance of her enjoying his company. Nevertheless, she had to get closer to the blackguard if she had any hope of reaching the gun.

"I fear I'm going to fall. If you won't slow the carriage, will you at least hold on to me?"

A smug smile lent his cherub face a grotesque appearance as he held his arm out to the side, inviting her to sidle up to him. How could she have ever thought him handsome?

She lowered her gaze as she scooted closer so he wouldn't see her repugnance and anticipate her move. Her spine stiffened when his arm wrapped around her back and his fingertips brushed her breast. Taking a deep breath, she laid her head against his shoulder.

His pleased chuckle made her blood run hot. Did he truly believe himself to be such a prize that he could abduct a lady and she would welcome his advances?

Tentatively, she placed her palm against his chest. His muscles twitched. "I knew you wanted me, too," he said in a husky voice and eased up on the ribbons. The carriage began to slow. She had to grab the pistol before he stopped the phaeton and realized what she was doing.

She slid her hand down his torso slowly, trying not to grimace.

"Don't be shy, Vivian," he growled, bearing his teeth. "Put your hand on it now."

She didn't wait for further permission. Her hand flew to the butt of the gun and she yanked it from the holster as the carriage rolled to a stop. Pulling the flint back to full cock, she aimed at his chest and scooted away when he froze.

His Adam's apple bobbed, his gaze never leaving the barrel of the gun. "Be careful. That's not a toy."

She carefully climbed to the ground while keeping the firearm trained on him. "I stopped playing with toys years ago, Mr. Collier. Right around the time I took up shooting. I am fully aware of the damage a lead ball would cause to your person."

With her feet firmly on ground, she backed away on shaky legs.

His face contorted with anger. "Get back in here now."

She lifted her chin as she took two more backwards steps. "You have no authority over me, sir. I am returning to my betrothed, and if you dare to follow me, I will prove my skill at shooting."

"You wouldn't."

She clucked her tongue. "Now, now, Mr. Collier. You have underestimated me once already. Perhaps you shouldn't press your luck."

His lips set in a thin line, and he glared.

"Nevertheless, I think it is likely Foxhaven will be a bigger threat once he learns what you have done. If you are wise—and I fear you are not—you will ride as far away as you can and never show your face at Irvine Castle again." She shook her head slowly. "I pity you, Mr. Collier. I have seen the duke at target practice."

The color drained from his complexion. "Now see here. I only wished to take you for a friendly turn about the grounds. Surely you wouldn't bother the duke over a small misunderstanding."

"Oh, I would, Mr. Collier. If for no other reason than to protect Miss Truax from you. She has no idea what a blackguard you truly are."

"Perhaps you are correct, but neither is the lady blameless."

Vivi pointed toward the lane with the barrel of the gun then aimed it at him again. "Go now before I change my mind and shoot you anyway."

"I didn't want you anyway, you stupid bitch," he spat. "I'll find another means of getting even with that arrogant prick. Tell Foxhaven—"

"Go!"

He snapped the reins with a snarl. The carriage clattered along the dirt lane, the wheels throwing up dust. She coughed as it filled her lungs, but she refused to turn her back until he had disappeared from sight. Once she could no longer see a speck on the horizon, she began her trek back to the castle. She glanced over her shoulder once more for reassurance then swung her head around in time to witness her slipper come down on a pile of manure.

"Hellfire, damnation, and curse the Devil's ballocks!" Those were horrid words for any lady to utter, but one deserved leeway when one was nearly abducted, stranded in the middle of nowhere, and her favorite pair of shoes ruined.

Gads. She gingerly lifted her foot, but her slipper didn't budge. She stood there for a moment balancing on one leg and contemplated her dilemma. The satin slipper was beyond repair, and the hem of her gown wasn't much better off. She wrinkled her nose. There was no way she would soil her gloves by rescuing a worthless shoe.

With a loud sigh, she continued the long walk back toward the castle with one shoe and one stocking-clad foot. She limped along the country lane, cursing Mr. Collier under her breath. How far had they traveled? She couldn't even see the turrets from here. She would be lucky to make it back to the castle before the afternoon.

Missing her meeting time with Luke was a certainty, which meant she would have a lot of explaining to do. As much as she would like to shield Owen from any unpleasantness, it was unavoidable now.

Besides, once Luke learned of Mr. Collier's foolish antics, a poor groom who had been dragged into one of her messes would be the last person on his mind.

Luke wasn't as likely to forget her sneaking off to meet said groom and landing in this dilemma, however. Even though he had been patient from the moment of their embarrassing encounter at the creek, she couldn't hope for his continued goodwill this time. He would probably help pack her trunks and send her to Scotland himself.

Vivi's bravado vanished and she deflated under the weight of her burden. Perhaps Luke would have been able to forgive her past, but he couldn't overlook this misstep. There was no telling how many witnesses had seen her leaving with Mr. Collier. And with the way gossip spread among the servants, most of the castle staff probably already knew about her encounter with the lousy rake. She never should have promised Owen that she would keep their past association a secret from Luke, even if she had intended to tell him eventually.

It was true what Ash said about good intentions paving the road to hell. She came down hard on a jagged rock. Pain shot up her leg and she cried out.

"Damn you, Road to Hell!"

Twenty-six

LUKE HAD GATHERED IN HIS STUDY WITH HIS MOTHER, Richard, and Johanna to await Vivian's arrival. Johanna's show of support after their conversation last night had caught him by surprise, but he was pleased by her attendance.

He glanced at the clock on the sideboard. Vivian was fifteen minutes late. Until this point, he had allowed her some latitude—having sisters, he was aware ladies often operated by a different clock—but it was time to seek her out. "Perhaps I should organize a search party."

Johanna sprang to her feet. "Allow me to retrieve Lady Vivian."

"Thank you, Miss Truax."

She swept out the door in a rustling of skirts. The three remaining occupants stared at each other in silence.

Richard crossed his leg over his knee and drummed his fingers against his calf. Luke strolled to the sideboard to pour his brother a drink. Richard had never possessed much patience. It was a wonder he and his wife got on as well as they did.

"What type of lady keeps a duke waiting?" Richard asked.

Luke returned with a glass of brandy. "A lady who knows how to keep her husband chasing after her skirts."

Their mother tsked. "Lucas."

"Forgive me, Mother, but I would dare say you are perfectly aware of what tricks a lady employs to keep her husband by her side."

"Never you mind my tricks," his mother said with a sniff.

She attempted to hide her grin by lifting her nose and turning her face away, but both he and Richard spotted it and laughed. It had been no secret their father had run ragged courting her and never strayed from her side in all their years of marriage. Edward Forest had been the subject of much ridicule at Brook's, but only when he wasn't present.

There was a knock at the study door before Johanna entered with Vivian's maid. Both women were frowning. He nodded toward the piece of paper clutched in the maid's hand. "Do you have a message from your lady?"

Johanna nudged her. "Go on now. His Grace has asked you a question."

"Not exactly." Winifred scurried forward and shoved the rolled-up paper at him. "It's a message to Lady Vivian. I swear I knew nothing about it, or I wouldn't have allowed her to meet him."

Luke stood up straighter and took the note. "Meet who?" He scanned the contents then glanced to Vivian's maid for answers. "Do you know the identity of O?"

She shook her head. "Well, maybe. But it seems unlikely, Your Grace. I don't like to speculate."

"Do it anyway."

She took a step back and fidgeted with her apron.

"I'm not angry with you, Winifred, but I can't promise how much longer my patience will last."

"It's the groom I spoke with you about last night," Johanna blurted.

Luke raised his brows at Winifred.

"It *could* be Owen, Your Grace. He served at Brighthurst House awhile back. I didn't know he was here until Miss Truax told me."

"And what would this man want with your lady?"

"I don't know."

Johanna rolled her eyes, likely thinking no one would notice.

"Do you have something to add, Miss Truax?" he asked, crossing his arms and glowering.

Her gaze shot between Luke and his mother. She stepped closer and lowered her voice. "Isn't it obvious she is involved with this man?"

"She is not," Winifred insisted. "My lady is a good lady."

Johanna ignored her. "If you go now, you will catch her in the act. Then you will see I am right about her."

His mother stood and took the note from him. "I'm inclined to agree with Lady Vivian's maid. Did you see who delivered the message, my dear?"

The maid shook her head. "No, Your Grace. I found it on her breakfast tray, but it wasn't there when I carried her breakfast to her."

His mother scanned the brief missive then pursed her lips. "Thank you, my dear. You may go."

Winifred chewed her bottom lip and appeared close to tears as she bustled from his study.

When the door closed, Mother waved the note toward Johanna. "Now that the help is gone, let's be honest, shall we?"

Richard took the paper, his brows lowering as he read the contents. "I don't understand. Honest about what?"

Mother's stare never wavered from her companion.

A pink flush stained the younger woman's cheeks. "I—I have no idea what has transpired, Your Grace. I swear it."

"I recognize the handwriting, Johanna. I would like you to explain why you sent a note to Lady Vivian arranging a false meeting with a servant."

Johanna's complexion drained of color and she swayed. Richard held her up when her knees buckled. "I was trying to help," she said in a weak voice.

"Devil take it!" Luke stormed the door. He had to find Vivian before she landed in trouble.

Once he had cleared the castle doors, he rushed for the stables. A groom was already running to meet him.

"Your Grace, it's Lady Vivian." He spoke in a hushed voice, but there was a hint of fear in his tone.

"Where is she? Is she hurt? Take me to her."

The servant fell in step with Luke to return to the stables. "Mr. Collier rode away with her in the phaeton. I tried to stop him."

"Which way?"

The groom pointed north toward the village. "The gentleman is reckless. I pray for her ladyship's safe return."

"Saddle my horse," Luke snapped as they passed into the stables.

Richard came up beside Luke. "Make that two horses."

His mother and a tearful Johanna were several strides behind his brother.

Luke held his fist stiffly at his side for fear of throttling Johanna. "Mr. Collier has taken Vivian. What does he plan to do with her?"

Her jaw fell open. "But that wasn't supposed to happen. He was to summon the groom."

"Dammit!" Luke slammed his fist against the stall. She jumped and fresh tears flowed down her cheeks. "I told you the blackguard couldn't be trusted. You will be held accountable, Miss Truax. And don't think you will come out of this lightly."

He stalked past her to where Thor was housed.

"He said he loves her," Johanna called after him. "He was going to offer for her hand once you were freed from the betrothal."

"Hush," his mother scolded.

Luke took the reins from the groom to lead Thor from the stables. "I never wanted to be freed from Vivian. I just didn't know until I met her."

Richard joined him outside with his horse in tow. They mounted and set off for the gate.

"I'll kill him if he has touched her."

"Understood," Richard said as they cleared the gate.

Luke urged his horse into a gallop and Thor obliged, tearing up the ground in a matter of seconds. From the corner of Luke's eye, he spotted his brother's mount keeping pace. Perhaps even Richard believed there were times when risking one's neck was appropriate.

When they topped the hill, a figure in the distance caught Luke's eye. It appeared to be a child, perhaps a village girl who had wandered too far from home. As they drew closer, he could see he had misjudged her height. It was a woman hobbling down the lane. A well-dressed lady with her bonnet askew and hair partially tumbling around her shoulders.

Vivian. He pulled back on the reins to slow Thor. Richard followed suit with his steed.

"Is that her?" his brother asked. "Good God! Is she armed?"

A flash of sunlight glinted off the barrel of a pistol in her hand. Luke tamped down the urge to laugh hysterically, because that's exactly what it would be. A hysterical response. Never in his life had he been frightened out of his wits.

He had explored the crags around Northumberland, hunted wild boar in the Black Forest, dove from the highest cliffs he could find, and stared down the barrels of pistols on several occasions when an opponent was unhappy with how the cards had played out. None of those things had ever scared him. Yet, the tiniest hint of danger to his little spitfire and he turned into a petrified nursemaid.

"Luke!" The tremor in her voice tore at him. He dismounted the moment he reached her, barely waiting for Thor to come to a halt.

Her hair was a mess, her gown was soiled at the hem, and she had lost a shoe.

"Have you been injured?" he asked.

"I'm fine."

He ran his hands over her head in search of bumps. There were no visible bruises or cuts.

She pulled free of his grasp with a harassed scowl. "I swear to you, I haven't been hurt."

He held his hand out for the firearm and she passed it to him. He set the flint so it wouldn't fire, and then lost control. "What the hell did you think you were doing?"

She blinked. "I—I didn't want to go—"

"God's blood, Vivian! Whatever possessed you to leave the castle without an escort? Do you have a damned death wish, because it would be easier to ask for my help?" He shoved a hand through his hair, trying to rein in his emotions. "If you ever do anything this harebrained again, I may just wring your neck."

Vivian's bottom lip trembled, but she held her ground. "Could we please discuss this at a later time, Your Grace? I have ruined my favorite slippers, torn my stockings, and soiled my gown. Besides, I'm at a decided disadvantage should you decide to strangle me here and now since you have taken my gun." She finished with a sniffle.

"Hell's teeth, Viv. You know I wouldn't harm a hair on your head. But I'll rip Collier limb from limb. Where is he?"

She pointed in the opposite direction. "He took off like the devil was after him."

Richard came up beside Luke and held his hand out for the pistol. "Allow me to give chase. He won't get far in the phaeton."

Luke surrendered the gun then swept Vivian against

him. She squirmed in his hold, but he refused to let
her go. She worked her arms free, wrapped them
around his waist, and snuggled her cheek against
his chest. His heartbeat refused to slow. If he had
lost her… "You are fortunate I don't take you over
my knee," he murmured before kissing the top of
her head.

God help him. All he had were empty threats,
because he would rather be on the receiving end of
a whip than see her harmed in the slightest manner.

"Perhaps you should take Lady Vivian to Shafer
Hall," Richard said. "Phoebe will have something
she can wear, and no one must know about this
morning's excursion."

Luke released her. "Come on. You'll ride in front
of me."

He tried to cover his weakness with gruff manners,
but when she lowered her head and sniffled again, he
only wanted to reassure her all was well. At this rate,
he would likely exhaust himself rescuing her from
scrapes. Of course, she had done a bang-up job of
saving herself today.

He mounted Thor then signaled for his brother
to offer her a leg up. Vivian climbed into the saddle
and sat astride, half on him and half on the horse.
He wrapped his arm around her waist to hold her in
place. Now that he had her safely within his reach, he
couldn't let her go. He tapped Thor's sides and they
set off for Shafer Hall, cutting through the meadow.

After a bit, she wriggled to adjust her seat and
nestled into his crotch. His body warmed with her
snugly against him, fitting him so perfectly in every

way. Perhaps she was too much like him. This was the origin of his fear. Nothing had ever held him back, and Vivian was just as reckless.

"What am I to do with you, water sprite?"

She gave her head a small shake and a hot tear fell on his hand.

Brushing her hair aside, he placed a kiss at her temple. "No more tears. I have you now."

⁓

Vivi fought back her tears for the remainder of their ride, trying to honor Luke's wishes, but she was filled with sorrow. What was he to do with her? Well, there was really only one answer, wasn't there? She didn't believe he had thought of sending her on to Scotland, though. Not yet, anyway.

When they rode up the circular drive of Shafer Hall, a footman came out to greet them.

"Welcome, Your Grace." He showed no indication that he found the Duke of Foxhaven's arrival unexpected nor did he seem surprised Luke had arrived with a lady riding astride before him. The young man even had the good manners to pretend he couldn't see her ankles and half her calves from her skirts bunching up.

Luke swung down from Thor then assisted her with dismounting as the butler and an older woman bustled out of the house.

"Your Grace, we were not expecting you," the woman said and patted her mobcap as if to reassure herself it was on properly.

"We won't be staying, Mrs. Aylmer. Will you please

show Lady Vivian to a chamber to set herself back to rights? My brother assures me Lady Phoebe is happy to supply a new gown to the lady as well."

Vivi heated through at what the servants must think of her state of dishabille and what had caused it.

The woman curtsied. "It would be my pleasure, Your Grace."

Luke regarded Vivi with a frown. "I must attend to an urgent matter, but I will send a carriage for you."

Her heart leapt into her throat. This would be his life. Cleaning up her messes and growing more disgruntled with her.

She grasped his arm without thinking. "Please stay. Can't we talk through this first?"

Luke shot a look toward the servants, silently communicating for them to leave them alone.

The staff returned to the house.

His glance fell to her fingers digging into his forearm. She released him. "I'm sorry. I wasn't thinking."

He lifted an imperious eyebrow. "That seems to be a common occurrence, Vivian. You are correct about the need to talk, but now is not the time. Richard may require assistance, and I won't leave my brother to face Collier alone."

"No, of course not. You should help your brother. I wasn't—" She bit off the last word. Reminding him yet again of her tendency not to think things through carefully wouldn't help her cause. "Will you come back for me instead of sending a coach?"

"It may take some time. Are you sure you wish to wait here?"

She nodded. The last thing she wanted was to spend

the afternoon with Luke's kin pretending she hadn't spoiled everything between them.

Luke escorted her to the double doors, left her in the servant's care, and returned to his horse. If Mrs. Aylmer hadn't hustled her inside, Vivi would have stood on the stoop to watch him ride away from her.

"Come along, milady. Ann will have you back to rights in no time, and I will have Cook prepare luncheon for you."

"Please don't go to any trouble."

"It is no trouble."

The keys at Mrs. Aylmer's waist jingled as they climbed the stairs and walked the corridor. She stopped at a door, turned a key in the lock, and entered a bedchamber. She crossed the room to fling the curtains wide, flooding the quaint space with sunlight. It was a tidy and welcoming room. "This chamber hasn't had visitors in a while, but I see to it the chambermaids keep it tidy."

"It's lovely," Vivi said. "May I take my meal in here?"

Mrs. Aylmer offered another kind smile. "If that is your preference, milady. Now, you rest. It appears you've had quite a time of it today. Lady Phoebe's maid will be in to assist you in a moment."

Vivi stood in the middle of the room after the housekeeper left. The furniture was too fine to spoil with her dirty gown. A young woman entered several moments later, carrying a few dresses.

"Mrs. Aylmer said I am to set you back to rights, milady."

Lady Phoebe's maid turned out to be a soft-spoken girl who blushed every time Vivi met her gaze in the looking glass. Once Vivi had approved her handiwork, the maid bolted for the door as quick as a fox with hounds nipping at her hindquarters.

Another maid entered minutes later with a footman and a tea cart. "Mrs. Aylmer thought you might like to read while you await the duke's return," the young woman said and placed two leather-bound books on a side table. "There is a library below stairs if you prefer something different."

"Thank you. I'm sure these will be more than satisfactory."

The maid beamed, leaving Vivi with the impression she had selected the books. When the servants left her alone again, she admired the lovely array of cold meats, cheeses, and fruit, but she had no appetite. She forced down a few bites to be polite, but her stomach rolled and bobbed until she feared she might toss up her accounts.

Standing, she began pacing the chamber until her feet ached. She plopped down on the bed. It was softer than it had appeared. She wiggled then stretched out on it to further test it for comfort.

Too bad she wasn't tired or else she could escape her racing thoughts for a while. She had no doubts Luke cared for her; perhaps he even loved her. He had been willing to give up his dream of exploration to please her. He had even embraced an existence that caused him great discomfort. She never should have allowed him to make those sacrifices.

She refused to bring shame upon his family too, any more than she already had. She wouldn't be a stain upon the pristine reputation the Forests enjoyed. It was unfair to take his sisters with her in her fall from grace, and there was no question she would fall out of favor with the regal women who had welcomed her so warmly last night.

Once word spread of her reckless ride with Mr. Collier, everyone would think her scandalous. A lady of poor Quality. Unfit for polite society. All the things her sister-in-law had predicted.

Luke deserved better than she was able to give him, and if he couldn't see it, she would have to be the voice of reason for him.

She curled up on her side and closed her eyes to shut out the shame threatening to overwhelm her. Quietly, she lay there until her thoughts began to slow, some evaporating like morning mist before she could comprehend them. Wisps of ideas unrealized until there was blessed nothingness at last.

Something grabbed her from behind. Vivi screamed, flung her elbow in a wide arc, and connected with flesh.

"Devil take it!"

Her heart was pounding loudly in her ears, but she recognized that voice. She flipped over to face her would-be attacker.

Twenty-seven

LUKE PRESSED HIS PALM AGAINST HIS THROBBING EYE; the hammering shot straight through to the back of his head. "I called your name," he said lest she think he had intended to frighten her.

"Oh, sweet strawberry jam!" Vivian bolted upright and scooted to the edge of the bed to tug his hand away so she could peer at his eye. "It's turning purple already. You can't arrive to dinner with a blackened eye."

He chuckled. "It wouldn't be the first time."

"This isn't funny. I have injured a peer of the realm. Is there nothing I can do right?"

"You plant a facer pretty well."

"Oh, don't be flippant, Luke." She touched the injured area around his eye.

It was unlike her not to see the humor in the situation. The encounter with Collier must have shaken her even more than he had suspected. He threaded his fingers with hers and pulled her hand away from probing his injury.

"Everything is fine. Just don't touch it." He placed a kiss on her hand to take away any sting his words might have.

She blinked up at him; her hair was mussed again from sleep. "I'm sorry. Did I break anything?"

"You have broken me from ever sneaking up on you again, but that's all."

She pulled her hand free of his and sighed, her shoulders sinking until she looked so dejected he thought his heart may rip in half.

"Did you find Mr. Collier?" she asked.

"You have nothing to fear from him now. He's being held at the castle."

He sat on the bed and wrapped his arm around her. She laid her head on his shoulder with another heavy sigh.

"I wasn't afraid of the blackguard. At least not once I had commandeered his firearm."

Vivian was brave beyond words, foolishly so. Just as he had been his entire life. Now he better understood his father's chiding. Luke wanted to take her to task for it, too, but his disapproval wouldn't change what she was inside. She lived life at a full-out gallop. It was exciting and marvelous to be in her presence. But her recklessness scared him to death. He had lost his father not long ago. Losing her would be too much.

He licked his lips, unhappy everything had come to this. "Vivian, I can't live this way. I cannot watch you every minute, and I refuse to treat you like a prisoner. I was concerned about you making small missteps when we arrived, but this is so much more. Do you understand?"

She nodded, her hair making a shushing noise against his jacket.

"Do you truly?" He captured her chin and urged her to meet his eyes. "This cannot continue."

Her silver-blue gaze lowered and her lashes fanned across her pale skin. "I understand. Would you allow me to write my brother?"

He paused, uncertain he followed her logic. "If you must, but what does Ashden have to do with our affairs?"

"I would prefer to leave straight from here, if he is agreeable. It's such a long ride from Brighthurst House."

Luke grasped her shoulders and held her where he could see her face. She bit down on her trembling lip. "What in God's name are you talking about? Where do you think you are going?"

"To Scotland. I've decided to take vows."

He couldn't be hearing her correctly. She wanted to leave? Had she gone willingly with Collier after all and then changed her mind? He regarded her closely, searching for clues to explain her state of mind. "I didn't think you wanted to take the veil."

Her eyes were large circles. "I don't, but what gentleman in his right mind would have me now? And I cannot go back to Brighthurst House."

He almost shouted that he would have her. Again and again and again. But he bit his tongue. He would be speaking out of anger, suggesting that she was nothing more to him than a good shag, and she was more. So much more that it hurt to be apart from her, even for a short time.

"That makes no sense," was all he could manage.

She rose from the bed and stood before him. "Luke, I cannot ask you to spend every day of your life in pain, and that will be your future if you marry me. Either the headaches will plague you or my mistakes will haunt you. Can you not see you would be better off without me? I make a mess of things everywhere I go, and today is a perfect example. Word of my excursion with Mr. Collier will have already spread. I'll be given the cut direct just like in Dunstable, only this time more people will be hurt. Do you want your mother and sisters to suffer my same fate?"

Luke laughed. He hadn't known her speech was going to end on a humorous note.

She glared, obviously misinterpreting his amusement. When she tried to stalk away, he caught her hand.

"Is that what you think will happen? No one would dare give Mother the cut direct unless the lady or gentleman in question wanted to become a pariah. And God help anyone who mistreats her chicks. She is a fierce mother hen."

"But the gossips will talk behind her back. And yours."

He shrugged. "I'm sure that happens now. People can be petty and jealous, but rarely to our faces. How refreshing it would be to have someone actually say something within my hearing instead of falsely flattering me then reviling me once I walk away." He cupped her cheek, brushing his thumb over her silky skin. "That day at the church picnic I knew you hadn't been taught to ignore hurtful words. I wanted to protect you from gossip as much as possible for your sake, not ours."

"I am bad for you, Luke. Why can't you see the truth? You need a genteel wife who will make you proud."

"You are exactly the kind of wife I need. I have been traveling the world in search of something that would make me feel whole again, and you were right here all along. *You* are what I need."

Tears flooded her eyes; her expression twisted with doubt.

"You also make me feel out of control, Viv, and I hate it. I want to keep you safely by my side. I want to love you into our dotage, so why won't you allow it? Do you have no faith in me?"

She eased away from him and swiped at her tears. "I don't understand."

"You know of my failings. How I turned my back on my responsibilities and my struggles with—". His throat tightened and refused to allow the last word.

"Oh, Luke." A soft glow emanated from her bright eyes, and she reached out to caress his face. "I have absolute faith in you. I wish nothing more than to spend my life with you, but you deserve more."

His heart stuttered before launching into a driving rhythm. She thought she was saving him, a misguided attempt to protect him. "You have everything I want, Vivian."

She sighed and let her hand hang by her side. "You only say that because there are things you don't know about me. Things I have done that could change how you feel about me."

"You are speaking of the groom."

She gasped. "How—?"

"I have known for some time, and I don't believe the rumors."

Her lips parted on a breath, tempting him to kiss her. "Just like that, you believe in my innocence?"

"I know you and I believe in you, but the question remains whether you believe in me, too. Upon my honor, I will protect you, my love. I will utilize every drop of power my title allows me to save you, but I must know if you trust in my capabilities."

She blinked, his words seeming to penetrate her stubborn head. "I have never doubted you."

"Nor I, you." He leaned forward until they were nearly nose to nose. "And someday, if you want to tell me what happened that day with the groom, I will listen with an open heart and mind."

"What is wrong with now?"

"*Now* I want to kiss you."

❧

Vivi gave up her arguments the moment his lips touched hers. His kiss was demanding and possessive. Her heart stalled then began to beat heavily, more vigorously as hope built inside her.

Luke wanted her. He believed in her. He promised to weather any storms for her.

Even if it was unfair to ask this of him, she couldn't deny the truth any longer. She would have no life if they were separated, and neither would he.

He held her tightly against him, his hand cradling the back of her head as his tongue swept across her lips. She moaned softly, opening her mouth to welcome the sweep of his tongue. He kissed her deeply, intimately until she could no longer distinguish what was her and what was him. They had merged into one.

Luke broke the kiss but didn't pull back. They were suspended there, mouths close but not touching. Her lips were moist and swollen; her pulse was fast and strong.

His thumb moved in a slow arc across her cheek.

"Stop me now, my love, for I haven't the willpower on my own."

There was no stopping for either of them. She needed him like she needed air to breathe.

"I don't want to stop." She flicked her tongue across his bottom lip, goading him. He cursed softly then seized her mouth again.

His fierceness fed her desire, challenging her to love him with the same passionate intensity. She climbed onto his lap. Cradling his head, she kissed him as deeply as he had her. How she loved his touch, his spicy scent, the brush of his dark hair against her wrists. Every inch of her was pressed against him, but it wasn't enough. She wanted to see the strength she could feel beneath his clothes.

She unknotted his cravat then moved to his waist-coat, shoving the garment down his arms. He released her long enough to pull his arms free.

"Undress me too," she said as she tugged his shirt from the waistband of his trousers.

Luke urged her to stand at the edge of the bed then spun her away from him. His fingers attacked the fastenings down the back of her gown and pushed it off her shoulders. With the last button released, the muslin slid down her body and pooled at her feet. He unlaced her corset and tossed it to the floor. Her petticoats followed.

"Turn around."

She did as he commanded. With his blue eyes ablaze, he grasped the hem of her chemise and peeled it over her head. She bent forward to release the ties of her stockings.

"Leave them on."

Her hand paused in midair and shook slightly. His demands excited her in a way she never would have expected.

He ripped his shirt over his head, messing up his curls, and then stood to unfasten his buckskin trousers.

Her stomach tumbled. "What should I do now, Your Grace?" Her voice sounded deeper, sultry.

He kicked off his boots, dropped his pants, and sat back on the edge of the bed. He extended his hand and she placed hers in his. "Come here so I may touch you."

His fingers curled around her wrist and tugged her toward him. Her thighs bumped against the mattress, and she cried out in surprise. He raised one brow and grinned most wickedly as his fingers walked up the backs of her legs to cradle her bottom. His lips grazed the valley between her breasts.

"I want to taste every inch of you, Vivian."

He began at the hollow at her collarbone, licking, and he stroked her body from hip to shoulder then back again. Her breasts felt fuller and moisture pooled between her legs. She captured his head and drew him to her breast, her nails lightly scraping his scalp. His tongue lapped at her nipple until she twisted in his arms, wanting to be closer. He sucked her into his mouth and lovingly circled her bud until it was hard and tingling. His fingers made lazy loops at the base of her spine, and tremors coursed through her.

An ache began deep inside her, a longing for something more than the pleasure she had known recently.

"I want…"

She didn't know what to call it or even what she was asking. She just knew she couldn't get enough of him no matter how closely she hugged him to her.

He gazed up at her, his eyes almost black. "And I want you."

His hand continued its journey down her belly and delved into her curls. She leaned into his tender touch with a satisfied sigh.

"Show me what comes next."

"Vivian," he said on a breath. He sounded as if he intended to argue, but she wouldn't allow it. Grasping his chin, she tipped his head back then leaned over him, her mouth hovering close to his.

"I want to know how to make love. Please, tell me what to do or I'll be forced to explore all on my own."

He grinned. "Is that supposed to sway me to do your bidding?"

"May—"

He pulled her onto the bed and she squealed. He rolled so she was beneath him and smiled down at her. "You are wrong again. When will you learn I play to win?"

"I—"

His mouth plundered hers until she lost awareness of everything except the most delicious details—the searing heat of his hand on her hip, the rapid beat of his pulse at his neck, his hardness pressing against her intimately.

His kisses trailed down her chin, her neck, and her chest. He took her nipple between his teeth and gently tugged.

"Luke!"

He drew back, his eyes filled with concern. "Did I hurt you?"

"No," she whispered. Her chest rose and fell more rapidly than before. Making love with him was exhilarating beyond anything she had ever imagined.

"I'm frightening you."

She shook her head. "Do it again."

A sly grin spread across his face before he lightly nipped her breast again. His fingers touched between her legs and she arched her back. He caressed and teased her body until she quivered from head to toe.

He shifted to kiss her again then placed his head close to hers. His warm breath feathered over her ear. "I'm going to bring you to completion now."

"No!" She gripped his shoulders and tried to hold him in place when he slid down her, but she didn't have the strength.

He settled between her thighs. "Yes, Vivian. And then I am going to take your innocence, because I am beyond the point of stopping."

She laughed, the sound airy. "I'm giving it to you."

"And I love your generosity."

❧

Luke's blood rushed through his veins. Vivian's taste on his tongue and her erotic sighs and moans made him harder than he could ever remember being. His sexual hunger for her was untamed and his control overtaxed. When she had appeared frightened by his fervor, he had felt like a scoundrel, but then she had held him captive with her liquid-silver gaze and told him to do it again.

He licked her again and again, sensing the tremors racing down her legs. Vivian's breaths came faster and harder. When she came, she cried out loudly, her legs clamping around his head. He thrust his fingers into her, feeling her body grip him. She released a long sigh and dissolved into the bedding, her arms and legs limp.

He feared she would still experience pain, but perhaps her relaxed state would make their coupling easier. Positioning his body above her, he kissed her forehead, her nose, her chin. "I love you."

"Me too," she whispered.

He smiled and brushed the back of his fingers over her soft cheek. Would she ever make the same declaration to him? Perhaps he didn't need to hear the words for there was no mistaking the affection for him in her gaze.

He prepared to enter her, uncertain if he should give her fair warning first. He kissed her again and surged forward while his mouth still covered hers.

She stiffened and tore her mouth from his. "Oh, my Lord! Gads, that—"

She snapped her mouth closed and stared up at him with wide eyes. He held still, his tortured breath stirring her hair. She felt amazing surrounding him, but he hated that she had to suffer for his pleasure.

He kissed her temple. "I'm sorry, darling. This is the only time it will hurt, I promise."

She shook her head. "I'm all right. It was just a bit...shocking."

"You are a horrible liar."

Her chin lifted. "I am *not* lying. And this can't be all there is to it, so please continue."

His laugh was strained, but he genuinely appreciated her pluck. Gently, he withdrew and slid back inside her. As he repeated the motion, she sighed and closed her eyes. Her hands brushed his buttocks and tension seemed to drain from her.

"Move your hips with me," he murmured.

When he thrust into her, she met him and sighed again. He stopped to kiss her then pushed into her once more. She quickly adapted her movements with his and soon he was lost in her. Her soft moans filled him with elation as she welcomed him, loving him back with her body. Her fingers clutched at his back, urging him to go deeper.

His thoughts abandoned him, all except one word repeating in his head. *You.* He had found what he had been searching for all this time. Vivian was his guiding star, leading him back to the life he had always been meant to live. She was his hope, his deepest desires, and his destiny.

"You are mine," he murmured moments before she sent him to his *la petite mort*. He surrendered to it, welcoming his temporary destruction, for his beloved Vivian would put him together again as only she could.

Twenty-eight

LUKE HADN'T REALIZED HE HAD BEEN HOLDING HIS breath, but when Vivian signed her name to the marriage settlement, it came out in a whoosh. She laid down the quill and accepted his mother's enthusiastic congratulations.

Richard clapped him on the back. "Well done, brother."

When Mother released Vivian from her embrace, she joined hands with Luke. Their fate was sealed, come what may. Vivian was his and soon she would have his name to prove his devotion. He lifted her hand to his lips, drew in her sweet scent, and marked her with a kiss.

Mother slanted a smile at him. "What an exhausting day. I am afraid you will have to excuse me so I might retire for the evening. Richard, will you escort me to my door?"

"My pleasure, Mother. I should collect Phoebe and make our way back to Shafer Hall."

When they were alone, Luke scooped Vivian into his arms and carried her to the settee. He settled on the upholstered piece with her on his lap and traced the rim of her ear with his finger. She leaned into his touch.

"How are you feeling?" he asked.

"The soreness is mostly gone and I feel amazing." She wiggled to around to face him, her eyes snapping with the curious energy he had loved from the moment they had met. "Will we share a bed often? I wouldn't like waiting long between visits."

Luke laughed, rejoicing in the fact Vivian was as passionate as he had judged her to be. "Try keeping me away." He nuzzled her neck, becoming aroused again. If he hadn't taken her innocence only hours earlier, he would already have her half undressed. "Perhaps I should send you to your chambers while I still have the wherewithal to do so."

"Soon." She played with the hair at his collar, her expression turning thoughtful. "Miss Truax wasn't at dinner. Has she been locked in her chambers like Mr. Collier?"

"She has been ordered to stay there until I can decide what should become of her." He hadn't felt right about imprisoning a family member and one-time confidant, but he couldn't look upon her without disgust.

"What do you want to do with her?" Vivian asked. "I hope you won't be too harsh with her."

"She conspired to ruin you and take you away from me. How can I be anything but harsh?"

"You said yourself she fancies herself in love with you. What she did is unforgivable, but I can understand her desperation. Mr. Collier is the true culprit, filling her head with lies and empty promises. Perhaps I would have believed him too if the situation were reversed."

"But you would never conspire to hurt another person."

She dropped her gaze. "No, I wouldn't. I simply ask that you give careful consideration before you decide her fate. People make mistakes."

He kissed her forehead. "You are too tender-hearted, my love. I promise the punishment will fit the crime. Nothing more and nothing less."

"What will you do with Mr. Collier?"

If Luke made Collier's transgression public, the man would have accomplished his aim to some degree. He wouldn't allow the blackguard to taint Vivian's reputation. The bastard had sought his revenge where it would most hurt Luke. Damn the consequences to Vivian. And Luke had been stupid enough to reveal his weakness to Collier. It would be easiest to take him into the woods and put a ball in him, but murder wasn't the answer even if Luke's rage called for blood.

"Lord Brookhaven has offered to take him back to London, but Collier's days of mingling with the *ton* are over. Without the viscount's support, he has no access to society, and Brookhaven has assured me he has already dissolved their friendship. If I find he has lied, I will challenge them both."

Vivian nibbled her bottom lip. "What about Owen? You won't say anything to Lady Stanwood, will you?"

"I see no reason to bring the countess into family matters. From all accounts, the man is blameless."

This seemed to put her concerns to rest, and she laid her head against his shoulder. "Thank you for believing me. If my brother had placed more faith in me, Owen wouldn't have been driven from his home."

"Your brother believed you, Vivian. But sometimes a man must make decisions to protect those he loves. I would have done the same thing if my sister were in a similar predicament. And he defended your actions to my father."

She sat up with a soft gasp, her cheeks flaming. "Your father knew?"

"He did not put any more credence into the rumors than I do. The only thing I would have done differently is deal with Mrs. Honeywell from the start. If Ashden failed you, it was in that respect."

"But he did attend to Mrs. Honeywell."

"He could have performed the task better. Rewarding her wagging tongue with invitations to join your brother and sister-in-law in Town was foolish."

"What would you have done?"

"It doesn't matter. She will give us no more trouble." He wrapped his fingers around the back of her neck and urged her forward for a kiss.

When they broke contact, she wrinkled her nose. "You do realize in most circumstances you will not be able to divert my attention that easily, but I care nothing for Mrs. Honeywell so I will let it go."

"I will take your warning to heart."

Luke escorted Vivian to her bedchamber and left her in the care of her maid then made his way to the chamber where Collier was being kept. He didn't trust himself alone with the bastard. He tested the door to confirm it remained locked then found his way to the master's chamber.

He hadn't decided what to do with Johanna yet, but perhaps his mother would have some guidance on the morrow. One thing he knew with certainty: she was no longer welcome in his home. She had already proven untrustworthy. He wouldn't be fooled twice.

✦

"Lady Vivian, wake up." A hand at her shoulder shook her violently. "She is here, Your Grace," Winnie bellowed.

Where else would she be but in her bed in the dead of night? Vivi rolled over to find her maid leaning over her. Long shadows blocked out one side of her face, her other bathed in dim light from the candle she held aloft. "Winnie? What the devil are you doing waking me at this hour?"

Heavy footsteps crossed the room and Luke appeared at her bedside still in his nightshirt. "Thank God, you are safe."

Vivi rubbed the sleep from her eyes and sat up. "What is going on? It's the middle of the night."

Her maid gave her a lopsided grin. "It's early morning, milady. The milkmaids are up."

"I am not milking cows if that's your reason for bursting in here."

Luke took the candle from Winnie and shooed her from the chamber. "One of the chambermaids discovered the door to Collier's room ajar. He is gone, and I feared he had taken you with him. I should have posted a guard outside his door."

None of this was making any sense. "Wasn't his door locked from the outside?"

"Yes, I checked it last night, which means someone had to take the key."

A gentleman cleared his throat at the threshold of

her chamber. Vivi yanked the covers up to her neck. "Lord Brookhaven?"

"Pardon the intrusion, Lady Vivian. Your Grace. I have just been informed by my driver that Mr. Collier has absconded with my coach. Apparently, Miss Truax woke my man and told him the coach needed to be readied for my departure, but when he wasn't looking, Collier jumped on the box and drove the team."

"Wouldn't it have been easier to saddle a horse and avoid detection?" Vivi asked.

Lord Brookhaven grimaced. "And less costly. My outrider was badly injured when he tried to stop Collier and received a boot to the jaw. The back wheel rolled over his leg."

"Oh, dear!"

Luke stalked around the end of her bed toward the viscount. "Perhaps we shouldn't speak of such things in the lady's presence."

"Forgive me, Lady Vivian." When the two men moved into the corridor, Vivi swung her legs out of bed, wrapped the counterpane around her, and hurried after them.

"Wait a moment." She caught up to them halfway down the corridor. "What about Miss Truax?"

The men turned to frown at her. She pulled the covers tighter around her.

"It makes no sense for Collier to steal a coach when a horse would provide a better chance at escape," she said. "And how did he convince Miss Truax to help him?"

Brookhaven scratched his whiskered cheek. "We should ask her. Will you send for her, Foxhaven?"

Luke met Vivi's gaze, understanding flickering to life behind his eyes. "He needed a coach for his passenger."

She nodded. "She's in danger. I know it."

"Damnation." Luke spun around and stormed to his bedchamber. Vivi lifted the counterpane so she wouldn't trip and dashed after him.

"Where are you going?" Brookhaven called after them.

"Miss Truax is in need of rescue," Vivi said then disappeared into Luke's chambers.

He had already peeled his dressing gown over his shoulders and tossed it aside before grabbing a pair of trousers from his wardrobe. "I should wring her neck."

Vivi let the counterpane fall to the ground and walked to his wardrobe, too. "There will be plenty of time for that once we find her." She eyed the trousers hanging on pegs and picked the smallest pair.

"What do you mean by *we*?"

She shoved her leg into the pants. "I am going with you."

"You most certainly are not." He paused after pulling his shirt over his head. "What the hell are you doing, Vivian?"

Her chin lifted an inch. "I can't ride astride in a gown, and a sidesaddle is out of the question. It will only slow us down."

Luke stalked across the room, grabbed her by the shoulders, and bent down to her level. "You are not going. I need you to stay behind and tell Mother what has happened."

"She needn't know anything until we return with Miss Truax. They haven't been gone long. We can catch them if we hurry."

"And why should I take you along?"

"Because I can shoot almost as well as you, but more importantly, she may need a lady when we find her."

The stubborn set to Luke's jaw eased a bit, and she knew he was considering her logic. She pushed harder to make him understand.

"I hope I am wrong about Mr. Collier's intentions, but if he treats her poorly, the presence of another man may be too upsetting."

"How do you know of these things?" he asked quietly.

"Even in Dunstable, we had men misuse women. Please, allow me to help you. I promise to listen to everything you tell me to do."

He scoffed and released her shoulders. "Another first for you, darling?"

She stuck her tongue out and rummaged in the wardrobe for a shirt, the pants falling low on her hips.

Luke tugged them up and pulled a sash from a drawer. "You won't be much help if you lose your pants along the way."

A wide grin spread across her face as he tied the sash tightly around her waist, securing the trousers. "You will need your own boots, so go get them."

Vivi dashed to the door, but stopped in the threshold. "Are you planning to leave me?"

"Hurry, before I change my mind."

She did as he bid and was slightly winded when she met him at the stairwell. As they walked side by side to the stables, he reached for her hand. "You may need this." Cold metal touched her palm when he pressed a small caliber firearm into her hand. "It has one shot, so make it count if you must use it."

Lord Brookhaven was waiting in the stables. "Seeing as how it's my property the blackguard stole, I want to be part of his capture. It isn't far to the border. I imagine that is his destination. He has kin in Glasgow."

Luke nodded. "Saddle the black stallion for the lady," he said to a nearby groom.

The servant balked when he took a gander of Vivi in Luke's clothes.

Luke's brows lowered dangerously over his intense blue eyes. "Make it quick."

"Yes, Your Grace." The groom jumped to obey, fumbling to release the bridle from a hook. Her mount was readied quickly, and soon she, the viscount, and Luke were riding toward the village north of Irvine Castle.

They traveled in silence, perhaps each lost in their own thoughts. Vivi should be furious with Miss Truax, but she was too worried for the other woman's welfare to hang on to her anger at the moment. She had seen the coldness in Collier's eyes. He knew nothing of compassion nor did he have any qualms about taking whatever he wanted. He had shown his character well enough when he had forced Vivi into the phaeton earlier. She hoped Luke's kin would escape the situation unscathed.

The sky grew brighter the farther they rode. Vivi had a feeling the promise of a beautiful, sunny day provided a poor indication of what was to come.

When they entered the outskirts of the village, thin threads of smoke were rising from the chimneys. One of the residents may have seen Lord Brookhaven's coach pass through if he was awake early enough.

"The inn is this way," Luke said and took the lead. "We will ask after Collier at the yard."

There was no need to ask anything, however. A sturdy coach with the Brookhaven crest sat in the coaching yard.

"Why did he stop here?" Vivi asked. For a man who strove to be nefarious, Mr. Collier was a dimwit.

"I don't know or care." Lord Brookhaven dismounted and turned the horse over to an ostler before strolling to his coach and sticking his head inside. "No one is here."

Luke swung down from his horse then assisted Vivi. "Stay outside while I search the inn."

"I think not. There would be no point in my traveling all this distance just to wait outside. I'm coming with you."

He grabbed her arm, and she thought he would stop her, but instead he linked arms with her. "Stay close to me."

Vivi quirked an eyebrow. "Won't this appear suspicious given I am dressed as a man?"

"No one who gets a good look is going to believe you are a man. Not with that arse."

"Oh!" She nearly turned a circle trying to get a glance at her backside.

He chuckled under his breath and held the door open for her to proceed inside. "You needn't draw more notice to it, but to satisfy your curiosity, it looks marvelous."

Her cheeks heated and she hurried into the inn, pushing her hat low to hide her face.

A man approached from a back room, his protruding

belly arriving seconds before the rest of him did. "Welcome, Your Grace. What brings you to the Wild Boar at this hour?"

"I'm seeking the gentleman who arrived in the coach outside. Did he take a room?"

"Aye, he was lookin' for a spot for his wife to rest. But he ain't here now. Saw him slip out back 'bout half an hour ago. Figured he might be lookin' to hire a driver and outrider since he managed to lose 'em along the way."

"And the lady was with him?"

The innkeeper hitched a thumb up. "She be restin' above stairs still. Last door on the left."

Luke paid the man several coins then motioned for Vivi to follow him. She peeked at the man from beneath the rim of her hat as she passed and met two narrowed slits for eyes.

Drat! He probably suspected she wasn't a man.

Vivi tried to imitate Luke's wider-legged amble, but almost tripped over the longer pants leg. Giving up the pretense, she scurried up the stairs behind him. He stopped outside the last door on the left and stared at it.

"I have kicked doors open in the past, but it can be painful. And then there would be the cost for repairs."

Vivi reached for the handle and pushed it open. She grinned up at him. "Obviously, I'm the brains of this match."

"Well played," he said with a wink.

Their playfulness disappeared when muffled sobs sounded from the dim room.

Luke slipped inside. "Johanna?"

There was no answer. Only louder cries. He

moved to the curtains and drew them open. Early morning light pushed its way into the room, revealing a crumpled heap on the bed. It was Johanna, and her legs were drawn toward her middle.

When Luke would have charged over to her, Vivi held up a staying hand. "Miss Truax, it is Lady Vivian and Luke. We have come to bring you home."

"I know who you are," she managed to croak out. "But I have no home any longer."

Vivi cautiously crossed to the bed so as not to startle her. "Your home is with your family. You are as much a part of the Forest clan as anyone."

She shook her head, another sob bursting from her.

Vivi moved to place a comforting hand on her hair. "We can debate this later. Are you hurt?"

She buried her face against the covers and cried even harder.

"Johanna, what has he done to you?" Luke came forward. "I swear he will pay."

"Leave me be," she moaned.

Vivi tried to catch his attention and flicked her gaze toward the door. His lips set in a thin line.

"Go," she mouthed and motioned for him to leave them alone. His frown deepened, but he left, closing the door behind him. She sat on the bed beside Johanna and brushed her hair behind her ear like Patrice had done for her when she was a young girl. She didn't ask any questions or lend any commentary. She had been on the receiving end of well-meaning comments in the past, and no matter the speaker's intentions, the words could hurt. She just allowed Johanna to cry until her tears began to subside.

"Why are you being nice to me?" she asked between sniffles.

"I don't know." Vivi sighed softly. "Maybe because I have made mistakes, too, and I know how horrible I have felt afterward."

Johanna held her hair aside and gazed up with narrowed eyes; her bottom lip protruded mutinously, reminding Vivi of a child. "Have you ever tried to hurt someone intentionally?"

She shook her head and swallowed hard. "Is—was that your intention? To hurt me?"

"No." Tears welled in the other woman's eyes and slid down her cheeks. "Not like this. He said he loved you."

Vivi concluded she referred to Mr. Collier. "I'm certain the scoundrel said a lot of things that were untrue."

"He told me he couldn't live without you. That he wanted to marry you. I feel the same way about Luke."

Vivi's stomach turned, and bitterness crept into the back of her throat. She didn't want to feel jealousy or anger, especially when she had won Luke's heart. But she had trouble ignoring that she could have been suffering Johanna's fate hours earlier. Vivi could be ruined and destined to a life of solitude because of Johanna's machinations.

The other woman rubbed the back of her hand across her nose and regarded Vivi warily. "I'm sorry. I didn't mean to…"

Vivi forced herself to speak calmly. "Why did you help Collier escape?"

Johanna hid behind her curtain of hair again. "We had an understanding. If I helped him, he would take me with him and give me his name. It seemed like the best prospect available to me. I couldn't stay with the duchess any longer. Not when His Grace plans to turn me out."

"You don't know that." Neither did Vivi, but would he have come looking for Johanna if he felt no responsibility toward her?

"When we stopped here, Mr. Collier said I had to prove my dedication. I didn't know what he meant, but then he brought me to the room. Then he—" She whimpered and Vivi wanted to have the man at gunpoint again.

She smoothed a hand over Johanna's back. "It's all right. You do not have to talk about it."

"H-he said I had failed." Johanna took a shuddering breath. "That he would never marry a loose woman like me, and then he left me."

Make that two guns pointed his direction. Never had Vivi despised anyone as she did that despicable excuse for a man. "He will pay for what he has done. Luke will see to it."

"It doesn't change anything. My life is over."

There was a soft knock, and the door slowly swung open. Luke eased into the room. "May I come inside? I have a proposition from Viscount Brookhaven. He hopes you will consider his offer."

"No," Johanna mumbled. "Please, I cannot show my face to anyone ever again."

Vivi grabbed Johanna's hands and pulled. "Oh, come now, Miss Truax. You are made of sterner stuff than this." Eventually, the other woman sat up on the edge of the bed beside Vivi, her head lowered and hair falling forward to shield her face.

Vivi nodded to Luke to indicate he should proceed.

"Lord Brookhaven feels responsible for your circumstances, at least to some degree. Had he not brought Jonathan Collier to Irvine Castle, none of this would have happened."

"I am to blame," Johanna said. "Please tell Lord Brookhaven I do not hold him responsible. I harbor no ill feelings toward him."

The door swung open wider, and Lord Brookhaven filled the threshold. "That is a relief, Miss Truax," he said with a smile. "If you hated me, it might make life a tad more difficult for us."

Johanna blinked up at him. "How so, my lord?"

He stepped into the room and closed the door behind him. "I think we may be able to help each other, Miss Truax. It seems you need a home, and I have need of a wife to manage my household."

Johanna gazed at him warily as if she expected he was playing a trick on them all.

"Uh…It's a rather daunting undertaking," Brookhaven said and scratched his whiskered jaw. "I can understand your reluctance. Perhaps you have heard tales of my offspring?"

She shook her head.

"Oh! Well, splendid. I had feared—" He waved his hand in the air like he wished to wipe away his last statement. "It doesn't matter. I bid you to say nothing until you understand the terms. My wife left me with six offspring, five boys, all of them as wild as March hares, and one sweet young girl, who may be mute. She is still a youngster, so there is a chance she may speak eventually, but I cannot say with certainty she will. I have had difficulty keeping a governess, and I haven't time to place another advertisement or conduct interviews. My duties call me away often, so there would be many days the children would be under your rule alone."

"Did you mean to say that you wish for me to be a governess to your children?"

"No, no. I have gone that route and every one of the women has left us. A wife seems the better bet."

Tight lines appeared around Johanna's mouth. "I see. A wife cannot leave so easily."

Lord Brookhaven pointed at her and grinned. "Exactly. You are a clever one, Miss Truax. In case you are wondering what you will receive in return, besides a roof over your head, I will provide a reasonable clothing allowance so you may dress as one would expect of a viscountess. And you will have ample pin money to purchase whatever you would like for entertainment."

The harsh lines in Johanna's face began to soften. "Do you want more children, my lord?"

He shrugged. "Not particularly, but if you find you are with Mr. Collier's child, I shall claim him as my own."

Vivi and Johanna gasped.

"So there you have it, Miss Truax. All the terms of my proposal. Would you like time to consider it before you reply?"

She stared at him with her mouth agape. Lord Brookhaven began to fidget with his cravat and shot a look at Luke. When a bead of sweat popped up on his forehead, Vivi elbowed Johanna in the side.

"Yes," she blurted. "I mean, I don't need time to consider. I accept."

Lord Brookhaven blew out a long breath. "Very well. Then I shall await you in the dining room. We should have a good meal before we set off for Gretna Green."

When the viscount left, Luke gave Johanna a brief nod then spoke to Vivi. "I will send for Brookhaven's servants. I'll be in the stable yard. Will you be long?"

"I want to assist Miss Truax with setting herself back to rights then I will join you."

"Very well."

Johanna's head dropped when he quit the room without a word for her. "He hates me now."

Vivi patted her leg. "Give him time."

Johanna took Vivi's hand in hers. "I don't deserve your kindness, my lady, but know I am your humble servant from this day forward."

She squeezed her hand in response. "Allow me to send for water and then we can start on your hair."

❧

Luke couldn't help but smile when Vivian came out of the inn and tugged up the waistband of the trousers she was about to lose. Even with her hair tucked under a hat and dressed like a bedraggled gentleman after a long night at the tables, she was breathtaking. He couldn't believe his good fortune in finding a wife who suited him so well.

Brookhaven would not be as lucky, but since the viscount seemed to be in the market for a house-hold manager, he hadn't made a poor deal. Johanna would manage his household, and Luke had warned Brookhaven he might find himself managed as well. Nevertheless, the viscount was a grown man.

"Shall we go, Lord Vivian?"

She wrinkled her nose at him. "I suppose we should before everyone begins to stir at the castle. I'm not certain I could explain my attire."

Luke linked his fingers and offered her a leg up. Once she was settled in the saddle, he squeezed her thigh. "The advantage to being a duchess is you need not explain yourself to anyone. A few days under Mother's tutelage and you will be well prepared to manage anyone who tries to tell you differently."

She giggled. "She is outspoken at times. I like that about her."

He mounted Thor and signaled him to begin the walk back to Irvine Castle. The return trip would take longer with Brookhaven's mount tied behind his horse, but Luke didn't mind. He was with Vivian.

"How many children do you want?" she asked as they rode side by side down the dusty lane.

"Not six!"

"But that is how many your mother bore."

"Yes, but my siblings are all terribly annoying. My parents should have stopped with perfection." He grinned at her. "You shouldn't mention that in front of any of them, mind you."

She laughed. "Your secret is safe."

Although she spoke in jest, he knew she was being truthful. He would always be able to trust her with his secrets, with his heart, and she could trust him to do the same, although he would love to tell his brothers of her antics at Brighthurst House. Richard and Drew would find the tales amusing, but it was also something special he and Vivian alone shared.

"Do you know what I thought when I first saw you in the spring?" he asked.

A pink flush brightened her cheeks. "I'm afraid to hear."

"I thought you were a vision, like the ladies I saw at my bedside at Twinspur."

She raised her brows. "Who came to your bedside?"

"I don't know. I couldn't see faces. I am not even certain they were women. They radiated with a warm light, and I felt everything was going to be all right again when they were there. I had the same sense when I looked at you."

She walked her horse closer and held out her hand. He linked his fingers with hers. "I thought you looked like Sir Launcelot on your stallion."

"From *Le Morte d'Arthur*? Vivian Worth, how would you have any knowledge of that scandalous tale?"

She shrugged. "My brother shouldn't have left the book sitting out. I am not responsible for my curious nature. You should prepare yourself, Your Grace. I fear I may scandalize you often."

"I hope so," he said with a wink. "But seeing as how you haven't done or said anything scandalous in the last thirty seconds, I'm not sure whether to believe you. There is a lake on our land. Would you care to join me for a morning swim?"

"My, that would be scandalous indeed, if we were discovered."

"I imagine it would, but where is the fun in playing it safe, dear Vivian?"

"Very well. Lead the way."

As he guided his horse ahead of hers, she cleared her throat. He looked over his shoulder to find her grinning wickedly. "Nice view, Your Grace."

He chuckled and turned back toward the lane.

"Luke?"

"Yes, darling?"

"I love you."

His heart grew to twice its size. Never could he have anticipated the impact of those three little words, but they meant the world to him. "I love you, too, water sprite."

Epilogue

Vɪvɪ ᴡᴀꜱ ᴜɴᴀʙʟᴇ ᴛᴏ ꜱᴛᴀɴᴅ ꜱᴛɪʟʟ ᴀꜱ ꜱʜᴇ ᴡᴀɪᴛᴇᴅ ʙʏ her husband's side to receive their wedding guests. She felt as if she might float off into the night sky without Luke's arm anchoring her to the ground.

When he had suggested they exchange vows before Vicar Ramsey and invite the entire village to witness their nuptials, she had been more than a little hesitant. She was certain no one would attend and she would be humiliated on what should be the happiest day of her life.

She had been wrong about the good people of Dunstable.

Every man, woman, and child had piled into the church that morning then made their way to Brighthurst House for the wedding breakfast. Perhaps it was curiosity over what type of gentleman would take the unruly Lady Vivian Worth as his wife. Or maybe it was simply because nothing exciting had happened in their small village for years.

Whatever the reason, the guests had arrived in jovial moods and seemed to have no memory of her past. Of course Luke's demands that Mrs. Honeywell personally call on every resident in the county to explain how she had made a grave mistake likely had something to do with the reception Vivi had received upon her return.

Now, the celebration had carried over into the evening with Mr. and Mrs. Honeywell hosting a dinner and dance as penance. What a change in attitude Vivi's elevation to duchess had wrought. Mrs. Honeywell had been dogging her heels at every opportunity that day, practically begging for ways to serve her. If Vivi were the vindictive type, she would have run the woman ragged trying to fulfill her requests. Instead, the dowager Duchess of Foxhaven had seen to the deed.

"Welcome to Lichefield Hall," Mrs. Honeywell gushed as Lord and Lady Eldridge moved down the receiving line. "How happy Mr. Honeywell and I are to open our home to the duke and duchess's friends and family. Mr. Honeywell and I have been close family friends with Lady Brighthurst and the new duchess for ages."

Vivi almost laughed aloud at the fib, but she covered her response with a friendly smile for the earl and countess. She had learned to employ a few tricks over the last few weeks, and she would have them perfected before she and Luke returned from their honeymoon and took up residence in London for the season.

Luke covered her hand with his and smiled at her. "Are you having fun?" he whispered in her ear.

"This is the best day of my life."

"This is just the beginning. It is my mission to make every day the best of your life."

"My, you will be busy, won't you?"

Luke fanned his fingers out over the small of her back, his firm touch making her feel protected and desired at once. "Fortunately for me you aren't difficult to please."

A fresh wave of exhilaration swept over her with the arrival of a new guest. "Oh, look! It is Dottie Kennicot. Or rather, Mrs. Quinn now. I wonder what she is doing in Dunstable."

"She's here to see you, of course. Vicar Ramsey's bride thought a reunion with your dearest friend would be a fitting wedding gift."

A thrill chased through her every time she was reminded of her cousin's happy circumstances. Not only did Patrice enjoy a peaceful and loving existence with the vicar, she suspected she was with child.

Vivi glanced up at Luke. "Did you arrange for Dottie to be here this evening?"

"Go speak with her. She has traveled a long distance." He gave her a gentle push toward her old friend.

She weaved through the guests gathered on the veranda and faltered in her step when Dottie met her gaze. They both stared at each other, frozen for a moment. Eventually, Dottie lowered her head and curtsied. "Your Grace."

Vivi rushed forward to grab her hands. "Oh, my molasses! We have been friends far too long for such nonsense."

Dottie's eyes filled with tears even as she laughed. "My dearest Vivi, I have missed you so. Can you ever find it in your heart to forgive me for turning away from you?"

No longer did she feel the sharp edge of rejection she had once experienced when she recalled those days with no friends to share her burden.

"You had no choice, Dottie. I have never blamed you. Besides, you are here now. Come, allow me to introduce you to my husband." Vivi linked arms with her and leaned close to speak in confidence. "He puts Sir Launcelot to shame."

Dottie giggled, sounding just like the young girl she used to be when Vivi had read the book to her in secret.

Toward the end of the night, Vivi felt lighter than she had in years. She had married her perfect match, made her family proud of her, and renewed a friendship she had missed more than she had known.

Luke motioned for her to join him. Reaching his side, she placed her hand in his and allowed him to lead her away from the other guests, down the stone stairs, and into the night. The same starry sky that had witnessed those precious moments when she and Luke were discovering each other now bore testament to their deep love and affection.

"Thank you for this day," she said. "I never thought I would come back here, much less be welcomed."

Luke put his arm around her shoulders and drew her close to his side as they walked into the meadow. "You needn't thank me. I would do anything to make you happy."

She pulled him to a stop. "You have never asked me what happened that day."

"I know everything I need to know," he said and wrapped her in his arms.

"Still, I would feel better if I told you. I stayed the night in the stable and Owen kept me company, just as Mrs. Honeywell said, but I promise, the only thing on my mind was Maggie."

"Maggie?"

"Yes, you have met her. She has sad, brown eyes and says moo."

"The milk cow? Why, in God's name, was a cow on your mind?"

"Because she was in labor. Why wouldn't she be on my mind?"

He shook his head and laughed. "How silly of me. Please, continue."

"Well, she had been laboring with her first calf all day and into the night. I couldn't leave her until after she had given birth. The poor thing was scared out of her wits."

"Only you would be concerned with the emotional welfare of a farm animal." Luke hugged her close and kissed the tip of her nose. "And you wonder why I am madly in love with you."

When his lips covered hers, her mind was at peace. Her past would stay in Dunstable, forever put to rest, while she enjoyed a future with the man she adored. And what an exciting future that would be.

Acknowledgments

I would like to take a moment to thank my dear friend, Lori, for her encouragement when I hit a snag in writing this book. She told me to follow my instincts, keep writing the story, and trust my editing team to point me in the right direction if I strayed off course. She was right.

I'm also grateful to my Sourcebooks editor, Leah Hultenschmidt, and assistant editor, Aubrey Poole. They provided excellent guidance, and their enthusiasm made this a fun experience.

I'm always thankful for my husband's support and willingness to talk through plotting. This time, however, he also shared his expertise with concussion management. I'm pretty lucky to have married a psychologist and all-around great guy.

About the Author

Samantha Grace is the author of several Regency romance novels. *Lady Vivian Defies a Duke* is the final installment of her Beau Monde Bachelor series. *Publisher's Weekly* describes her stories as "fresh and romantic" with subtle humor and charm. She writes what she enjoys reading: romantic comedies about family, friendship, and flawed characters who learn how to love deeply.

Samantha is a part-time hospice social worker, moonlighting author, and full-time wife and mom. She enjoys life in the Midwest with her husband, two witty kids, and a multitude of characters that spring from her imagination. Samantha is happily working on her next project. To learn more about Samantha's books and upcoming appearances, you can visit her at www.samanthagraceauthor.com.